Karma Days

A JOEY HOPKINS STORY

RENDER WILDE

The characters, events, and places in this book are fictitious. Any similarity to real persons, living or dead is coincidental and not intended by the author.

ISBN: 978-1-949735-77-2 (sc)
ISBN: 978-1-949735-59-8 (hc)
ISBN: 978-1-948928-08-3 (e)

CHAPTER 1

Thou shall not steal.

A simple commandment. A simple thing to accomplish and comply with, or is it? Owen Canton closed his Bible and meditated on it. He thought of himself as a good man, yet he struggled with himself with the true basics of trying to live without sin. He found that it was just impossible in the world we live in now.

His life had been thrown a curve ball in the last few months. It seemed after living such a rich and rewarding life over the last twenty years, that a debt had come due. The first thing to disrupt his life was the murder of his wife. She had been on the way home from the market when she encountered a drunk driver. The man had run her off the road into a shallow ditch. The whole event had been caught on a security camera. Owen had been forced by the police to view this footage more than once. It is not an easy thing to do – to watch someone come up to the side of your car, break the window out with a pistol, then point said pistol at your wife and assassinate her.

The police wanted to know if he recognized the assailant. Owen had no knowledge of the man. They tried to view the angle that Owen might have hired this man. He had not done such a thing. Maybe he was a rival or had an ax to grind with her or with him. Owen told them he had no known enemies. He was just a writer who wrote stories that the public seemed to love and connect with. He had written ten books and made the bestseller list five times. He thought his only sin at that time might have been that he kept too much of the money he had made and that maybe he should have given more to charity.

Although his name had been dragged through the mud by the media, once he had been cleared of being a possible suspect, he was free from any possible connection with the murder of his wife. The public had their opinions on his guilt or innocence which weighed heavily on poor Owen's soul. He was innocent, yet he felt he had to defend himself, clear his good name. The media had stolen his innocence; he wanted it back. He was a writer, so he decided to tell a story of a man who had been wrongly accused of a crime and what it did to him. He got about ten pages into the story when the second tragedy befell him.

His father loved fishing down by the river that ran along the railroad tracks. Back in Central New York where Owen's parents live, an active rail line runs with over twenty trains a day passing through this small community. Many people fish on the other side of the river, but the big fish had staked out the railroad side of the river. Owen's dad wasn't afraid of the tracks. He felt safe and secure around the tracks and it was worth the risk for those big bass. As long as he kept his head on a swivel and his ears open to the sound of the whistle, he felt he was safe. Never in Owen's wildest dreams would he have imagined that his father would step out in front of a raging train and kill himself. His father loved life and had too much to live for. He never would have committed suicide. It was hard to take when the authorities notified him of the dreadful incident.

His story would have to be put on the back burner. His mother was devastated. On the other hand, his brother, who was born with an intellectual disability, simply thought that his father had just taken a trip and would be back soon. Some mean folks just called him retarded, a moron. Owen thought the disability was caused by the prescription drugs his mother had taken leading up to the time she found out she was pregnant, which after having Owen, the doctor told his mother that she would never be able to have children again. Years later, she had Todd, a miracle for sure. Owen was already ten years old, so he always felt like an only child. Since Todd needed a lot of care, Owen was pushed to the side, his needs were secondary to his brother's. To say he resented his brother would be close to the truth. He loved him, yes, but he needed his parents' love as well, but felt it was all given to his brother. Owen became very independent and it didn't come as any surprise that he left home at a young age and never returned except for the holidays.

Now he was preparing to rush home to comfort his family that was shrinking by the minute. First his wife, now his father in less than ninety days! He had always wished that he had children, but his wife had two miscarriages which had taken a heavy toll on both of them. They decided not to tempt fate and put an end to their hopes. Best to just live without children than face that severe pain once again.

He decided to drive because he didn't know how long he would be gone, could be a week or a month, never could tell. He had never had to bury a parent before. While he was packing his SUV for the trip, his neighbor had returned home early from work. The man was a contractor for the city, doing work maintaining roads and new construction. Owen thought he was a thief stealing hardworking taxpayer money. His house was huge, and Owen thought he owned every toy that a grown man would want to possess. Now he was arriving home in the middle of the afternoon with the most beautiful woman Owen had ever seen. He was mesmerized by her beauty from the moment he saw her. A feeling that he just had to have her overcame all his thoughts. He sat transfixed on his tailgate just staring across the street wondering what it would be like to hold and love someone as desirable as the woman that had just entered his neighbor's house. A plan began to form in his head, a selfish cock-blocking plan. He just had to meet this woman. Maybe she would be a bitch with a nasty attitude, and he thought that would serve his neighbor right.

His name was Richard Ekhart, but everyone called him Dick. Owen thought that that was just what he was, a big Dick. This woman needed to be saved from this despicable person. She needed to be with someone more like him – a mature and stable man, someone that would love her and not treat her like some trophy he had acquired playing the game of life.

Owen crossed the street and knocked on the door. He could hear giggling and some playful banter coming from inside. When Dick answered the door, his shirt was unbuttoned and hung open, revealing some impressive pecks and six-pack abs. Owen never even came close to having a body like that. He sucked in his pot belly and asked if he could borrow a straight slot screwdriver. Dick smiled at him like he was some lost puppy and invited him in.

"I'll be right back dear. Owen here needs a tool." He laughed at his joke and hurried to the garage to retrieve the needed tool Owen had asked for.

Up close this woman looked even more beautiful, if that was even possible. She sauntered up to Owen and introduced herself.

"I'm Lori Stenville. You're the writer Owen Canton! I've read all your books. I just love them. I can't wait to read the next one."

She sounded so excited that Owen felt thrilled when she sat down beside him on the couch, sitting so close they were touching. She kept touching his arm as they were talking, and he kept staring into her baby blue eyes that were enhanced with just the right amount of makeup and color, making them stand out in near perfection.

The sound of someone clearing his throat brought Owen back to the here and now. Dick was standing in front of him with the screwdriver in his hand almost like he was ready to use it as a murder weapon. Owen shot up off the couch startling Lori, made some lame excuse that he had to go, and headed for the door.

He stopped when Lori called out to him.

"Owen, I want you to have this."

He turned toward her as she handed him a business card. Owen felt that she held it in his hand for just a bit longer than she should have, and with their faces mere inches apart, his lips yearned to kiss hers. He caught himself beginning to lean in for that kiss, managed to thank her, and hurried across the street breathing hard. He chastised himself for nearly stealing a kiss right in front of Dick. The chemistry he felt for Lori was so strong and he felt like she could sense it as well.

He looked at the card she had given him. It was a business card. She did drapes and home interior design. Did she want to try to get him as a business client or did she want him to have her number? These questions would have to wait for an answer. He had a long drive ahead of him.

As he was pulling out of his driveway, he glanced over at Dick's place and saw her in the window, measuring it for some new curtains or something like that. She was watching him, this he knew for sure. He felt her eyes on him all the way down the street. It had only been a few months since he became a widower, it was well-publicized in the media. If Lori were a fan like she said she was, she would know this. Owen felt a small pang in his gut, like maybe he had a small chance with this woman. She seemed so nice and personable. Someone he would most certainly enjoy spending more time with. He decided he could use some new drapes in the living room. He would call her for sure and set up an appointment once he returned.

CHAPTER 2

Lori stood on a small step stool and took measurements of the front window. She had intentionally started on the front of the house so she could observe what Owen was up to. As he departed his house, she thought she might have caught him sneaking a peek her way. The little girl inside of her was thrilled, the spirit not so much. They had much work to do. That work was about to start when she felt his hands reach around her and cup her breast. He pulled her back out of the window and into his arms, snuggling his face into her neck and breathing deeply of her perfume, which she had intentionally applied a liberal amount to her neck to get him to do just this thing. The mouse had taken the bait. Now that he was in her trap, it was time to exterminate this rat.

Richard had a history of being a womanizer. His conquests of women had found a few of them missing, never to be seen again. He knew where the bodies were hidden, and he was about to confess to what he had done. He was unaware of this at the time, but he sure as hell was about to find out.

Lori let him have his fun, and instead of screaming out against the unwanted touching, she embraced it and played it up as if she were enjoying herself. Richard was completely taken off guard and he relished the thought that he would not have to fight this girl to have his way with her. He let up his guard and loosened his hold just enough for Lori to gain an advantage. Momentum had swung her way and she finally took full advantage of it. All those years of mixed martial arts training came back to her and within seconds Richard was completely at her mercy. She was on top of him maintaining a dominant role. Richard never knew what hit him and he was loving every minute of it. It was all part of Lori's game. She played him like a fiddle, making him fantasize that he was about to have a night he would remember for the rest of his life. He would most definitely remember this night, Lori was going to make sure of that.

They rolled around on the floor exploring each other's bodies, kissing and feeling, touching and rubbing. Richard was breathing heavily with the thought of a sexual experience that was sure to follow all this foreplay. Lori beamed with delight and smiled. She congratulated herself on a job well done. First off, she had survived long enough to get him to bend to her way. Many women that had come before her had not been as fortunate. Secondly, she was about to put her plan into action. This required him to fully trust her, which she seemed to have accomplished.

"Richard, let me up. I want to get a condom out of my purse, and I need to visit the bathroom. Let's take this to the bedroom. I so need this, and you're going to give it to me, my stud," she said in a very seductive way, one that would get him hightailing it to the bedroom ready and waiting for her return.

She reached into her purse for the special prophylactic. The outside label read, "For her and his pleasure, guaranteed." She knew that this special rubber, once in place would put this big brute of a man right in his place. He would be ready for action just long enough for her to watch the real fun.

He led her to the bedroom on the first floor. It had its own private bathroom, complete with a jacuzzi tub. She squealed with delight when she saw it. This was just too perfect. Her gaze went up to the ceiling and she silently thanked the Lord for the privilege of letting her be his tool for revenge.

Staring back into the mirror, she saw the sweet girl who just a few weeks ago was lying in her own feces barely alive, suffering from low blood sugar that was about to claim her life. This girl was the perfect vessel for her, much better than her first experience when she had stepped into a sex doll by mistake. It had been her first time taking a body and the doll looked so real. She had been trapped inside that darn doll for weeks until a minister cast her out and freed her to get a real host.

This time, she had been so excited to have such a perfect specimen that she stepped into the body before the soul passed, and with the healing power of an angel, she saved her life. Now they shared the same body. She could feel the girl's soul trapped with her inside this body. Although the girl was grateful to be alive, the real Lori was not very enthused with the arrangement. That was just too bad. The spirit needed her to carry out God's will. When she was done with her, she would be released and would either succumb and pass as she had been found, or she would go on to live a very healthful and fulfilling life. That was not her choice, that would be up to a higher power than her. She was the spirit Karma, and Karma was a bitch.

Lori opened the door and peered out. Richard had the rubber in place and was smiling broadly. His tool was at full attention, ready and waiting for her. Lori giggled to herself, opened the door, and went to him. She ran, skipped to the bed, and jumped on top of him.

"I need you so bad. I'm so hot," she cooed. He responded with a slur of words. She peered up at him as the drool ran out of the side of his mouth and dribbled down to his chin.

"What's the matter, baby? You're not having a stroke on me, are you?"

She placed her hand on his tool and felt it start to subside. Soon he would be fast asleep as the powerful sedative took effect. She cuddled up to him and made sure he knew how disappointed she was that he was unable to perform for her. It was all part of the mind game.

Once Richard was out, she grabbed her phone and called her assistant. His name was Ryan and he had been working with her for some time now. He was another angel who would hop from one body to another. Unlike her, he waited until the soul left the body before he would take possession of it. He said it was less complicated that way. As the days would go by, she would learn exactly what he meant by that statement. Lori had a huge crush on Owen, and it had almost ruined her plan to take this a-hole down. Karma knew she would have to be more careful in the future. She liked this body and planned on using it for the foreseeable future.

Karma had given Ryan a set of instructions when she called him, and like a good soldier, he followed them. He pulled the van that advertised the business into the driveway and began to unload the materials they were going to need: lengths of nylon rope, a set of handcuffs, suction cups for the floor of the tub, and a hundred pounds of ice. He went to the back deck after giving the items to Lori and removed the propane tank from the grill. Ryan had a special device that when attached to the tank, would release the gas in a slow deliberate manner. It was perfect for filling a house up with gas while giving them plenty of time to make a getaway.

Ryan assisted Lori in getting Richard into the tub. Once he was in place, Ryan set about finding some candles to give the bathroom some ambiance. Nothing like a lit candle and some propane to give your night the bang it needs. Lori proceeded to hog tie Richard in place inside the tub. She ran the nylon rope through the two suction cups she had placed on the floor of the tub. Then she tied his legs together at the ankles and secured them to the suction cups. This would ensure that he would not be able to get out of the tub and escape the ice water that he would be kneeling in. It was important to place him in a kneeling position so that he could pray to God before he died and beg the Lord for forgiveness.

She ran the rope between his legs and around his handcuffed hands. He would be given just enough slack that he might be able to extinguish the candles by splashing some water at them. Next, she placed a collar around his neck and ran a length of rope in three directions, ensuring that he would be unable to just put his head into the water and drown himself. The handgrips around the tub were perfect just for this sort of thing. Satisfied that she had accomplished everything, she called for

Ryan and he gave her the thumbs up. She opened a pack of smelling salts and woke sleeping beauty.

Richard's head bounced around a little and as reality started to settle in, he slowly realized that he was indeed screwed. Lori sat on a stool beside him, talking about what little pleasure he had given her.

"I was so looking forward to having a romp in the hay, and you fell asleep on me."

Lori laid it on heavy that she was not happy with his performance. A debt had to be paid. Richard just thought she was a sick and disturbed person. He tried to explain but since he was clueless that he had been drugged, he was at a loss for words. So, he just stuttered out an incoherent explanation.

"I don't need or want your excuses. We are going to play a game now. Since you are in the position that you are in, you have no choice but to play with me," she said while taking her blouse off and placing a nipple to his lips demanding that he get to work.

Richard began to suck and lick at the offered breast while begging to be released from his bondage. Lori had heard enough, sat up, and began to run cold water into the tub. She walked out of the bathroom and returned with a ten-pound bag of ice in each hand. She placed them down before him and exited to grab the other bags. Once she had all the bags in place, she opened them and poured them into the tub with Richard. His tool shriveled into a tiny child-like size which Lori had to comment on. She degraded him and made him feel petty and insignificant. This is what he did to all those women that he had raped and murdered. Karma had come to town and he had a debt that needed to be paid. He would pay it in full tonight, this she was going to ensure.

Lori turned the water off and listened to Richard's whining about how cold it was. It triggered something in her subconscious. Maybe it was the little girl talking to her, but that little girl wasn't pleading for his mercy, she wanted to degrade this subject even more than what was already happening to the poor man. Lori called out to Ryan and asked him to bring Black Betty in. It made her think of the song by Ram Jam of the same title. Richard was going to love this.

Ryan came in a few minutes later holding the vile thing by two fingers with a look of disgust on his face. Lori waved him off and grabbed the dildo from him. She began to tease Richard with it, telling him of all the places such a thing could end up in. She rubbed it on his cheeks and got it close to his lips.

"Maybe you would like to suck on this for a while, or better yet, how about I ram the damn thing up your ass, would you like that you big Dick? I bet it would fill you up nicely and make you feel just like the women you violated before you killed them!"

Lori had lost her composure and was screaming in his face. This was not Karma. This was the little girl inside her taking control. Karma had to throttle her back and regain control of the body. This was definitely going to be the last time she was going to take a body that hadn't passed yet. Although there was something that she liked about it, the thought that she might have to fight the will of the person inside of her while dealing with insane lunatics was frightening.

Karma decided that Black Betty was going to be used to get some peace and quiet in her life. She pinched Richard's nose, and as he opened his mouth to yell, she inserted Black Betty. Now his screams and whines were muffled. It was much better, and it seemed to satisfy the little girl inside of her. The real Lori.

Lori leaned over and saw sweat on Richard's brow. She thought this was unbelievable, with him sitting in ice water. It was time to confess, give up the location of the two missing women, and end his time here on earth. She reached into her bag of goodies and removed a box cutter. It was time to unpack this package a few cuts at a time. She began just above his eyebrows so that the blood ran down into his eyes. Nice deep cuts that bled profusely, blinding her captive. She added a few more around his body, turning the water a crimson red.

Lori leaned in and whispered into his ear.

"I know what you did to those girls. I'm going to place a cellphone in your hands, and when I do, you are going to confess to your sins. I want you to send a text message to a police officer friend of mine. His name is Mahoney, one of Richmond's finest. I want you to tell him where you hid the bodies and I will know if you're lying. I will read the text message and if I determine you have lied, I will inflict some severe pain upon your body – the likes you have never felt before. Nod your head if you understand what I have said to you."

Richard breathed heavily and nodded his head that he understood. She grabbed a face cloth and wiped the blood from his eyes but had to hold it there to keep any more from blinding him while he typed in the message. His first attempt was a complete and total lie. She reached down between his legs and cut across the tip of his flaccid penis. This got his attention quickly. The next cut would be a whole lot deeper and complete. He frantically typed the real location and confession to the murders of the two missing women. Lori gazed at what he wrote, took the phone back from him, and hit send.

"Now was that so hard my little dicky? Which by the way, you should be grateful that you still have after the pitiful lie you typed in the first time. We still have a little time for fun before the cops get here. I thought we would start by praying. I see you are already kneeling, so let us begin."

She removed the face cloth and the blood flowed back into his eyes.

Lori typed in several songs for Richard to listen to while he waited to die. The first song was "Create in Me" by Rend Collective. This song was to cleanse his soul as he asked for forgiveness. The second song was by Matt Maher called "Lord, I Need You." The last song was going to be his deciding factor, whether he had decided to give himself fully to God or die an unforgiven sinner, "More Love, More Power," an intense song by Jeff Deyo. Something to get his heart pounding as the end neared. She handed the phone back to Richard after hitting the play button.

"It's in God's hands now whether you live or die. If you do get saved, remember not to remember who did this to you. I have got to go now, but I won't be far away, and I have a lot of connections you don't know about. Good luck and make sure you ask God to save you. He is your only hope now," she said and laughed as she lit the three candles placed around the bathroom and walked out, closing the door just enough to let the gas pass through.

Ryan set the regulator to a slow-release and instantly you could smell the fumes from the propane begin to seep out. Lori wondered who he would call to come save his sorry ass. She had an idea who it was going to be. Officer Mahoney would not act on the text message until he had confirmed that the bodies were indeed hidden where the text message said they were. At least that was what she hoped. It would be a shame for him to get blown up when he walked in the house looking for Richard with a lit cigarette in his mouth.

She drove out to the gate while Ryan sat in the passenger seat. This community was gated and had a guard manning the gate twenty-four seven. The street gangs and violence in the city demanded it. She knew the guard was armed and was not the least bit shy to use his weapon.

She stopped at the gate to ask him a question.

"I have another job I need to measure out, but it seems that Owen Canton isn't at home. Did he say when he would be returning?" she asked in her flirtatious manner that she knew would get most men to give her anything that she wanted. This body was amazing, and men were just drawn to its beauty. Karma took full advantage of it.

"He said that he was taking a trip to New York and wasn't able to give me a return date. He asked me to keep an eye on his place, even tipped me handsomely to do it."

The idiot just gave away too much information. Lori rolled her eyes behind her sunglasses.

"I'll be back to install the blinds at the Ekhart residence next week. Until then, take care and have a nice day."

She waved to him and pulled off. She wanted to make sure this guy remembered her and what time she left. It would be a few hours before all the excitement began.

She drove down the street and found a nice quiet place to park. Ryan had brought some sandwiches which they ate in silence. Once finished, she knew he would start in on her. He never disappointed her.

"Lori, why do you always have to kill them? Can't you just make their lives miserable and leave it at that?"

She patted his hand, made a couple of soothing noises. He just wasn't able to understand how the Lord worked. Each one that ended up dead had made their own choice. They would be saved if they denounced evil and gave themselves to God. These arrogant fools always chose evil.

They made their own bed, so they got to sleep in them. She always gave them a chance, just like Richard. He had the means to save his own life. The phone was in his hand. He could call 911 and be free in less than fifteen minutes, but he would never do that, because she knew he would be looking to pack a bag and get out of town as soon as possible. Once the cops found the bodies with his confession text, he would be toast. The question was going to be, who was he going to call?

Fifteen minutes later, they saw a pickup truck with Ekhart Construction stenciled on the side go flying by, heading for Ekhart's house. It was his foreman, another one she needed to visit. Poor Richard had chosen badly, his fate had been sealed. She wondered if he had even listened to the music that she had provided for him. Lori doubted it. She put the van in drive, and they drove back into Richmond. Later that night, she got her next assignment as she watched what happened in a gated community just outside of Richmond.

Officer Mahoney was giving an interview. He was guarded at what he would reveal as it was an ongoing investigation and she wondered why they even had him speak at all. Her next assignment shocked her and the little girl inside her. Owen Canton was next up. Now, this was getting interesting. What was his sin that required the likes of her? When she viewed the information on her phone, she gasped. It would not be a normal assignment.

She yelled out to Ryan, "You're going to love this next one."

They were about to make a lot of people pay for their indiscretions. Owen was going to be the funnel in which it was dealt out. His life was going to be very chaotic in the days ahead, many choices needed to be made. Would he choose the right ones? This they were about to find out.

CHAPTER 3

Richard Ekhart was having trouble seeing and his hands were shaking so badly from the cold that he could barely hold onto the cellphone. He had pondered dialing 911 and have the bitch arrested for what she had done to him, but he knew his fate had been sealed when she made him confess to the multiple rapes and murders of those sluts. He had covered his tracks well and knew he hadn't made any mistakes. How did she know about what he had done, and worst yet, that he had lied when he wrote the first text message? He figured that they would look in the location he had said and would find nothing, then come looking for him and free him from this hell.

The stupid songs she had programmed just made him angry and he muted them. The blood in his eyes made it difficult but he was able to send his foreman a text and have him head this way. The man was an asshole, but he did what he was told and kept his mouth shut when Richard would make deals that were just a bit on the shady side. The politicians got their cut and he usually walked away with a nice payday. His foreman would have his hand out looking for his cut, and that was okay, because the idiot never even got close to what he was owed.

He wanted to send another text message, but he dropped the phone in the water. The first traces of fumes began to make their way into the bathroom. He needed to extinguish those candles in a hurry, if not, he wasn't going to be around to make his escape. He tried to splash water toward the candles. That worked on the one that was closest to him, but he was unable to get enough slack in his hands to get much momentum to reach the other two candles. He tried to stand up but was only able to get a few inches higher than he was because his ankles seemed to be caught on the floor of the tub. He tried to view what was holding him in place, but he was unable to see because of the amount of blood in the water. He began to feel weak and lightheaded, probably from the loss of blood and hypothermia. If he was unable to get out of this tub soon, he knew his chances of survival were limited at best.

The sound of one of his work vehicles backing down the driveway gave him some form of hope. Jerome was a large black man that had a chip on his shoulder. He was his only hope. The only one he could have called. Thoughts of Jerome standing over him and laughing started to pass through his mind. Hell, Jerome might even take a leak in the tub and leave him to die. Thoughts of having taken advantage of the man started to make him nervous. He should have treated the man better. He vowed to himself that he would, but he knew it was all a lie. What was done was done. He was paying the price for all of it right now.

Jerome was outside, checking out the situation. He saw his boss's truck but little else. The big Dick had sent him a text asking him to come to his place. It was an emergency. Tell no one. It was a hot September day. He was covered in sweat from hours in a ditch putting in drainage pipes with a few other co-workers. They were none too pleased with him when he said he had to go. They thought he was bailing on them. He would have taken any excuse to get out of the sun and grab a little AC in the truck. He texted Richard he was on his way, left his fellow workers to finish up. This would not be the first time his idiot of a boss had gotten himself in a predicament. Jerome was getting tired of bailing his ass out and covering for his misdeeds. If he wasn't in need of all the money that steadily flowed his way, he would tell Dick to go to hell and let the bastard fry.

He had stopped to grab a six-pack, finished two of them by the time he reached his boss's place. He popped the third one and began to look around. The key to the house was hidden inside a false rock in the garden. If you didn't know about the rock, you would never know it was there. He grabbed the key and entered the house. The first thing he noticed was the smell. A propane tank was placed in the center of the room with a regulator that allowed the gas to slowly escape. He turned the gas off. He stood up and grabbed the tank, and walked back outside. He inspected the regulator, decided that he wanted it for himself, removed it, and tossed it into the back of his truck. He placed the propane tank back on the back deck. He looked around to see if he was being observed, and noticing nothing, he walked back inside, closing the door behind him.

The fumes were strong in here. He thought about opening some windows to ventilate the place when he was distracted by a sound from upstairs. He reached into his pants and removed a buck knife. Opening the knife, he ascended the stairs to search the second floor. Finding nothing, he returned to search downstairs. The bedroom door was closed. With his knife in hand, he slowly entered and searched the area. Another door to his left was ajar, and he thought he heard noise from within that space.

When he entered and saw what was within, he nearly fell on the floor laughing. This was the funniest thing he had ever seen. Zipping down his zipper, he had to relieve himself before he pissed his pants. He used the toilet and saw the relief in his boss's eyes.

The same stool that Lori had sat on was now occupied by his foreman. Jerome didn't seem in that much of a hurry to release him from his confines.

"What have you gotten yourself into now Dick? Boy, you sure are a mess. When you texted me, I was grateful to get out of that heat, but it seems I've landed right back in the fire here with you. Would you like to explain?" he chuckled.

"Well, I guess you would if you weren't sucking on that great big fat black dick. I sure hope you don't expect me to replace the fake one with a real one."

Jerome was cracking himself up. He reached into his back pocket and pulled out his smartphone. Looking around the room, he noticed the two burning candles and put them out. He sniffed the air, turned, and opened the door to get a little more ventilation into the bathroom.

"I have just got to get a picture of this for the boys. They are never going to believe this shit."

He put the camera up to his face, centered on Dick's body, and decided it would come out better if he used the flash.

"Now, smile! We want this to be a picture to remember for the rest of your life."

He pressed the button, the flash went off, and he got some real good shots of his boss. He was snapping one after another and was backing up to get a view of the whole room. He reached behind himself to feel for the wall and his hand came close to the doorknob. By opening the door after he had extinguished the candles, he had let in a large amount of gas fumes. A static flash from the doorknob to his finger was all it took. It was the spark that made the place go up in flames.

If Jerome had left the door open to the outside and aired the place out a little, both of them might still be alive. If Jerome hadn't been looking to embarrass his boss, and maybe have a little blackmail photo to go with it, they might have lived. If Richard had asked God for his forgiveness, he might have been saved, but none of that happened. Karma had struck again, and she is such a bitch.

CHAPTER 4

Owen had been on the road for about four hours now. He was almost in Pennsylvania. The mistake of thinking 95 was going to be the fastest route had shot his nerves to hell and back. The DC drivers were completely insane. He had been doing eighty miles per hour and almost been run off the road several times. He decided he would divert from his route and head for the mountains. Dealing with all the tractor trailers on Route 81 was better than all this traffic and massive tolls on 95. He headed around the outskirts of Baltimore, his sights set on Route 83. He almost made it in one piece.

Owen had his eyes fixed ahead of him in four lanes of heavy traffic. It never stopped those idiots who thought they could do ninety miles per hour in heavy traffic. His eyes caught sight of a BMW racing up from behind him. He had a semi to his left, cars to his right and an opening in front of him which the BMW was racing for. In that instant, Owen realized that he was going to get hit. No way was the vehicle going to be able to cut in front of him without hitting something. He hit the brakes hoping to give the car the space it needed. The driver must have realized at the same time it had run out of space and braked hard, swerving into the side of Owen's SUV. If Owen had not panicked and braked hard, the accident might have been avoided, but the same could have been said about the driver speeding in heavy traffic. The BMW careened off the side of Owen's SUV and ended up under the trailer of a semi-truck. The sound of metal bending and glass breaking, along with tires screeching across the pavement was all Owen could hear. He never heard the screams of the BMW driver just before he lost his head.

The police arrived shortly thereafter. Owen's trip had been delayed. His vehicle was not damaged enough that he no longer could drive it, a few dents along the entire driver's side. He was still able to open his door. The BMW was totaled along with its driver. A lawyer was on his way to the hospital where his pregnant mistress was giving birth to his illegitimate son. Owen had not known any of this, but Karma did. The lawyer's wife had a huge life insurance policy on her husband, one that paid double if he died in an accident. She just became a very wealthy woman.

The accident had cost Owen enough time that he decided to get a room for the night before finishing the trip. He was tired and shaken from the day's events. When he checked his cellphone for messages, he found one from the Richmond police. An officer named Mahoney was trying to get ahold of him. He needed to ask him a few questions. Owen returned his call trying to figure out why the Richmond Police would want to talk to him and ask him questions. He found out just what this was all about.

"This is Owen Canton. I'm returning your call," Owen said nervously.

Mahoney paused for a minute, asked him to hold on as he puffed on a butt while looking through his paperwork.

"I wanted to ask you some questions about your neighbor, a Mr. Richard Ekhart. Do you know if he had any enemies and did you see anything suspicious at his house today before you left for your trip?"

It was a simple question, one that Owen wasn't sure why it was being asked. He thought he would answer with a question of his own.

"Has anything happened to Ekhart? I'm not sure about enemies, but the only thing I saw at his house today was a lady who does window and home design. He came home early so she could measure his windows. I left before she did," Owen rambled on in an apprehensive manner.

Mahoney let Owen wait long enough that he called out over the phone, "Are you still there?" Mahoney answered that he was, he was just checking something out on his computer.

"We checked out the lady, she is clean. You might want to call her. I'm sure you're going to need some new window treatments yourself," he chuckled.

"What do you mean by that?" Owen inquired.

"The explosion across the street from your house did some damage. You might want to contact your insurance company, maybe a contractor to get some plywood to cover the windows until you can get them replaced," Mahoney said nonchalantly.

Owen had many questions for Mahoney after that. He was quite excited about what had transpired after he left. Mahoney answered that it was an ongoing investigation, nobody was ruled out just yet, that included Owen himself. This perturbed Owen to the point that he raised his voice, maybe cussed a few times. He was concerned for the girl, Lori. He thanked Mahoney and apologized for his gruff manner over the phone, made the excuse that it had been one of those days. He hung up and immediately called Lori. She sounded like he had just woken her up. He stared up at the clock, it wasn't even ten in the evening yet. Maybe she went to bed early and was an early morning riser.

"Hi, it's Owen Canton. Sorry if I woke you up. I heard there was an accident at the Ekhart house, and I wanted to make sure that you hadn't been injured in the explosion."

"Well, I appreciate your concern, and as you can hear over the phone, I'm alive and well. Has something happened that I should know about?" she asked this as if she hadn't known what had taken place that day.

Owen went on to explain and give her the details. Lori seemed genuinely oblivious to what had taken place, you never would have known that she had orchestrated the whole day from talking to her.

They talked for nearly half an hour. It was Lori's plan. Get Owen to trust her. Soon he would invite her to come live with him. She just had to bide her time. With a big smile on her face, she hung up. Another call was made, this one to another person on her long list of subjects to be dealt with.

"He is on his way, Andy. I hope you get your revenge. Once you do, come visit me. I'll show you the time of your life," she giggled as she hung up.

The plan was all coming together, she was such a troublemaker. Andy was just a pawn in the game. He never realized he was. He just wasted his life away after Owen had stolen his one true love. Alcohol abuse along with a drug addiction had ruined a once promising mind. Now he spent his days vowing revenge on the one man that had ruined his life. If he had looked in the mirror, he would have seen it was the reflection in the mirror that was responsible, but he needed someone else to blame, and that man was Owen Canton.

Karma had been his doctor several months prior, told him of his terminal cancer and how much time he had remaining in his life. She even told him where he could find his one true love, trying to get him to reminisce and maybe pay her a visit before he died. He went to Richmond in search of her and in a drunken haze, he had run her off the road and put a bullet in her head. Andy then fled back to New York where he hoped the authorities would not track him down and arrest him. He would give it a few months, then return and finish off Owen. He wanted Owen to suffer first, know what it was like to be heartbroken when the love of your life was stolen from you.

Karma couldn't let Andy return to Richmond, so she sent Owen to him. It was all part of the plan to reform Owen, get him to see the light. She knew Andy would try to kill him when he returned to his hometown, especially with her encouragement. With a smile on her face, she reached down and pulled the covers over her head. The real Lori was pitching a fit inside her head. The plan was revealed to her and that seemed to calm her down, or so she thought. A thousand what-ifs emanated from her mind to the point she had to get up and take a sleeping pill. It was extremely difficult to explain to someone who didn't understand how the universe worked, how the universe did indeed work. All she did was set the stage. What happened after that was all in God's hands.

Owen was also restless. After talking with Lori, he called his insurance company and told them he was out of town and what had taken place in his neighborhood. They ensured him that they would send out a contractor to board up the broken windows along with an insurance assessor. His claim would be handled, there was nothing for him to worry about. He thanked them and tried to lie down to get some sleep. His sleep was met with a variety of nightmares, each one more intense than the previous. He kept seeing his father stumble around the railroad tracks fighting off some perceived demons. The nightmares were so intense that he would wake up in a cold sweat. Then he would get up and stumble around the hotel room, use the bathroom, and pace around some more. He didn't know who or what to turn to. He wasn't a true believer in a higher power, for that surely would have helped if he could have prayed to his God. Instead, he turned to himself, tried to talk it out, and reason what was happening to him. This was a dead end. No answers were forthcoming.

He tried to sleep once again, but the nightmares returned. In frustration, he showered and got an early start on his trip north. The sun had not risen yet, his stomach was empty and protesting, and his eyes felt like lead weights. After a couple of near misses with some semis, he decided it might be a good idea to get some coffee and something to quiet his growling stomach. A truck stop was just ahead at the next exit, it had a diner that was open twenty-four seven – a good place to grab something.

As he was slowing down to take the exit, a tractor trailer blew by him, startling him. He glanced up just in time to see a buck bolt from the woods trying to cross the highway. The truck sent the deer airborne. The deer sailed through the air in slow motion straight towards Owen. His eyes bulged open as wide as they could get as the deer landed right on top of his hood. Owen sat transfixed, staring into the deer's lifeless eyes staring right back at him through the windshield as he skimmed off the guardrail, putting a fresh set of dents on the passenger side of the SUV.

He slammed on his brakes and got the vehicle back under control and somehow managed to get it stopped along the side of the highway. Another vehicle pulled over to assist him. Two men exited the car and began to make jokes as Owen examined all the fresh damage to his SUV. They were not trying to be mean-spirited. They meant no harm. They were just trying to calm Owen down. Owen was in a place in his mind that was unable to perceive it that way, and he lashed out at the men that were just there to offer some help and make sure he was okay.

Perturbed with his attitude, they pulled the buck off the hood of his SUV and loaded it into the back of their pickup truck saying it would be a shame to waste such a beautiful animal. They would put the beast to good use.

Owen waved as the men tore off down the highway. His focus was centered more on his SUV, as each mile toward his destination seemed to be taking on more and more damage. He determined that he could still make it the rest of the way. His intentions were to get his father buried, investigate what truly happened to him, and return to Richmond as soon as possible. His book deadline was quickly approaching and if he didn't have a manuscript to present to the publisher soon, he might not have a publisher to give the next manuscript.

Shaking his head, he got back into the SUV, started it back up, and headed for the next exit. The diner was just off the exit and to the right. He needed to get some caffeine into his body and get his mind straight. Some food and coffee just might be what the doctor ordered.

His vehicle was a mess, he was a mess. Something was trying to prevent him from going home. He could feel it in his bones. He told himself to turn around and return to Richmond, but he never listened to common sense. Stubborn in his ways, he trudged on. First coffee and food, then on to New York, where fate awaited his return.

CHAPTER 5

Karma was busy getting things prepared for Owen's return. Lori was going to be the perfect person for this job. She just had to find a way to be able to manipulate her and keep her under control. She didn't need Lori blurting out all the juicy details of what was about to happen to him.

Karma decided to let Lori have a little freedom and be herself while she remained hidden in the background. The first thing was to explain how Lori had suddenly become free of the diabetes that had once ruled over her life. Karma had a plan.

"Lori, I know how much you love Christian music. I found a church that has this band that I know you are just going to love. Try not to pay too much attention to the pastor there. He thinks of himself as a want-to-be comedian, but he has a good heart. If you don't want the diabetes to come back after I leave you, then you must do this for me. Do you think you can do this for me?" Karma said inside of Lori's head.

Lori sat in her chair petting her cat. He was a stray that had adopted her many years ago. It started as a simple handout of some tuna, followed by Lori buying some cat food. Soon the tomcat was at her door every day and would sit in her window meowing loudly until she got up and put some food out for him. Once winter got there, she opened the door on a cold day and the cat rushed inside. He never left.

Now he was part of her life. When Karma controlled her body, the cat didn't want anything to do with her, but now that Lori had control back, the cat was back in his favorite place, in her lap. Lori liked this situation. It felt like she was getting back to normal. It was one of the things that help persuade her to do Karma's bidding.

"What do I have to do?" Lori inquired to the spirit that resided in her head.

"I want you to go to the church and ask the Pastor to heal you. He will refuse, but the man who leads the band will offer to help you. His name is Peter. He might have his three children with him, if he does, all the better. Once he heals you, you will be free from this disease for the remainder of your life. Should be a piece of cake," Karma lied confidently.

"Will I live long enough to enjoy this newfound freedom once you depart from my body, or will you leave me in disarray? Or even on my deathbed or possibly in a jail cell doing time for murder?" Lori had serious concerns and they were well-founded.

"Come on Lori, would I do that to you? Seriously, I have only your best interest at heart," she said while pondering just how she would leave this sweet girl. Her fears could very well turn out as she perceived them. Karma would have to be careful about how she did things.

"I'll give you the rest of the day to yourself, I have things to tend to. If you need me, I'll be right here."

She laughed. Lori was not amused.

"Thanks for letting me be myself for a day. What church is it that you want me to go to?" Lori inquired.

Karma gave her the address and told her to go tomorrow. They would be there practicing for a concert that they were about to perform for the President of the United States.

"Have fun and be sincere. I promise you this is going to work out. You will see. Trust me." The words of a car salesman trying to get some sap to buy a junk car and say it's a wonderful and dependable car.

Lori worked around her house doing some chores that Karma had refused to do herself, like clean the toilets and wash the bathroom floor. She put all the dirty dishes in the dishwasher and got that started, grabbed a duster, and worked in the living room dusting all the places dust liked to accumulate in there and the dining room. Once finished, she grabbed her car keys and headed out. Karma observed from a distance. She wanted to see what Lori was up to.

Lori headed for downtown, parked, and began to walk into the heart of Shockoe Bottom. She headed straight for the Hot Stuff Restaurant and ordered an open-faced chicken sandwich. She ordered it to-go and made her way across the street, past the farmers market and over to an area where a canopy was set up with some picnic tables. Once in place, she ate and waited.

This place was infested with snakes, and not the kind that slither around eating mice, no. These were the tattooed kind that fed on innocent people that ate alone and seemed to be helpless, just like Lori was presenting herself. It didn't take long for one to find her, a girl that was as pretty as she was didn't have to wait long for any kind of attention.

Karma realized what Lori had done a bit too late to prevent her from doing it, the sly little bitch had gotten one over on her. Now she was going to have to deal with three assholes determined to get themselves a piece of ass and they may or may not let her live. Karma needed her alive and well. She took back control as the men approached.

"Hey, little lady, what brings you to this part of town? I bet you it was me," he laughed and his cohorts laughed along with him, arguing it was them that she had come to town for.

Karma knew this to be true. The little bitch knew this was going to happen. The pink crop top, the short white shorts, and white running shoes, her hair tied back in a high ponytail. It all made her a very inviting dish on this hot September day.

"Hello boys! Looking for a little fun? Well if you are, you came to the right place."

This got the idiots all worked up with a fresh round of laughter as they anticipated an afternoon of fun, which Karma was about to dish out. She took another seductive bite of her sandwich, licked her lips.

"This is so good," she exclaimed. "Maybe you boys should go get yourselves one and join me for some lunch."

One of the braver assholes utters, "We'll just have some of yours."

He reaches for the sandwich to pull it from Karma's hand and gets his first big surprise. He realized way too late that he was playing with the wrong prey. The sound of his wrist snapping was the first thing his two friends heard. The foot to the head was the next thing one man saw as the other was bent over, holding on to what was left of his junk. The speed in which it happened was incredible. Unless you had been watching, you never would have seen what happened. Three gangbangers were now lying on the ground in severe pain, wondering what the hell had just happened to them as they watched this not-so-innocent girl walk away.

Karma could hear Lori in her head yelling that she was a badass now. Lori sounded extremely excited about this. Karma began to wonder if this might not have been a trip to exact a little revenge on some people that might have taken advantage of Lori in the past. Yet another thing she was going to have to be careful of. Sharing a body was beginning to become complicated. Ryan was right, wait for the soul to leave the body, then take control. It was much simpler that way. Too late for that now. She would just have to deal with it until it was time to move on.

Karma got Lori back to her car and gave her back control.

"Don't ever do something reckless like that again, do you understand me?!" she shouted to herself making it look like she was crazy to anybody that might have been strolling by.

Her door flew open and a very large bearded man sat down beside her. Karma felt the whole car tilt toward the passenger side. Lori just gasped, reaching for mace that she wasn't carrying in her purse.

"Calm down, I won't hurt you," said the bearded man. "I wanted to tell you I saw what happened and I just wanted to meet you."

He put his hand out and introduced himself.

"I'm a pastor at a church on the other side of town, name's R.J. Ted. May I ask what is your name young lady?"

Lori didn't know what to say. She was looking for Karma to come to her aid. Karma was nowhere to be found at this moment.

"My name is Lori Stenville. I just came to get some lunch when those jerks tried to assault me," she stuttered out.

"I was running to help you out, but you had the situation under control before I made it more than two steps. That was some amazing shit I might add. You trained in martial arts?" R.J. inquired.

Lori never had any training in anything other than ballet and track. She was the furthest thing from a fighter. What Karma had done to those men had sent a thrill through her body. She felt a power in her she never knew existed.

R.J. waited for an answer that wasn't coming. Lori didn't know what to say to the man, so she remained quiet, shaking slightly from the adrenaline rush. He just stared at her, making her uncomfortable.

"I don't know who you are or why you're in my car, but I would like to leave now. Can you please leave so that I can do that?" she asked in a pleading way.

"I'm sorry if I've frightened you. I just wanted you to know that I was amazed by your fighting abilities and wanted to let you know that if you wanted, you could join a group of my friends that are fighting evil in this world. We would love to have you join us. It's a never-ending battle, but we are making headway, this I can assure you. Let me pray for you and then I'll leave, would that be alright with you?"

Lori shook her head that it was alright. R.J. prayed and made her laugh out loud. He was so funny. She just had to know.

"Are you having a rehearsal tomorrow at your church for some upcoming concert?"

"Why, yes, I am, how did you know?" R.J. asked, fascinated.

"I need more than just your prayers. I'll be there by tomorrow, I promise. Now, get the hell out of my car before you break it!" she said jokingly.

As R.J. removed himself from her car, making it creak back into a horizontal position, she thought it might not have been a joke at all. The guy was huge. The car was grateful, and Lori had a big smile on her face. She was going to be healed and she was going to do everything possible to stay alive and not let Karma ruin her life. She began to formulate her plan.

CHAPTER 6

Owen was back on the road headed for New York. His belly was full, and his mind was wired with several cups of coffee. The first thing he wanted to do was stop at the railyard in Selkirk and talk to an old classmate that had gone to work for the railroad. His friend had done well for himself and was now in management. He thought he was a trainmaster now, or some title close to that. He searched his memory, but it was coming up with nothing. He thought he should have tried to keep a closer relationship with his old classmates, but time and distance have a way of making that complicated. His only connection over the last ten years was Facebook. His schedule hadn't allowed him to spend all his time keeping up with what was going on back home. He hoped his old friend would understand.

His GPS said he was only about half an hour out when the call of nature from all that coffee made him search for a place where he could relieve himself. He found a gas station that had a restroom and a convenience store. It would be perfect. He could take care of his business and grab a few things for the road. He found a spot on the side of the store and entered. A cheerful woman welcomed him to the store. She seemed to be close to her fifties but still had some of that youthful vibrance in her demeanor. He asked where the restrooms were located. She smiled and pointed him in the right direction. It felt to him like she might have been checking him out as he proceeded to the back of the store. He was currently the only customer she had.

He was at the sink cleaning his hands when he heard a ruckus coming from the front of the store. The friendly woman was screaming, and he thought he might have heard a slap or two before another scream of pain reached his location in the safety of the restroom. The day he was having might have been what caused him to do the next stupid thing he did. He exited the restroom with a chip on his shoulder and an ax to grind.

The first thing he saw was what looked like a drug-addicted youth holding a gun to the woman's head, demanding she open the cash register. He told her she was going to open the safe because he knew damn well yesterday's receipts had not been picked up yet. The lady was not being cooperative, and this was making the youth violent. Maybe she thought Owen would come to her rescue, or maybe she was just wired that way, feisty and ready for a good fight. Either way he looked at it, something was needed to be done.

He slithered to a spot where he could get a better look without compromising his cover. A quick search for a weapon revealed that he was down to throwing some candy bars at the guy, maybe hit him over the head with a bag of Ruffles. It was futile. No weapon was to be found. He opened a bag of Skittles and improvised. When you have nothing to work with, work with what you have. He had Skittles.

"Let her go asshole!" Owen announced in a forceful voice, his hand full of the candy.

The young punk looked over at him and laughed. Owen didn't look or appear to be a threat. He was just an average built middle-aged man. No scars or threatening tattoos, nothing that said he was a badass and you better beware if he came after you. He put the gun firmly to the lady's head and announced he would blow her brains all over the store if he didn't back off. It was too late. Owen had already committed to his game plan. He kept right on walking toward the punk with determination in his stride.

With a nervous look on the youth's face, he once again warned he would kill the bitch. Owen was waiting for the gun to be pointed in his direction. The closer he got to the man, the more convinced he would do just that. He got his wish.

The punk pointed the gun at him, Owen launched the handful of Skittles and dove for cover. A deafening shot rang out, nearly hitting Owen as he sprang up from his duck and cover and threw a roundhouse punch that connected with the punk's chin. Owen watched in horror as the man's eyes rolled up in his head and he fell to the ground. Owen was expecting to have to wrestle the young man and try to disarm him. He never in a million years thought his punch would knock the little bastard into next week.

The cashier was quick to grab some zip ties from the rear of the store and secure the punk's hands and legs. She kept giving Owen grateful looks as she worked. Her hair was slightly ruffled, and she had a couple of red splotches on her face where she had taken a couple of the slaps, but other than that, she was in good shape. Owen grabbed the gun and gave it to her, his next big mistake of the day. She took it from him and slapped the punk a couple of times to try to revive him. The woman got right into the punk's face, looking him right in his haze-filled eyes.

"Not so tough anymore now are you, pussy?" she waved the gun in his face threatening to kill the young man.

"I should put a bullet in your drug-filled brain and claim it was self-defense. My friend here will back me up. Won't you mister?" She said this as she turned to Owen to verify that he would indeed back her up. Owen thought he had just made a bad situation even worse by handing the gun to this crazy hate-filled woman.

"Why don't we call the authorities and let calmer heads prevail. Miss, please give me the gun," Owen requested.

"Are you insane? This punk will be back on the street before you get to wherever you're going to! Come back here and finish the job. We finish this bastard off now with some old-fashioned country justice."

She pointed the gun at the young punk and prepared to fire the weapon. Owen hit her hand as she pulled the trigger and the bullet ended up on the floor beside the young punk. The youth was so scared he pissed his pants.

The gun came up and now was pointed right at Owen.

"Mister, if I were you, I would mind my own business. If you don't want to be a part of this, then I suggest you get your ass out that door right now, because this is going to happen. I can't have these criminals coming in here and threatening my life and business. You know what I mean. This guy will be the message to all those punks that this is not an easy target, and I'll thrive here in this location once the message is sent."

Owen was sure she was serious, but what could he do? She had the gun and the power. He wasn't going to try to take the gun away from her. The woman had been through so much already today. He walked out the door to the screams of the youth that was tied up and sitting on the floor.

"Help me Mister, please! Help me!" was the last thing Owen heard just before the shot rang out as he was driving away.

He sure hoped she wiped his prints off the gun, for he knew without a shadow of a doubt he would have some officers visiting his home in due time wanting to know why his fingerprints were on a murder weapon. He contemplated calling the cops. Tell them what had happened, but in his heart, he knew she was right. The justice system was a joke. These criminals were running rough shots throughout the country. Maybe a little country justice was what the doctor ordered.

Trying to get your head right after that was not an easy task. He was still deep in thought when he pulled into the railyard. The local news had a story about a store off the highway where a young man had been shot while trying to commit a robbery. The store manager had fought the assailant and was able to wrestle the weapon free, but it had discharged and fatally wounded the assailant. They made her out to be a hero, but Owen knew she was a murderer. It made his stomach turn, and he bent over thinking he might lose all his breakfast. The feeling passed, thankfully.

Owen went inside the office and asked where he might be able to find his old classmate. A male clerk made a call and directed Owen to an empty office. It would only be a few minutes before his friend arrived.

He was served coffee and asked if he might want a Danish, as they had a few leftovers from the morning. Owen declined, thanked the clerk for looking out for him. His stomach would not have been able to handle it. The coffee was just making his indigestion worse. He left it on the desk unfinished.

Wade Smith came walking in a few minutes later and gave Owen a big hug. He was truly excited to be reunited with his old friend from school who had become a successful writer. They talked about some old classmates that had met with one tragedy or another. Wade said he was sorry to hear about his father and after some small talk they got down to why Owen had made this visit.

"I know there are cameras on all the locomotives. I was wondering if you could show me the video from the locomotive that killed my dad."

Wade made a whistling noise, raised his eyebrows.

"Are you positive you want to see that video? These things are disturbing to me when I have got to watch them. Not sure what it would do to a family member to watch his own dad get spattered by a train. Maybe you should think about this before you take on investigating your father's death."

"I'm positive my dad would never commit suicide. I need to see the video to confirm this. Something else had to be going on. Wade, I beg of you, let me see what happened so that I can have some peace. If he committed suicide, I need to know that was indeed what happened."

Wade paced the room trying to decide what he was going to do for his old friend. He walked out of the office and left Owen alone, never saying where he was going or if he was coming back. A few minutes later he heard some shouting and a few cuss words. Owen was sure something had been thrown across the room. More noise could be heard, yet Owen sat patiently waiting. He was done interfering in any situation, just look what it got him just this morning. His stomach did a few more flips. He was in desperate need of some Tums, or something that would help quiet the acid that was destroying his insides.

Wade walked back into the office with a laptop in his hands, his brow covered in sweat, his face flushed. He grabbed a radio from a recharging stand and motioned Owen to follow him.

Once outside, they climbed into a company vehicle and sped out of the railyard. Wade remained silent all the way, Owen just sat there and kept quiet. He figured Wade had stepped on a few toes to get what he requested, and he didn't want Wade to have second thoughts on what they were about to do. He had been made to watch the execution of his wife because the police needed to know if he could identify the man. The viewing of his father's death was a completely different story. Owen didn't need to do this. He wanted to do it so he could understand what had happened to his dad in his final minutes. Both videos would leave their own mark, but Owen knew he had to do it. Something just wasn't right, and he needed to get to the bottom of it.

They drove into town and Wade found a diner that had a liquor license. He needed a beer and he was sure Owen was going to need one after viewing this video. They walked in and grabbed a seat further in the back, away from the view of the street.

Wade didn't need anyone to see him drinking while he was on duty. These railroaders would snitch on a trainmaster in a heartbeat for retribution for all the things trainmasters would do to them. Wade was just doing his job with all the tests he would have to perform on the guys, but they would think it was just harassment, which occasionally it was. The pressure the company put on these management guys to get failures was intense. If an accident happened, it got even worse. The company would go back and start to see if the trainmasters were doing a proper job, writing up guys for stupid little knit-picking violations, keeping the employees on their toes. It was all a game that everyone had to play. No one could follow the rules one hundred percent. The job would never be completed if they did, everyone knew this, so the game was played between management and employees, with neither of them ever winning.

Wade opened the laptop as he took a big pull of the draft the waitress had just placed on the table. Owen looked on at him in amazement. He was having a hard time believing Wade would drink while on duty. The draft in front of him was beginning to sweat, and it sure did look inviting. After a few minutes of waiting for Wade to find the video, it was too much for Owen to handle and he grabbed the mug and downed it. He called over to the waitress to bring another round. Wade looked up, raised an eyebrow, but continued to search the laptop. He found what they were looking for when the second round of beers arrived.

Owen watched the train move down the track at about forty miles per hour. Track speed at that location was forty-five according to Wade. It rounded a curve and there was his father running from something. Owen watched as his father kept looking over his shoulder as if he were being chased. He was sure his father never saw the train because he was shouting at somebody over his shoulder and wasn't looking as the train rounded the curve.

This was clearly not a suicide as Owen had deduced. His father was trying to escape some threat or person. He was literally running for his life! The threat hadn't gotten him, the train did. Whoever it was, won the day. They had killed someone without actually doing it themselves. Why hadn't the cops come to the same conclusion as he had? It was like the lady at the store said. The system was a joke, you needed country justice to make things right.

Owen grabbed his beer and finished it. Wade patted him on the back and ordered another round. When they finally got up to leave, the table was covered in empty mugs. Wade was going to have to keep a low profile for the remainder of the day. He needed to go someplace and sleep it off. Owen's vehicle was at the railyard. It was going to be a while before he was going to get to continue his trip. His father's funeral was the next day, and this trip hadn't been the fastest or smoothest he had ever taken. He was just several hours away from his old home. It wouldn't hurt to hide out with Wade and let him sober up. This is what he told himself as he tried to work out just what demon his father was fleeing from. He would arrive at his old house later that night. His brother and mother would be patiently awaiting his arrival. So many questions bombarded his mind as he waited for his old friend to wake up. This trip had been a nightmare in the making. He was going to be so thankful when he would finally be able to return to his home in Richmond. He looked forward to the peace and quiet he surely missed. His only fear was that he had enough aspirin to deal with his brother and mother. Together, they could be quite a handful.

Several hours later, Owen was driving the company truck back into the railyard. He was running out of time and his friend was just about sober enough to sneak back into the railyard so the two of them could make a clean getaway. If everything had gone as planned, no one would have been the wiser, but Karma had an eye on Owen now. And when Karma has you in her sights, watch out, and that's exactly what Wade screamed just before the company vehicle was struck by an RCO conductor operating a locomotive that was running through the yard.

Owen wasn't even near a track, and still they were struck. The locomotive had derailed. A distracted RCO conductor wondered who the new guy was, driving the company vehicle through the railyard. He was concerned that he might be getting set up for some test or worst yet, they were trying to get him for something he had done previously. He was so distracted he missed lining the switch for his intended route and ran through the split rail that protected this portion of the track and yard. The locomotive just kept going and derailed just like the split rail was designed to do. The conductor was launched through the air right into the company vehicle that he was so concerned about.

Wade was infuriated with the conductor and his bad luck. He saw his whole career going up in smoke. No good deed goes unpunished, he thought as he gripped the conductor by the neck, squeezing with all his might. The damage to the truck was minimal, but the damage Wade was doing to his career was severe. Owen had to do something before Wade killed the conductor.

"Get back in the truck Wade. I'll take care of this one," Owen said as he grabbed Wade by the shoulder and pulled him off the frightened conductor. He had to pry Wade's hands off the poor man's throat, and physically force Wade back into the truck. Owen turned to the conductor. The man was frightened, yes, but he also was very pissed off now and wanted a piece of his boss. Owen had to pretend he was somebody that the conductor might fear. Someone that could cost everyone their jobs if they didn't shut up and listen.

"I will deal with this trainmaster. After I'm done with him, I want a written statement from you as to why you tried to kill me," Owen pointed at the derailed locomotive.

"This is totally unacceptable. This never should happen. None of this should have happened today. If you want to keep your job, then you better figure out a way to get this thing back on the rail before I get back!" Owen was putting on his best performance he could muster under the circumstances.

The conductor was calming down, and he began to understand the situation. He was being given a way out, one in which he might not get fired. He rushed up to the cab of the locomotive and grabbed the radio, and made a few calls to some friends in the car department. He asked them to bring some re-railers. They needed to cover up another derailment.

Owen heard all this conversation on the radio in the truck. Wade heard it as well. He slammed his fist into the dashboard and cussed, wiping the spittle from his chin. He looked over at Owen.

"What kind of black voodoo have you brought upon us, Owen? I think you should leave before this whole thing gets completely out of control. I'm sorry for the loss of your father and the incompetence of the police. I sure hope you find what you're looking for, but I've done all I can do for you."

He patted Owen on the shoulder and asked him to leave his damn railyard and never come back.

Owen had to agree with him as he jumped into his SUV and sped away from the railyard. One look at his vehicle was all you had to see to know that Owen's life was in complete shambles. There wasn't a minute of the day he wasn't dealing with another problem or mishap. It wasn't going to get any better either. He was on his way to his childhood home – the place he had fled from so many years ago. The place where there was no peace and quiet. His mother and brother fought constantly. His father always stood up for his brother, and his mother would stand up for him. Always, someone was bickering and complaining about the other. Owen didn't have the best relationship with his brother. Ten years is a lot between a sibling, and he felt they never really connected. His brother's disability only complicated things further.

Owen took a deep breath just before he drove down the street that led to his childhood home. He took another deep breath as he walked up to the door, and yet another when he rang the bell. The door opened and it began.

His brother Todd hadn't seen him in a few years. Owen had been making excuses as to why he was unable to return to New York. Some of them were made up, and some were true. The fact that his wife couldn't stand to be around them might have been a factor in his decision to stay away. Maybe it was just another excuse he was using to keep from getting this kind of welcome.

The door flew open and Owen ended up on his back with his brother on top of him. His brother wasn't exactly a small person. Intellectually disabled didn't mean he was physically disabled. His brother's sheer size was much greater than Owen's. His brother had to outweigh him by at least fifty pounds, and we're not talking fat pounds. Todd was all muscle. Something he did to himself to prevent the bullies from picking on him.

Owen fought off his brother's excitement the best he could. It was like dealing with an excited St. Bernard. He even thought his brother might be licking his neck and face.

"Stop it, Todd. I'm excited to see you as well. Can you please let me up?" Owen pleaded with his brother.

If his brother didn't want to let him get back to his feet, he knew he wasn't going to be able to force him. Owen tried to remain calm and keep his patience. Several minutes later, his brother helped him to his feet and ran through the house loudly announcing that his dear brother had finally come home. He watched him run the entirety of the house, open the back door, get into his Ford pickup truck, and speed away. He was honking his horn and screaming out the window that his brother was home for all the neighbors to hear.

His mother was in her usual place; in her rocking chair staring out the window at the awesome view the Adirondack mountains provided. She never got up. She just called him over to her side.

"I'm so glad you finally came home to visit. I would come to see you, but I've grown much too old to travel anymore these days. You could at least call your poor mother once a week."

Owen apologized to his mother. He told her he would try to do better.

"I know you're a busy man and all, but family is very important. Speaking of which, I would like you to take that crazy son of a bitch with you back to Virginia. You see what I have got to put up with, and now that your father is gone, God rest his soul, your brother has been completely out of control. Just look at how he acted with you today."

His mother was practically begging him to take his brother back with him. If Owen had his way, that was never going to happen. He loved his brother, but to deal with him on a daily basis, now that was too much for him to handle. He wanted to explain this to his mother, but now was not the time.

"The funeral is not until tomorrow afternoon now. It got pushed back because some big-shot politician in the area met his demise with a moose. Now the jackass gets the morning service and we're pushed back to the afternoon. Why couldn't that asshole be given the open spot in the afternoon and leave our service as is? I can't stand the way the system works for these rich criminals."

His mother was hot, and not a pinch of sympathy was going out toward the politician she was furious with. Owen had to laugh to himself that his mother referred to the politicians as criminals. He thought his mother had always been out of place here in New York, seeing that she was a right-winger and she lived in the land of the left. He let her vent, listening half-heartedly.

Owen had pulled up a chair and was chatting with his mother for almost an hour when his brother finally returned. Todd looked at his brother and waved, but never even thought about coming into the room where his mother was seated. The feud between the two of them must really be contentious if his brother wouldn't even come into the same room with her. Yet another problem Owen would have to deal with before he departed.

Owen was getting hungry, so he offered to make supper for all of them. His mother wished him luck with that. When he opened the refrigerator, he knew exactly what she meant with that comment. The freezer was just about bare, and the lower section wasn't looking any better. He would have to do some shopping, he mumbled out loud to himself. His brother couldn't have thought of a better idea and dragged him out to his truck and offered to drive him to the market.

His brother's disability was a strange one. Intellectually he was slow, his speech was slow, his behavior could be outright bizarre, yet there seemed at times when his brother was the smartest person in the room. It was like a bridge that had collapsed and most of the information on the other side was unable to get across, but some of it were able to make it and come out on the other side in bits and pieces. His brother could function like a normal person, but he just had a hard time communicating with people and getting his message across. Often, Owen felt sorry for his brother, wished that there were some sort of cure or medicine his brother could take. In the end, he knew it was futile. His brother would always be the way he is, and Owen grew to accept that, at least he thought he had. His frustration with his brother would come out whenever they were together for more than a few minutes. Todd wasn't the easiest person to be around. There were times when he would fly off the handle, yelling and screaming at the slightest provocation. Other times he could have bullies in his face threatening to kill him and he would just smile and laugh and think they were joking with him. The signals from his brain were muddled and often sent the wrong message, causing Todd's strange behavior.

The ride to the market had Owen sitting on the edge of his seat. Todd drove a parts truck for some automotive company, so he knew his brother had logged thousands of miles since he first got his license, but today he swore his brother had gotten it from a Cracker Jack box. When they arrived at the market, Owen quickly jumped out of the truck and cussed his brother out. Todd just stood there bewildered at what his brother's problem was. He knew he hadn't hit anything along the way. Confused, he followed his brother into the market and immediately began to look for all his favorite foods. He had a craving for a peanut butter and banana sandwich.

As the two of them walked down the aisles, Todd would put things in the basket and Owen would put them back on the shelf. This went on for almost twenty minutes and after a major temper tantrum, Todd was able to refill the basket with the items that he had originally put in it. Owen was searching the pharmacy aisle for some extra strength Excedrin. He knew he was going to need it.

His brother was now insisting that they go fishing in the morning before the funeral. He knew all the best spots and assured Owen they would be back in time for the service. Owen was thinking this was a major bad idea, but his brother was so excited to have him back in town that he felt he owed it to his brother to give him some of his time. Explaining this to his mother was going to be the reason for the headache medicine, so he grabbed a second bottle.

His mother had a knack for being a bigger pain than his brother. He already longed to be back on the road to Virginia, at least there he knew all his problems could be dealt with in a calm and reasonable matter. Here in New York, it was always filled with mayhem and chaos which were difficult, if not impossible to deal with. He downed the first two pills and prepared himself for the fight that he knew was to come. His mother was going to be so thrilled when he told her what his plans for the morning were going to be. Now all he had to do was get back to the house in one piece with the way his brother was driving.

Owen closed his eyes, gripped the door handle tightly in his hand, and silently prayed to a God that he had given up on recently in the past. No God would do these things to a person, like the events that were taking place in his life at this moment. He had once heard that God wouldn't burden you with more than you could handle, but Owen felt he was way past that point. What Owen didn't know was, God gives you these burdens to make you stronger, and Owen was about to get very strong – very strong indeed.

CHAPTER 7

Lori found the church she was looking for. It looked more like a warehouse than a church, but it had a large sign out by the street saying this was indeed the place she had been searching for. Upon entering the front door, she was greeted by a receptionist who informed her where she would be able to find Pastor Ted. He was out in the sanctuary working with a youth group. Lori looked in the direction the receptionist pointed and thought she heard the bouncing of a basketball. Confused, she entered through the door to find a large room bigger than the size of a basketball court with a stage at one end, and rows of bleachers along the sides of the wall. She looked at her feet and saw the floor was a multi-sport court good for playing all kinds of sports. Right now, the pastor was in the middle of a game of basketball with some black teenagers. They were tall and skinny, and he was broad and bulky. He was also the only white person on the court. She guessed this was his way of working with the youth of the city, playing basketball with them. In her mind, she was trying to figure out how playing basketball was teaching them anything about God.

R.J. noticed her about the same time one of the teens went and dunked on him. R.J. took a face full of basketball shorts as the two of them crashed to the ground. Lori could hear him yelling about some offensive foul as the other boys whooped, hollered, and razed him about getting dunked on. Lori was in tears with the way they carried on and gave each other a hard time. The one-liners R.J. came up with had all the boys in stitches, and Lori had to find a seat before she fell to her knees from laughing so hard. It got R.J.'s attention and he begged off from the boys to tend to her. This got him some more razing and a round of wolf whistles. He just waved them off; he had business to attend to.

"What may I ask do I owe the pleasure of your company today, my young lady?"

He grasped her hand in his big paw and greeted her like she was royalty. Lori blushed slightly, but she got right down to business.

"Do you believe in healing? I'm in need of the Lord's healing touch. I was wondering if you could pray for me and ask the Lord to heal me."

This got R.J. to raise an eyebrow.

"The Lord works in mysterious ways, my child. Sometimes, he shines a light on you and heals your mind and body. Other times people feel like he abandoned them and left them to wither away and perish. There is no telling what he has in store for each of us. I can't say to you with complete confidence what the Lord has planned for you. All I can do is pray over you and hope he takes pity on your soul and works his wonders within you."

He stared into Lori's tear-filled eyes as he gave her this speech, his own thoughts wondering what this poor girl could possibly want to have healed. He thought maybe she might have a terminal illness or something else that she felt desperate enough to come to him asking to be saved.

"What exactly would you want the Lord to heal you of? You appear to be in great physical shape and your mind seems sound to me," R.J. inquired of her.

Lori responded with an outburst of tears. It took her a few minutes and R.J. gave her all the time she needed. Finally, Lori was able to reveal why she came here today. R.J. took it all in and denoted that this may be more mental than physical. He might be able to work with that. The craziness she was toting about a spirit named Karma and how her mind and body had been invaded. How she had been on her deathbed with uncontrollable diabetes and now didn't need a single shot of insulin. R.J. listened and the more she went on, the more he felt he would never be able to help this poor child.

"Wow, that is quite a tale. How is it that this spirit allowed you to come and visit me today? If you say as you do that this spirit has taken over your body and mind, why would it allow you to come and seek to be freed from it?" R.J. was trying to be sympathetic, but he was having trouble with her story. Then she explained.

"Karma has another one that has her distracted right now. She told me he will be a major player in some war that is going on in the world right now. You might know him. His name is Owen Canton."

R.J. was convinced she was going to say Joey Hopkins, and when she didn't, he let out a big sigh of relief. R.J. didn't think he could deal with Joey battling Karma to death. His eyes fixated on the wall where the bullets had penetrated during his last super bash. He blamed Joey for all that chaos. He blamed him for everything that happened that night. What if it was Karma that had come to visit them that night? He shuddered to think about it. Suddenly all R.J. wanted was for Lori to leave.

"I will set up something with some friends of mine. We will need all of us to rid you of this spirit. Are you sure you want to do this? This is not a spirit to be taken lightly. What if she gets mad and takes it out on all of us? I want to show you something."

He dragged Lori to the wall he had been staring at and showed her the patches. He told her the story and the mayhem that had followed. He walked her outside and showed her the parking lot and explained how the bodies of many innocent people lay about the lot, dead and dying.

"This spirit shows no mercy and I'm scared to death of her. Maybe it would be best if you found someone else to take care of your problem."

He left her in the doorway, slid back inside, and locked the door so she couldn't pursue him. Lori had indeed scared the hell out of him.

Suddenly, Karma made her first appearance of the day in Lori's mind.

"I told you. The two of us are stuck with each other for a while. Better get used to it. We need each other. By the way, I had nothing to do with this place getting shot up. That was all Jesus and his grand plan. I just had the people that were into human trafficking panic. They were the intended target, and they all got just what they deserved. The people in the parking lot were collateral damage. If they had been inside, they would have been protected. No one inside died that night."

Lori listened to Karma explain to her that the ones that had been inside were worshipping God and Jesus while the people outside were worshiping their football gods. Those gods provided no protection from the bullets that flew about the parking lot, while the one true God provided protection for all of those who were worshipping Him inside the church.

"It was quite the night. Too bad you weren't here to experience it all," Karma giggled as if she had had the time of her life, which Lori figured she had.

The drive back to her apartment had her longing for a bottle of wine. She stopped and got her a couple of bottles of red wine. Karma insisted they were better for her if she was going to drink. When she opened the door, Ryan was waiting for them. He was in a panic. He quickly explained what was happening in New York and what was going to take place in the morning. Karma giggled once again and opened a bottle of wine.

"It's time to celebrate Lori. The fun is about to begin and you're going to be a big part of it."

Lori had no idea what fun Karma was referring to. All she knew was that when Karma was excited, people tended to meet their maker. She flipped on the stereo and turned to K- Love, a song by Jeremy Riddle was playing, "The Lord is my Shepherd." She prayed for whoever Karma had her sights set on, then she prayed for her own body and soul, which she so wanted to be able to take control of.

Then Karma got her drunk. She stopped caring and just let the world do what it was going to do. A surfer would look at a tidal wave and think they had found the perfect wave. The people on the beach would know that the end was near. Lori wondered what it would look like to the surfer as he watched the faces of the people on the beach look into the face of their demise. She felt like she was the one riding the wave, and she didn't like what she was seeing. The look on R.J.'s face told her all she needed to know. Karma is a bitch.

CHAPTER 8

"Wake up Owen! We got to go before mom wakes up." Owen's brother sounded so excited, he wished he felt the same way.

The argument with his mother last night was not what he wanted. He had tried and failed to get his mother to see where he was coming from and how this was going to be a good thing for Todd. He might even be manageable at the funeral if he had spent his whole morning spending time with his brother that he so missed. His mother was miffed and threw a few things across the room. She broke a few more things on her way to her bedroom and slammed the door shut behind her. He waited until midnight to see if she would come back out. Resigned to the fact that she wasn't coming back out tonight, he went to bed and slept fitfully, tossing and turning throughout the night. Bad dreams had woken him several times. He might have slept better in his own bed, but he doubted it. His mind just didn't want to shut down, and now his brother was waking him before the sun had even made its appearance in the sky.

The two boys snuck out of the house and were on their way as they watched the sun appear on the horizon. As fast as his brother drove,

Owen was surprised to see they always seemed to have a car trailing at a distance behind them, even when his brother had taken some back roads that led up into the mountain to one of his favorite spots.

Owen got out of the car and stretched. He looked for the car that had been tailing them. Nothing came up the road this far. They were alone as far as he could tell. Owen finally became less paranoid and started to relax. He took a deep breath of the mountain air and immediately began to sneeze. Damn allergies, he thought. He then swatted at the first mosquito and thought the same thing about the bugs.

He sprayed himself with some Deep Woods Off and took some of his allergy medicine along with a couple of pills to cure the headache that he was sure his brother was going to give him. Once these things were accomplished, he was ready to set out.

Half an hour into the woods and still, they hadn't seen a bit of water. He began to wonder if his brother had a clue where he was leading them. He tried to call out to his brother, but Todd had put some distance between them, and Owen was constantly trying to keep up.

Off to his right, he heard something in the woods. It sounded like a kitten calling for its mother. Curious that a cat could be up here in this secluded area, possibly abandoned and dying of starvation, he left the trail to search for the animal. He loved animals and the last thing he wanted to see was a poor kitten starving and trying to survive.

He made his way around a ridge of rocks and found what he was looking for. Two small kittens with bobbed tails were just outside a small cave. They seemed so small and frightened. Some a-hole must have discarded them out here to die or be eaten by some predators looking for an easy meal.

Owen sat next to them and pulled out a piece of his tuna sandwich which turned out to be peanut butter and banana. His damn brother must have his sandwich. Owen broke off a piece and fed the kittens. They were hungry and didn't care what he offered them. It was food.

After a few minutes, Owen decided he better be catching up with his brother. As he walked away, the kittens followed him. They wanted more food. Owen put the rest of the sandwich on the ground and snuck away only to see them once again a few minutes later. He might have made a mistake in giving them something to eat. He picked them up and returned them to the cave where he had found them. As he turned to walk away, he found he had another problem. Their mother had returned, a fresh kill in her mouth where a car had run over a poor bunny rabbit. Her paw was injured, and roadkill was the only thing she could catch in her condition.

The first thing Owen realized was he had just befriended a pair of Bobcat kittens. The mother might be injured, but she was still formidable. The big cat let out a cry that reverberated throughout the mountainside. Owen sure hoped his brother heard and was on his way to rescue him. As they stared at each other, each wondering what the other was going to do, Owen noticed the shard of glass the bobcat had stepped on. He thought he could get it out if only the big cat would allow him to do it for her. They circled each other and the mother dropped the bunny for the kittens to consume. Then, she focused on Owen.

Owen sat and tried to be timid and non-threatening, like he was just a friend to help. The kittens meowed to their mother as if saying he was a good guy. Owen thought this might be a good thing before the big cat gouged out his eye and clamped down on his throat, ripping it to shreds. Just the thought of the bobcat doing that to him sent shivers up and down his spine. The mother got closer to him and when it was within arms reach, sat down and licked its injured paw.

Owen slid slowly toward the animal and reached for the paw. The bobcat issued a warning to him. He responded by saying he had no intentions of hurting her. He said it in a soft and non-threatening way as if that made any difference in what he was about to do. He thought to himself this was the stupidest thing he had ever done. Later that day, he would think differently.

The cat's paw was in his hands when his brother made his appearance. He saw him on top of the ridge looking down on him. The bobcat's back was to Todd. Owen looked his brother right in the eye and tried to get him to back away. He pleaded with him while making non-verbal eye contact. This was not the time to be a hero. Wait until the bobcat had him in its grips, then kill the damn thing. Owen was looking at his brother, pistol in hand, aiming right at him and the bobcat.

Owen gripped the shard of glass in hand as he dove for cover. The glass came with him as he heard the explosion of the pistol and felt the whish of the bullet barely missing his head. The bobcat scrambled for safety. The kittens ran back into the cave.

Somebody behind Owen let out a blood-curdling scream.

Owen's face was covered in dirt. He wiped the dust from his eyes to see someone flopping on the ground in severe pain. He recognized the man almost immediately from the security cam video the cops had forced him to watch of his wife's assassin. The man still held a wicked-looking knife in his hands. One that he was planning on using as soon as Owen had finished with the big cat. If the bobcat didn't kill Owen, this man had planned on doing it.

Seeing him in person, Owen realized who he was. This guy's name was Andy, the last boyfriend his wife had before she dumped him to go out with Owen. The guy said Owen had stolen his future wife from him and had vowed revenge. That had been many years ago.

Did the guy wait ten years to finally decide to act on his plan of revenge? Nobody took any of his threats as anything but a jilted and bitter man. The guy was harmless, or so everyone had thought.

Todd ran up to Owen all excited. He was jumping up and down saying how he had saved Owen from the bad man. The bad man, as Todd had put it, was still very much a threat to all of them.

"Drop the knife and I'll try to help you," Owen pleaded with Andy.

"Screw you!" he spat out at Owen. Then, he spat out a mouthful of blood.

"You're going to die if I don't stop the bleeding and get you some help. I can't do that with you holding onto that knife. Please let me help you," Owen begged him.

He didn't want to have to explain how his brother had shot and killed a man on the side of a mountain a few hours before his father's funeral service. Better this guy survived so he could explain it himself as to what he had done and what his attentions were towards Owen.

Todd handed the gun to Owen and ran off to his truck shouting over his shoulder that he had a shovel and an ax in the bed of his truck.

Owen just shook his head, looked at Andy, and said, "My brother thinks you're already dead, wants to hide the body. Get rid of the evidence. Let me help you."

Owen pulled out his cell phone to call 911. He saw he didn't have a signal. His brother was on the way back to finish off this guy and Owen didn't have a clue as to what he was going to do.

Andy waved him over, asked him to come a little closer. When Owen did, Andy tried to throw the knife at him. It bounced off Owen's leg harmlessly. This gave Owen his opening, tore off Andy's shirt, and made a compress from it. Todd had caught him in the lung. He could hear the air escape after each breath Andy took. It was bad, but he thought this was a survivable wound.

"I killed your wife, ran her off the road, walked up to the car, and put a bullet in the bitch's head. I loved that woman and you stole her from me. Both of you broke my heart. I've never been the same," he cried as Owen tried to save his life. The confessions continued.

"I came back and caught up with your dad. He was out fishing along the tracks. I chased him out on the tracks and let the train do my dirty work."

The bastard started to laugh. Owen's blood pressure began to rise. He did all he could to contain his anger.

"I knew his death would get you back into the old neighborhood so I could finish you off as well. Your damn brother seems to have spoiled my plans for now, but you'll both go down for killing me, so I'm still going to win in the end!" Andy let out a choked cackle, spat up some more blood.

"Why did you wait so long, and then decide to act out? Why now, you piece of shit?" Owen found himself gripping Andy's throat and squeezing, blocking off his airway.

It took everything he had to let go. Owen got up and paced around. He wanted to punch something, just lash out and make the hurt go away. The more Andy riled Owen up, the harder it was to keep his cool.

"I found out I have cancer, it's terminal. If I was ever going to get payback, it had to be now and soon. It's Karma, Owen! Payback for what you did to me. My life was miserable after you took everything away from me. Now, you get to feel what I felt for all those years," Andy proclaimed gleefully.

Owen lost all control. The pistol his brother brought was within his reach, now it was in his hands. And the next thing Owen realized after he heard the shot was that he had pulled the trigger and shot Andy point-blank in the forehead, just above the eyes. Kill shot.

Owen stood above the man that had come to kill him. His would-be assassin lay on the ground with a fresh bullet hole in his head. He felt justified and guilty all at the same time. On his hands and knees, he cried out to God in anger.

"How could you do this to me, Lord?!" he screamed.

I've tried to live my life the best I can, yet you want to destroy me! Why?" he cried.

One of the kittens came over to console him. He almost picked it up and tossed it across the forest floor, but he stopped himself when he looked up and saw his father's ghost staring down upon him.

"Owen, my son. You have avenged my death. Thank you. I come to bring you a message, one I hope you take to heart."

His father stood before him as an apparition, but Owen could clearly see it was indeed his father.

"I want you to take care of your brother. Your mother was never able to deal with him. I know you can even if you don't want to," he smiled as he said those words.

"This problem you see before you will all disappear." He waved his arm about the area.

"All I need you to do is strip his clothes off and bury them where your brother says. Next, I want you to contact Lori, I believe you have her number in your wallet, don't let her get away. This is extremely important. There are things the two of you are about to do together that will be vital to how the end turns out. Take care my son and remember to praise God. Think of him like you would a coach. He is only making you do all those wind sprints to make you stronger for the game ahead. He doesn't hate you. He loves you. Always remember that."

Owen wanted to say something to his father, but as quickly as he had appeared, he was gone. He stood up as his brother returned with the shovel and ax in hand.

"You shot him in the head. Cool. He was a bad man. We can chop him up and bury him in different places." Todd was on a roll and ready to hide the evidence. Owen almost felt sorry for him.

"Were not chopping him up. Get his boots and clothes off. We can bury them, leave the rest for the animals. They will clean this mess up, not us," Owen declared coldheartedly.

The two of them walked away and Todd led them to a stream that was mostly dried up.

"The beavers made a new dam just upstream from here. The old dam is still intact about a mile from here. We were headed for the new pond the beavers made. Good fishing up there. We bury the clothes here next to the stream, then walk up and break up the dam so it flows back to the old one. This area will then be covered in water and the dogs won't be able to sniff out his stuff. Now start digging, we have got to make the hole deep."

Owen looked at his brother in disbelief. Todd just shrugged and said to Owen. "I'm going to break up the dam, so you better get busy."

Owen dug until the hole was several feet deep. He thought he heard the water coming so he quickly deposited the clothing in the hole and started to fill it in. He found a rock and placed it over the spot as the first rush of water made it to him. Within minutes the stream grew tenfold and the hole with Andy's grave clothes were underwater just as Todd said it would be. A song by Stephen Mcwhirter called "Grave Clothes" began to play. He could hear the music all around him but couldn't find the source from where the music emanated. He spun and saw his father. He waved to Owen and gave him a salute and was gone once again, leaving Owen thinking that he just might be going crazy.

Todd came running down from where he had broken up the dam. They made their way back down having to pass by where Andy's body had once laid. It was gone. It was like he had gotten up and walked away. Todd made a mention of it, but Owen was lost in thought.

He was thinking about his basketball coach and all the wind sprints he forced the team to run. They ran until they couldn't run anymore, then they would run some more until you felt like you were going to lose your lunch. Some guys did just that. Then, game time came and in the last quarter, the ones that were in shape were ready for the battle to the end, while those that weren't, were unable to compete and finish the game strong. The rumors of a pending apocalypse, the end of times, all this started to play in Owen's head. He thought that maybe he was being trained to deal with these pending end times that were just around the corner, waiting to show their ugly head.

Todd brought him back to reality with what they had just done.

"You know Owen. This would make a great story. You should write it, bet it would be another bestseller," his brother touted excitedly.

"Todd, you must listen to me now, this is very important. If you don't want to spend the rest of your life in jail, then please, I beg of you, forget this ever happened and never again make mention of it. Do you understand me?" Owen peered into his brother's eyes to see if the message had gotten through.

"You killed him. It wasn't me. I have nothing to worry about," Todd said as if he hadn't even been involved in a single thing that had taken place that morning.

Owen learned an important lesson that morning. If you were going to kill and then cover up a murder, don't do it with an intellectually disabled person. He thought he was so going to jail. Owen sat back, closed his eyes, and swallowed two more Excedrin. His father had asked him to take care of Todd. Owen thought if he wanted to stay out of jail, he might just have to do just that. The taking care of part might have been misinterpreted.

CHAPTER 9

As soon as Lori was asleep, Karma slipped out of her body and made her way over to where Ryan had been staying. She had made a grand entrance and startled poor Ryan. He hadn't been expecting her to show up in spirit form.

"You give up on the girl? Are you finally ready to find a suitable body to use now?" Ryan inquired.

"No, I just needed to talk to you without her listening in. She went to the preacher that cast me out of the doll and talked to him about removing me from her body. Can you believe that? She asked the dumb fool to heal her from me," Karma ranted in an unbelievable faked huff.

"All the things I've done for that girl, you would think she would welcome me possessing her body. Once I leave her for good, the diabetes is going to take back over, and she'll be as good as dead."

"You told her she was cured of the disease. Why did you lie to her? She might be more accepting to your being there if she knows you're the reason she's still alive."

"I lied to her because I shouldn't even be sharing her body, but this girl is special. I think Father led me to her, wants me to include her in what we need to accomplish over these next few months. I sent an email and all I got back were the next three missions we need to take care of. None of my questions were answered."

"You know what that means, right? You're being brought to a crossroads and must make the choice in which path to follow. I'm glad I don't have to make this choice. I'm just your assistant. You're the boss," Ryan laughed.

"Very funny. I'm so screwed. Damned if I do and damned if I don't. I really would like to see this girl survive. I'll just have to take her with me on a few missions so she can see what exactly we do."

"She has already seen what you do. Remember what she did with you with the rapist? You said she enjoyed it and kind of took control."

Ryan was making sure Karma knew what she was getting herself into.

"Don't forget when she went downtown and lured those gang members out for you to kick butt on. Remember the power she felt afterward, how she just glowed in the afterlight. You could be creating a monster. If I were you, I might reconsider what you're about to do," Ryan cautioned her.

"I got this."

As soon as she said that, a song came on the radio by the group called Love and the Outcome. Fittingly, the name of the song was, "You Got This." Karma and Ryan stared at each other and broke out laughing. The message had been received. They were on the right path.

Karma made the arrangements with Ryan to be at Lori's apartment bright and early. They were going on three missions, each one dealing out discipline to those that were in much need of it. To let them go without the proper discipline would be to say their behavior was acceptable, which it had not been, that was why Karma was called to set the record straight.

The morning came way too fast. Lori was awakened by a large bang in the kitchen. Not knowing what had caused such a ruckus, she grabbed her weapon out of her nightstand and slinked out of the bedroom. Mace in hand, she made her way down the hall to find Ryan making some breakfast.

"How did you get in my house?!" Lori demanded to know of Ryan.

All he did was hold up a smartphone and say he got there with it as he continued to prepare some eggs and toast. The explanation didn't satisfy her, and she was prepared to mace him if he didn't come up with a better answer. Karma had to intervene.

The voice in her head explained how the phone worked. Lori had never heard of such nonsense. Karma decided that the first mission would be a way to show her how it worked.

"You bring the Brucellosis?" Karma asked Ryan.

He nodded his head and held up a vial for her to see.

"We'll do that mission first. Give me your phone."

Ryan handed over his phone and told her that breakfast would be ready by the time they returned.

Karma looked at how she was dressed, shrugged, and giggled. If this guy wakes up while we're there, he is going to get himself an eyeful, she thought.

Lori was wearing a sheer Teddy that she liked to sleep in. It would get a man's attention in a hurry. She hoped this guy wasn't an early riser. The dog might be a problem as well. They were about to find out.

Karma gave the name to Lori to talk into the phone. His picture popped up and she could clearly see he was fast asleep. The dog was lying by his side in the bed. This would have to be an in and out type of job. Karma instructed Lori how to get back as they were not going to have a lot of time in the room. She was sure the dog would wake the intended person that they were there to dish out some old- fashioned karma to.

Lori asked what his crime was and what exactly they intended to do to the man as she stared at him sleeping peacefully.

"We are going to infect the dog and the man with this bacteria. It masks itself as the flu and is rare here in the States. The dog came from Africa, the man acquired it in a house fire. He is a fireman – a prejudiced one. The day he got that dog, a house fire had consumed this house where a family from Africa had recently moved into. While this man was inside making sure everyone was out, he rescued the dog and left a baby boy to die just because the boy was black. We are going to set the record straight with this guy. His next few months are going to be absolute misery. He might even die from the symptoms if the doctors don't figure out what he has. Are you on board with this, Lori?"

Lori shook her head, the anger in her was about to the boiling point. They would teleport in, infect the man and the dog, then bounce right back out. Ryan handed her two syringes that were ready to go, wished them luck, and returned to butter the toast.

Two minutes later, Lori was back, a fresh dog bite on her arm and a huge smile on her face. Karma made her go to the bathroom to get some first aid treatment for her injury. Once they returned, Lori told him all about how exciting it was to dole out some justice to folks that were in dire need of it. She wanted to know what the next one was. Ryan raised an eyebrow and thought Karma might be right. Lori liked this stuff just a little too much. Soon she would tire of it like they all did eventually. This was a short-term job that weighed heavily on the soul. To see what people were capable of doing to one another was not an uplifting and exciting thing to experience. To punish them for what they had done, sometimes that was exciting, but mostly it was sad. The pain and sadness that they inflicted was almost as bad as what the person had done to another. Always, they were given a choice to repent in the end. Some took it, but others never repented and went to the other side in disgrace. Satan always welcomed them with open arms. They belonged to him now.

Ryan wiped some sweat from his brow with a paper towel. The next one was going to be a little more complicated. The last one was going to be downright dangerous, but this was what Karma wanted. To teach Lori how it was done.

"Let's eat, and I'll tell you what we are going to do next."

He pointed to her arm and asked to see it. The dog had gotten in a solid bite to her forearm. It appeared to be a defensive reflex on Lori's part to protect her body with her forearm.

"I gave the shot to the dog first, my mistake. He lunged at me as I was giving the fireman his shot. I just threw my arm out in front of me so I could complete my task. I learned my lesson. We were gone before the guy even opened his eyes. Now enough of my injuries, tell me what's next up on the docket."

Ryan rolled his eyes, took a bite of his toast and a sip of coffee before he explained the next mission.

"This next person is a woman with a lot of wealth and power. She acquired all of this by being the biggest thief in the country. She has murdered two former husbands, then cheated and stolen the wealth of two other former spouses in nasty divorce settlements. We are going to pay her a visit as she drives her Mercedes-Maybach GLS to her weekly hair appointment. Like always, we will give her a chance to repent before she meets with a tragic end. You need to be able to teleport out of the car before she crashes, or you will die alongside this woman. The road you will be traveling on is full of switchbacks and cliffs as it meanders its way off the top of the mountainside where she lives in abundant luxury. Usually, she has someone drive her to these appointments, but we made her driver sick with a stomach bug and he is now unavailable. We have a little bit of time before she heads out. Would you like another cup of coffee?"

This one sounded easy to Lori, but something bothered her. The woman had acquired all her wealth from marrying rich guys. Those guys could also be some of the biggest scums of the earth as well. Most rich people made their money off the backs of others. So, wasn't it also part of Karma to have them lose a portion of their wealth to a gold digger wife? He also said she had murdered two husbands. She wondered how this woman had accomplished this. Was it by poison, or did she hire a hitman?

Lori wanted to ask these questions, but time had run out. It was time to go. They were headed for the great state of Maine. This was the woman's summer house. She spent the winter months on the beaches of Florida. She had grown up in Maine, loved the area, and decided to have this huge house built up here for the four months of the year when you could get up to the home. The winters were not a time of the year when you would want to stay in this house. A blizzard could have you snowbound for months. This lady needed her quiet time, but months on end was not what she desired.

Lori was hidden in the back seat when the woman got into the car. Her perfume immediately enveloped the entire car. Lori thought it was a nice scent and wanted to know what it was before the demise of this woman. Hopefully, it would not be too expensive, and she could purchase some. If not, maybe the woman had some on her and she could take it before the big crash.

Karma had to remind her to focus, they had a job to do. Karma thought Lori was right though, it was a very pleasant scent. She found herself also reveling in the odor and lost focus, enough to let Lori take the lead.

They were traveling a little faster than they should have for these roads. The more experienced driver might have been able to warn her that she was going too fast, but he was on the toilet emptying his bowels thanks to something Ryan had put in his breakfast bowl. Lori popped her head up from the back seat just as the woman was about to navigate a tight switchback that bordered a hundred-foot cliff with just a guardrail for protection from a misstep. If she had been going a little bit slower, the guardrail might have been able to hold back the heavy and solidly built car. The sound of steel upon steel permeated the car as they teetered on the edge of death.

The Mercedes hung on the guardrail, suspended as if it were being held in place so that a final judgment could be made. The stark fear on the woman's heavily made-up face was priceless. It was time for Lori to make her spiel.

"Lovely day, isn't it? A most beautiful day to spend your last day on earth," Lori gloated as if she wasn't in any danger at all. The woman looked at her in total and utter disbelief.

"We're about to die and all you're concerned with is what a beautiful day it is?! What are you, some sort of a nutcase?" the woman exclaimed.

"You need to take time to stop and smell the roses before your time comes to an end. I thought we could talk while we still have a few moments left to confess to a few things and ask for God's forgiveness. What do you think? Would you like to confess to anything while you still have the time?" Lori said with a bright and cheery smile on her face.

The car creaked and swayed and felt like it might want to make its way the final few hundred feet down the mountain. The woman gasped and began to speak her confession.

"I did it, okay?! My first husband used to hit me, dominate me. He thought I was only there to service his needs. I couldn't stand the man. I asked for a divorce which he denied me, and then he called me a whore. He would slap me around just to prove to me he could. I had to do something."

"I made a deal with a pool boy to kill my husband. I then made a deal with a gangster from Miami. He turned out to be my second husband. He had to go as well. That was an easy one. I just gave the feds all they needed, and they did the dirty work. I thought the gangster was just going to scare the boy off. The kid had been blackmailing me after he killed my first husband by putting a bullet in his head. Instead, he killed the boy and blackmailed me to marry him. I had no choice! I set him up because I knew he wouldn't let the feds take him alive."

Lori was seeing a pattern in this woman. Many bad choices had led to a life filled with misery. She was caught up in a web of deceit and darkness made of her own free will. She could have handled her situation a lot differently than she had. The woman had gotten the life she deserved.

"Have you ever had God in your life? If you had, I think you might have been able to deal with your issues in a different manner. We still have time to ask him into your life. Would you pray with me and ask him for your forgiveness?"

"We're about to die and you want me to ask God into my life?! Are you kidding me? We need to get out of this damn car before it goes over the edge!"

The woman was adamant that they get out. She started to make a move for the door which shifted the weight of the car. Lori had tried to get her to see the light. Time had run out. She felt the car lose its grip on the guardrail and begin its descent to the rocks below. The last thing she saw as she teleported from the car was the sheer look of fright on the woman's face as she realized she had just blown her last chance at redemption.

Back at her apartment, Lori felt sympathy for the woman. Ryan knew she would. This wasn't the easiest job in town. Many of the people that were dealt a taste of Karma were sympathetic. He hugged her and told Lori that it was the way of the world.

"You'll never get used to it, but maybe you'll understand what we do and why," he explained to her.

"This last one is going to be the roughest of all. That's why we saved it for last."

Ryan pulled out a Sjambok. It was a leather whip about fifty inches long and made from the hide of a hippopotamus. He handed it to Lori to see and feel.

"This is what the next man you're going to visit today used on his daughter because she dared to become a Christian. He whipped her continuously with it trying to get her to denounce Jesus and reclaim her Muslim faith. She never gave in to his will and he beat her to death. He stood over her dead body and spit on her and her faith. Today he will get a taste of his own medicine and we will ask him to denounce his Muslim faith and become a Christian. He will never do it, but he has some other issues that we will have him face as well. If and only if, he says he will convert to Christianity will we allow him to live. This was the choice he gave to his daughter, now it will be his choice."

"We're going to kill him?" Lori was aghast.

"To give you a simple answer, yes. He is a hypocrite of the worst kind. He pretends to be devout to his faith, but he makes a mockery of it while no one is looking. You will see when we arrive. I will be going with you on this one. He is a dangerous man, and he must be dealt with accordingly."

Lori listened to what Ryan was telling her. This whole time Karma had been silent. Her thoughts were back in the Mercedes as she listened to Lori speak to the rich woman who wanted to get out of the car before it fell off the ledge. She felt like the woman wanted to get to safety before she asked God into her life. God had made the decision to end the discussion. His will, His way. He knew her better than any of us. A song by Stars Go Dim started to play in her head. It was called, "You Know Me Better."

Karma had to agree that God knew what was best and could see into the heart like none of us could. She thought about her own life when she was alive and all the things she had done in the short span of it. It ended with a knife wound to the back, two quick pokes that took the life out of her. It was a wonder she wasn't in the grips of Satan. God had other plans for her, and now here she was, dishing out Karma to all those people that were just like her when she was alive. Her saving Grace was asking for Last Rites before she passed. She was denied, but she wanted them. She had never known God in life. Why she wanted her Last Rites was confusing, but something deep down inside her knew there was a higher power that she would have to answer to and she wanted to let Him know that she wanted to be forgiven.

Back to reality and ready for this last mission of the day. Lori was chomping at the bit. Ryan had told her what a despicable man they were about to deal with, and Lori wanted to get in the muck and dish out some good old-fashioned karma. You go girl, she thought to herself.

They arrived just as the creep was about to give another younger Muslim a lick on his lollipop. The man they were after was on his hands and knees, about to service another man in his locked office. This was all the motivation Lori needed as she wielded the Sjambok and drove it right down between the two of them. The younger man went right down to the ground and remained there for a very long time. His uncircumcised penis was going to be sore for weeks to come. Lori set her sights on the older gentleman, the one that had scurried under his desk and was now pointing a loaded pistol in her direction.

The man's name was Khalid, and he worked in one of the high-risers in New York City. His profession was a lawyer, but he managed an underground sleeper cell that was bent on the destruction of the Western race. He had used his culture to get away with murder and did just a few months in jail for the brutal beating and death of his daughter.

Lori was undeterred by the pistol, which could have ended her life. With super speed and agility, she swung the Sjambok at Khalid's hand as she dove for cover. The whip hit his hand as he pulled the trigger, lodging a bullet in the far wall just above Ryan's head.

In a flash, Lori was on her feet and was standing above Khalid. He was holding onto his hand and weeping. The pain in his hand was so intense he was unable to even pick the pistol back up with it. He lay on the floor begging for mercy, so Lori gave him some. She hit him several times across his back and thighs. He screamed out in pain, once again asking for mercy and trying to understand why this was happening to him. Lori explained.

"It's come-to-Jesus time for you, Khalid. Your daughter sends her regards," Lori said as she hit him several more times.

"I want you to understand something. You murdered your daughter because you believe she lost her faith in your God and had chosen another. Well, let me tell you something. My God goes by many names, one of them just might be the one you worship. Or he might not. The thing is, she was devoted to a higher power, one that stood for goodness and decency. Not one that commanded total and complete control of your entire life!"

A few more swats from the Sjambok followed her speech.

"My God is sending you a message now. He is disappointed in you and your hypocrisy. I am his messenger and I am his judgment." Lori hit Khalid at least a dozen more times as hard as she could swing the Sjambok. It was so bad that Ryan had to pull her off and get her to calm down.

"We take him to the roof now. Hold on to him and me at the same time," he instructed Lori as he held his phone up and teleported them to the roof.

The day was windy on the roof, the clouds gray above as if a pending storm were on the horizon, which it was. Flashes of lightning lit up the sky, and the building shook with claps of thunder. The storm was moving in fast. It was time for Khalid to experience what his culture does to homosexuals. Lori and Ryan grabbed Khalid and pulled him over to the edge of the roof. The beating he had taken at the hands of Lori took any fight he had out of him. They each grabbed a leg and hung him over the edge.

"Muhammad says to take them to the highest mountain and toss them over the edge. Do you think that you should be treated this way for your offenses?" Lori yelled to a frightened Khalid – a man who was sure he was breathing his final breaths.

"I have sinned against my God and yours as well," he begged Lori to forgive him and pull him back from the edge. "I have seen the errors of my way. I will do better in the future if you let me live, I promise this to you."

Lori looked over to Ryan and motioned with her eyes that they should pull him back and let him live. Ryan stared back at her and shook his head. It was now up to Karma. She would be the deciding vote. Lori begged her inner spirit to let him go, so she did, and Ryan did as well. They watched Khalid plummet sixty stories to his death on the sidewalk below.

"He was lying to save his ass, Lori. That man was never going to change his ways. He deceived you. I thought you knew better," Karma tried to explain to her. Lori just walked away in disgust.

"Take me home. I'm tired and want to take a nap. This has been a day of revelations. I want to go home and process it all," Lori spoke in a dejected and solemn tone.

Ryan searched her eyes for signs of Karma within. All he could see was Lori. Karma was hidden within and wasn't making herself known at the moment. Maybe the two of them were feeling the same way about the day. It had been a few days since they had to do any of the big projects. Ryan was convinced that Karma had gotten herself way over her head with Lori. He would have to file a report and ask for guidance before they took on another project.

They teleported back to Lori's house and she disappeared to her room. Ryan cleaned up the breakfast dishes and was about to leave when a knock came upon the door. He peered through the peephole to see a massive bearded man standing on the other side of the door. The man was huge and intimidating. Ryan was tentative to open the door, but he did.

"May I help you?" Ryan asked.

"Yes, my name is Pastor Ted from the New Hope Church downtown. Some people refer to it as the no hope church, but I disagree. I find hope in all things, and one of those things is young Miss Stenville. She asked me to help her excise a spirit, and I'm here to let her know that I've decided to help her with her little problem."

"I'm afraid she's not feeling so well right now and is taking a nap. Can I have her call you when she wakes up?" Ryan reluctantly said, knowing this was going to be a major problem.

"Well, I would say that would be the proper thing to do, but seeing as you're one of those spirits, I'm not sure she will get the message."

Ryan feigned indignance, as if calling him a spirit was a crime or something.

"It's okay, my boy. I've dealt with the likes of many of you in my time. Some of you are good, and others are not. A friend of mine has trouble with one, still not sure which category he falls under, good or bad, but the spirit has helped us more than not, so I guess he would fall under the good."

Ryan wasn't ready to admit he was from the spirit world, but invited Pastor Ted in anyway. He offered him a cup of coffee. They sat and talked about what was going on in the world for nearly an hour. Ted had many stories about some guy named Joey Hopkins. Told Ryan to avoid him if at all possible. Joey was a walking time bomb and anytime spent with the man drew you right down into his world of chaos. Sometimes he thought Joey might be from the spirit world with as many times as the man had almost died yet got back up time and time again.

Ryan wanted to go, and the pastor seemed like he wasn't in any hurry to be anywhere else but right here with him. He tried to be polite and asked pastor Ted to stop by again tomorrow, but the man never made a move to go, even asked for some more coffee. Ryan excused himself and went in search of Karma. He lightly knocked on the door and found her hiding behind it.

"Is he gone yet?" Karma inquired.

"No, and I don't think I could get him out of the house even if I wanted to."

"This is not good. What are we going to do?"

Lori took over. "We are going to have a talk with him, that's what we're going to do. Excuse me please," she said as she brushed past Ryan on her way to talk to Pastor Ted.

Ryan pulled his phone out and went home, not to his place but the one in the sky. They had a major problem and he needed advice as to what to do. He was met as soon as he arrived. The mission had changed, a huge problem needed addressing and he and Karma were going to be a focal point in all of it. Ryan sat and listened to what needed to be done. He asked if Pastor Ted was going to be a problem or was the man harmless. This caused much laughter among his peers. Ryan didn't get the joke.

"He is the least of your problems," one of Ryan's mentors explained to him.

"He recognized me as a spirit as soon as he saw me. I denied it of course, but he knew."

"That is because he is a man of God, and he sees what others cannot. You are an angel. You have an aura that is not easily hidden. It was not surprising he saw right through you. Fear not, for he is on our side. Your main problem is going to be to keep Karma under control. When she combined with Lori, the balance was thrown off within her. Karma and Lori will both fight to control her body and mind. It will be like playing with dynamite and a short fuse. You're going to have your hands full. Good luck with that."

"What can I do that I haven't already done? Karma is insistent that she keep the body. She refuses to find another!" Ryan whined, trying to find an answer.

"She is where she is meant to be. You will see. I can't explain what you need to do. You must figure that out on your own. Know this, the battle between good and evil is going to pick up a notch, and it's going to get downright messy. Do your job and be ready to help our people down in the trenches. Good luck."

Ryan watched his mentor walk away, feeling like he had just wasted his time on this trip. Everything that was posed to him he knew about except for the part where the mission was changed slightly. One of God's people needed to be punished and helped all at the same time. Lori was there to help him. Karma was there to punish him. Owen Canton was going to be in for a rough stretch.

CHAPTER 10

Owen ran with his brother back to the truck. Todd threw the shovel and the ax back into the bed of the truck and tossed his keys to Owen.

"I got Andy's wallet and keys. I'm going to take his car down the road about ten miles to a place where there are some hiking trails. Follow me," Todd instructed.

Owen watched his brother reach into the bed of his truck and pull out a gas container. By the way he lifted it, it appeared to Owen to be about half full. He had a bad feeling about what his brother was about to do. He yelled at him, but it was too late. His brother was already tearing away from the shoulder of the road. With no choice, Owen got in the truck and tried to keep up with his brother.

The speed in which they were traveling was sure to get them pulled over if they were to pass a police officer. What would they do then? Owen cussed to himself for getting into this situation in the first place. He started to pray for the first time in months, asking God to guide him and help him make it through this mess he had gotten himself into. All of a sudden, the radio came on as if it had just found a signal and began to play a song by Carrollton called "Leaning In." Owen listened to the words and began to understand. This is what it was going to take for him to see the light. He started to feel better about himself and then the music stopped like before, trying to find a signal in this mountainous region.

He pulled up to find his brother walking down the road from a car that was fully engulfed in flames. The black smoke could be seen for miles. Owen knew that in a matter of minutes the place would be inundated with emergency vehicles and police. He stopped the truck. His brother got in with a shit-eating grin on his face.

Owen was in disbelief. His brother was giddy.

"What have you done? Are you crazy?! Do you want to get caught and arrested?" Owen was beyond himself.

"DNA – had to get rid of any of my DNA. Best way to do that is to burn it away. I did – I'm not stupid Owen. Everyone thinks I am, but I'm smart."

Owen had his doubts. He thought his brother was an idiot. In a huff he got them heading back home. His brother Todd had pulled his hat over his eyes and was taking a nap. Owen thought he might not sleep for a week. The stress from the day was giving him chest pains. He felt his stomach churn from the acids that were eating away at his insides. The thought of just confessing and getting it all off his chest had passed his mind several times. The thought of his brother in prison made him keep his mouth shut. He didn't think his brother would last a week in jail. His mental capacity would not be able to handle it. Owen thought he might not last as long as his brother would. At least his brother was strong and fit, where he was just a man who sat in front of a computer typing up stories about make-believe places while getting fat and flabby.

They arrived back at the house with a couple of hours to spare. Owen's mother greeted them at the front door with a look of disdain. She was not pleased with the behavior of her two boys. Both of her boys passed by her saying nothing, with their heads hung low as she berated them all the way to their separate rooms. Once Owen had showered and got into his suit for the funeral service, he prepared himself for the onslaught from his mother. Thankfully, she was in her room preparing for the service. Owen sat with Todd and tried to instill in him that they never mention anything about what happened in the woods today. Todd said okay and as soon as someone asked how the fishing was that morning, Owen was sure he would give the fine details of the morning's events. He grabbed a cup of coffee and found his father's liquor stash. The coffee needed a little boost. He gave it the boost and added a little extra to that. Two more Excedrin and he was good to go. He thought he might even let his brother drive them to the funeral parlor. His death was imminent anyway, why not go in a fiery crash.

As Owen waited patiently for his mother, a knock on the door brought him back from his reverie. Owen was suddenly fearful. No one that he knew of was expected. He glanced out the window and saw the sheriff's car in the driveway. His heart immediately sank. How could they know what happened in such a short amount of time – unless his brother had blabbed to someone already? Resigned to his fate, he answered the door.

"Owen, so good to see you again," a warm greeting from the sheriff. The man even gave him a hug. Not what Owen was expecting. Maybe being wrestled to the ground with the cuffs being applied to his wrist, but he definitely was not expecting a hug.

Owen stood there stiffly not knowing what to say. The sheriff's smile faded slightly with discomfort in not being greeted in kind. It was an awkward moment.

The sheriff's smile returned, and he asked, "How was the fishing? Your mother was convinced you boys wouldn't get back on time, so she asked me to take her to the service. I was almost late myself."

"We didn't catch a thing. Todd took me to this old beaver dam. While we were fishing, the dam collapsed and all the water ran downstream, draining out the pond. I told Todd we didn't have time to find another spot, so we came back early."

It was the closest thing to the truth that Owen could come up with without revealing the truth of what happened that morning. He could feel his hands shaking and had them stuffed firmly in his pockets.

"I had to go out to the state park to investigate a car fire. By the time I got there, the car was a complete loss. No driver to be found. The plate was still intact. Belonged to a friend of yours. Remember Andrew Dotson? I bet you do," he said with a knowing smile.

"Yeah, I remember him. No doubt you do as well, since you're the one who arrested him when he tried to kill me."

"He never recovered from you stealing his girlfriend. You married that girl, didn't you?"

"I did. She was recently murdered. The cops made me view the security cameras with them. I had not recognized the man until last night."

Owen turned and sat heavily on the sofa.

"I saw him at the market when I was getting some items for dinner. He never saw me. I almost didn't recognize him. He has changed so much in the last ten years." Owen stood straight up and put on his best performance.

"You find that son of a bitch and lock him up. You have no idea what he put me through these last few months. I was accused of having my wife murdered for Christ's sake!" Owen sat back down and sobbed real tears, not fake ones like his performance had been.

The sherriff approached him and put a hand on his shoulder.

"Don't worry. We'll find him," the sheriff softly said to him. "But just in case we don't find him alive, you better make sure you have an air-tight alibi for this morning," he added.

As he said this, his mother entered the room and whisked the sheriff away, leaving Owen staring at them in disbelief. If Owen didn't know any better, he would have sworn his mother was having an affair with the sheriff. They walked to the car like they were two lovers on their way to the chapel. Owen had to wipe the tears from his eyes and stare at the two of them carrying on as they entered the cruiser. He was sure the sheriff would bend down and give his mother a kiss. Fortunately, he hadn't done that, for if he did, Owen wasn't sure how he was going to react.

Todd walked into the room wearing a suit and running shoes. The suit was black, the shoes were white. Owen just rolled his eyes and said, "Let's go, you're driving." His brother shrugged, put on a goofy face, and led the way.

"Todd, is mom seeing the sheriff? They sure seem close."

"Mom and dad were not getting along. She doesn't like me. Dad stood up for me. Dad slept on the couch a lot. He didn't mind. Sometimes I would sleep on the couch when his back would bother him. I didn't mind as well."

Owen began to put a picture together. Would explain why his mother wanted him to take Todd back with him to Virginia. Also, it would explain why his father had asked him to take care of his brother in the hallucination he had in the woods. If Todd were out of the picture, she could start her new life in peace and finally be happy. Owen wanted his mother to be happy; he wanted to be happy again as well. With Todd in the picture, he wasn't sure if that was going to be possible.

The earlier funeral had run late with massive crowds to send off the late former Senator Harrison. Owen knew his father's funeral would be put on the back burner until the crowd dispersed. His father wasn't as important in the scheme of things. Owen tried to quell his anger, but he was having a hard time with it.

"Todd, it's going to be a least an hour before dad's service can even begin. Take me to the bar down the street. It's time we share a drink together and talk about our future."

Todd never tried to argue, just drove screaming like a banshee all the way. Owen was grateful it was just a block down the street. He thought he never would have survived a five-minute ride with his brother acting the way he was.

Upon entering the bar, Owen wondered if the place were actually open for business. It was dark and gloomy, and they were the only two in the place. A rough-looking young man came out a door from behind the bar, most likely the entrance to the kitchen where the place offered up food to go with your beverages and greeted the brothers. One look at the two brothers brought a look of disdain from the man.

"If you're with the party for the old man, then take your business elsewhere. That guy was a crook and the people that hang around him are all worthless pieces of shit. Now get out, before I go back and get my shotgun and run you out of my place!" he shouted, saliva dripping from the side of his mouth.

Owen was prepared to find another place, but his brother had other ideas.

"Damn right, that asshole was a piece of crap. He wanted to take my guns away just because I'm not right in the head. Can you believe the gall of the man?"

Todd was getting worked up and starting to show it with his massive built frame. His muscles stretching his suit to the breaking point. Any second Owen was convinced the hulk would appear with his suit hanging from his body in shreds. Apparently, the bartender felt the same way, lightened up, and invited them to have a drink.

"What can I get you boys? A beer, whiskey, a coke for your brother maybe," he said hopefully staring at Owen.

Todd yelled out that he wanted a cold beer. "Give me an Exit 40 Pale ale!" he said while slamming his fist on the counter.

Owen had no clue what that was, but he ordered the same. Music was playing in the background and Owen could hear it was tuned to a classic music station he would listen to when he was back in town. He liked this station because they would play music he hadn't heard since he was a young child. It would bring back many pleasant memories of his youth. Now he heard the riffs of George Thorogood and the Destroyers. They had just begun, "One Bourbon, One Scotch, One Beer." Owen looked up in time to see the bartender turn the radio up and bring them their beers.

"I have an idea," he said to them. "I'm so sorry I treated you guys like worthless scum when you entered my place. My treat. Let's do what the song says. One Bourbon, one scotch, and one beer."

Owen thought that was a very bad idea, but Todd was all in for it. He got up on his chair, shouted out, and pumped his fist in the air. Owen just hung his head. This was going to be a very long day. He determined he would just drink the beer.

The bartender set all three of them up with the three drinks. With shots in hand, the bourbon was the first to go. Owen had no intentions, it just happened, down the hatch it went. The scotch was next to meet its maker followed by a hardy gulp of the beer. Before Owen knew what had happened, Todd had ordered another round. The song was still playing in the background. It was a long song, or so Owen remembered; he wasn't sure. His head was spinning before round two was through. Another round was called for.

They exited the bar just a little bit tipsy. If they were asked to walk a straight line or recite the alphabet, it wasn't going to happen in the next hour or so. They decided to walk the block or so back to the funeral parlor where the services were just about to begin. Owen looked up to see his mother's stare of discontent. Owen knew he had screwed up badly, but he couldn't have cared less. He giggled to himself and fell flat on his face. His brother had to help him back to his feet and got him seated in the back where Owen proceeded to snore loudly. Even Todd was embarrassed by his brother's actions.

After the service, Todd told his mother he would take his brother home. She told him to pack their stuff and be gone before she got home the next morning. She would spend the night at the sheriff's house. Todd was confused. Why did he have to pack his stuff? He wasn't the one who disrupted the funeral. It was all Owen's fault, he thought. His mother explained it to him.

"I have got to move on with my life, so do you. Owen will be more than happy to take you in. He has that huge beautiful home in Virginia. Your poor brother is living all by himself now, he needs you. Be a good boy and take care of him. Just look at him, Todd. Can't you see how much he needs somebody to look out for him?"

Todd looked over at his brother. Owen had slid out of the chair and was lying face-first on the floor, still snoring loudly. Todd had to admit to himself that Owen did need his help. He liked it here in New York, didn't really want to move. To save his brother, he thought he would do as his mother asked and go with him back to Virginia.

"Okay mother, I'll have him packed and ready to go by the morning. Is the sheriff going to be my new daddy? If he is, I have this ticket that needs to be taken care of. Do you think you could get him to fix it for me?" Todd handed the ticket to his mother. She snatched it from his hand, turned, and walked away without another word. Todd could tell when he really ticked her off, and this was definitely one of those times. He wondered if he would ever see his mother again. The way she was acting, he doubted that she would ever want to see him or his brother ever again.

Todd picked up Owen like he was a sack of potatoes and carried him down the block to his truck. Owen was making some muffled noises, but Todd wasn't paying any attention to him. His eyes were filled with tears. He flipped Owen off his shoulder and placed him in the front seat of his truck, hitting Owen's head as he was doing it.

"Todd, we have got to get to the funeral. Were going to be late," Owen slurred.

"Owen, we have done enough damage for the day. It's time we got back to the house and get ready to begin our journey. You and me Owen – we're going to be a team."

Todd slapped him on the side of the face, gently trying to get his brother to focus. The slap left a big red welt and Owen's eyes rolled back up into his head. Out like a light. So much easier to control this way, Todd thought. Maybe the slap wasn't as gentle as he thought.

CHAPTER 11

Lori entered the parlor and greeted Pastor Ted. He stood when she entered and smiled at her. They stood feet apart just gazing at one another, neither of them knowing quite what to say to the other. Finally, Lori broke the silence and offered to get R.J. a coffee.

"That would be nice. I would like to talk to you about what we discussed the other day."

As R.J. said that, he glanced around the room.

"Is she here, right now?" He nervously searched the room with his eyes trying to see if he could pick up on where Karma might be hiding.

Lori giggled at R.J.'s antics. "Pastor Ted, you don't have to look far to find her. Just look right at me and you will see her hiding behind this veil that appears before you." Lori swiped her hand across her face. When her hand finished the swipe, Karma revealed herself to Pastor R.J. Ted. Lori had lost all control. Karma had taken over.

"So good to meet you, Pastor Ted. I've been meaning to pay you a visit for some time now. I see that you have the drinking under control lately, but I know that you're weak and after today, you just might be needing something to keep your hands from shaking so much. Would you like me to get you a beer instead of a plain old coffee? Maybe I could add a little quicker picker upper to the coffee? Give it a little kick as you would say."

R.J. could see he was staring at Lori, but it wasn't her he was staring at, it was Karma. The one thing or spirit he wanted more than anything to avoid. His sins were many, and he knew that his punishment was way overdue. A song began to play in his head. Tree63, "Overdue."

"We finally meet, or have you been visiting me all along, because I feel like we're old friends who haven't seen each other in a while. Yes, I have beaten my alcoholism, but you already know it is a daily battle. Is that why you started right out of the gate by tempting me with it?"

"Why R.J., you know me so well. I have other things that I know you struggle with even more." Karma sat Lori's body down on the couch as close as she could get to him, almost sitting on his lap. She reached up and pulled her shirt down to reveal a breast, giving R.J. an eyeful.

"How about a little playtime, big boy? I know you would just love to dive into these sweet and perky breasts. Maybe go even further like old times when I posed as those Russian women. I know how much you loved those girls. Too bad that they're all dead. Maybe we could have found out just how much they loved you?"

Pastor Ted stood up quickly. Karma had rattled him to the core. It still haunted him to this day. He would get so drunk he could barely remember leaving the bar with a lady by his side. When he would awaken, she would still be by his side, but no longer breathing. It had happened three different times. All the girls had been strangled to death. He was sure he hadn't been the one to end their lives. He had many enemies that were trying to set him up and take the fall for something he had not done. The fact he couldn't remember had always been the one doubt on his mind as to whether or not he was indeed guilty of crimes he may or may not have committed.

"I have got to go. It was nice meeting you Lori, but I need to get a few errands done today and I'm behind schedule," R.J. said, now breaking out in a cold sweat. He couldn't get out of the apartment fast enough. Karma let Lori take back control, laughing hysterically at the way she had rattled the big guy.

"I'm so sorry, Pastor Ted. She is so strong. I have a hard time keeping her at bay. Can't you see why I need your help? Please help me!" Lori was clinging onto Pastor Ted's waist as he dragged her toward the door.

"I don't know if I can help you without destroying myself all over again. I know a man that might be able to help you. Let me ask him if he would be willing to try. As for me, I'm way out of my league with this one. I must go now."

R.J. pried Lori's hands from around his waist and quickly sprinted down the hall for the exit. Lori remained on her knees crying tears that no one was able to see but herself.

"Why do you want to be rid of me, Lori? I thought you liked me being inside of you. You told me how powerful you felt now. How you could take care of yourself in a tricky situation? Beat up punks that were trying to rape and harass you? Now, you're trying to get that fool to free you from me. Trust me on this one – that man has so many issues he can barely help himself."

"He is willing to help me. I just need to give him time to work up his nerve." Lori pouted.

"I think I've heard it all now." Karma laughed.

"You made a huge mistake. You have no idea what you've just dragged yourself into. I hope you're not into a quiet and peaceful life, because if you were, it's all over now. He will bring in a man that will make you wish that you had just put up with me. I'm not going anywhere by the way. I like it here."

"I'm sorry you feel that way. I would like to have my life back and my freedom. I don't care to be controlled by you. For now, I'll deal with it, but let me warn you. As soon as I can find a way to be rid of you, you're gone! Do you understand what I'm telling you?!" Lori screamed defiantly to no one in the room but herself. She fell back onto the couch and cried for a few hours.

Karma let her cool off a bit. She must admit to herself that she was a little hard on the pastor, but she knew why. He would bring the man Karma was so looking forward to meet, a one named Mr. Joseph Hopkins. Good times were just on the horizon. Ryan was just finding out about it, but she had known even before she had entered Lori how it would all play out. It was all part of the plan. There were so many people out there that needed her services, and Joey was going to point the way.

* * *

Owen had the headache of all headaches. His stomach felt like he was ready to lose his lunch. He tried to help his brother load the SUV, but for the most part, he was useless. He kept asking his brother what their mom had told him. This was a day when Todd was having an issue with his speech and getting his point across. All Owen knew for sure was their mother was quite displeased with their actions yesterday. Owen couldn't even remember being at the funeral. He sure hoped his father would forgive him. He knew or at least hoped his mother would forgive him. With what he was getting from his brother, his mother was not pleased at all with them and had demanded that the two of them be gone before she returned. The fact that she had stayed with the sheriff all night hadn't sat well with Owen. His father had not been in the grave for more than a few hours and then he discovers his mother is spending the night in the house of a single man. He began to wonder if his mother had been sleeping with the sheriff. Maybe they were having an affair and that was what was going on between his parents.

Owen began to pack his stuff in his SUV. His brother was hastily packing his red Ford 150 pickup. He just grabbed a handful of trash bags and started filling them with all the junk in his room. Owen was going to help him, but his brother shunned him away. With little left to do, Owen walked around the living room, glancing at old family photos when suddenly his brother frantically called out to him. Owen ran back into his brother's bedroom to find him struggling with a handful of weapons. Guns to be precise, and lots of them. Shotguns, rifles, several pistols of various makes and calibers. The granddaddy of them all, an assault rifle. It was an FN FNC with a folding stock. He struggled to imagine why his brother would need something like this.

"Help me with these weapons. Grab the ones on the bed, I've got these. I'm going to put them in your vehicle, keep them out of the weather. In case it rains on the way back to Virginia, they will be safe."

"Don't you need paperwork to take these weapons across state lines?" Owen inquired of his brother.

"Just the one." His brother smiled. "That one isn't even legal in this state. If they knew I had it, those corrupt politicians would come and take it from me." He handed the assault rifle to Owen with a big smile on his face.

"This one kicks some ass, and they would never want it in the hands of someone like me, now would they?"

Owen agreed. He never wanted it in the hands of his lunatic brother as well.

"Maybe we should leave it here. We have plenty of guns for you to play with. Leave this one here." Owen quickly found out that was the wrong thing to say to his brother. The rant and tirade went on for what seemed like hours but was merely five minutes or so.

"I will not leave this gun for that lousy, two-timing Sheriff Delahunt. He comes in here like he owns the place, pushes dad to the side, and has his way with mom. No sir, he's the last person I want to ever take possession of anything I might have owned." His brother broke down and sobbed on his shoulder. Owen was beginning to see a picture of some of the things that had been going on up here in New York. Most of it he would have rather not known about. He grabbed a few guns from his brother and told him it was going to be alright.

"Let's get rolling Todd, we have a long ride ahead of us," he said as he walked from Todd's room with a handful of weapons that he put in the backseat of the SUV. Todd followed him with the rest and brought a blanket with him. Once on the floor of the backseat, he covered them so that anyone who passed by would not be able to see the back was full of guns and think his brother was ready for a war. The war that Todd knew was coming. Any idiot could see it was just a matter of time before the evil politicians were going to try and take complete control and steal all the freedom he had left. Todd had chosen to go down fighting before he would ever let them take his guns or his freedom.

Once they were all packed and ready to roll, Todd told Owen that he would catch up with him. He wanted to go to the hospital and say goodbye to his girlfriend.

Owen thought that if his brother had a girlfriend here, then there might be hope that he could find one in Virginia, then maybe she would whisk him away and he would have some sanity left once his brother was gone. If only that was what his brother was talking about.

"You have a girlfriend. How long you two been going out together?" Owen asked. His brother chuckled at that comment and got red in the face.

"We're not exactly going out. We see each other at the hospital, and she gives me my prescriptions. She's the nicest person I've ever known and sometimes I dream that we're together, so that's why I call her my girlfriend."

Owen suddenly felt sorry for his brother.

"Have you ever been with a woman, Todd? Or have you just dreamt about it?"

His brother took his sweet time revealing the answer to the question Owen already knew the answer to. His brother was a virgin and would live with him for the rest of his life. Owen stared up at the sky and silently asked God what he had ever done to make the situation he was suddenly finding himself in.

Please God, he said to himself. Why me, God? Owen prayed while his brother explained to him about his non-existent love life which Owen barely heard as God spoke to him through a song. "Believe (Waiting For An Answer)" by the Afters. It played on and on even though Owen had never heard the song. It just kept playing in his head.

Owen heard himself tell his brother he would meet him somewhere on Route 81. He preferred to go over the mountains rather than fight the traffic on 95 and all those tolls.

"Just give me a call and we'll meet up for dinner in a few hours."

His brother nodded his head that he would call him.

Owen backed out of the driveway and began his journey back to his once peaceful home in Virginia where peace and quiet were now just a memory. He still had the aspirin and took a double dose. His headache was the least of his problems now. His brother was going to be more than a handful that he was sure he wasn't going to be able to handle by himself. The deadline for his new book had come and gone and he had written maybe ten pages thus far. He knew his agent would be hounding him for the next manuscript that Owen had no idea what to write about. His head was a complete blank, an empty sheet of paper that needed something written upon it. Now just what that something was going to be was the issue for Owen.

He spent the next five hours in deep thought, right up to the time when his front tire exploded. He fought the wheel to keep from crashing once again into the guardrail. His SUV had enough dents and scratches in it to last a lifetime.

Once he had the vehicle on the shoulder, he began to breathe once again normally, or as normal as he could muster after another hair-raising event on this trip from hell. He got out and checked the damage to his front tire. He must have hit a pothole and it was enough to bend the rim and blow out the tire. He had a spare on the back door, but all the tools to change it were under a ton of Todd's stuff that he had crammed into the back of his vehicle.

Owen was deliberating as to what to do when the flashing of blue lights caught his attention. Not now, Owen thought to himself. His first thought was he was carrying his brother's armory in his backseat. His second thought was he was going to jail.

The police officer was as friendly as he could be. He got out and checked the damage to Owen's SUV.

"Looks like you bounced off the guardrail. You okay, son?" The officer mistakingly took the previous damage to his vehicle as something that had just occurred.

"No, officer. That damage you see was from a deer a trucker hit and sent flying through the air. It landed on my hood the last time I drove through here heading north. Scared me so bad I lost control and kissed the guardrail. Seems the trip back is going just as smoothly as the trip north."

The officer walked around the SUV and pointed to the other side. "You spin out and hit the guardrail on both sides?" he inquired.

"No sir, that was from when I was on I-695 and had a car sideswipe me. That driver ended up under the rear of a tractor trailer truck. The guy was dead on scene is what the officer who responded to the accident had told me."

"Sounds to me like you've had a trip to remember. Bet you'll be glad to get back home," he chuckled. The officer was back around where he was looking at the front tire. The flat tire was on the traffic side of the SUV.

"Dangerous side to change the tire on. Looks like your vehicle is stuffed full. Going to have to empty everything out to get to your jack. Let me call a tow truck for you and have them come out and change it."

Before the officer could turn and head back to his cruiser and call for that tow truck, his brother had made an appearance. A brother that was panic-stricken that the cops had pulled his brother over so they could take his guns. Owen knew as soon as he saw the red pickup that things were going to go from bad to worse in a hurry. His only alternative was to save the officer's life. With no time to warn the man, he forcibly pulled him over the guardrail, practically tossing him as they plunged over the top of it. There was no time, it had to be done.

Owen found himself on top of the officer on the other side of the guardrail as the sound from his brother's screeching tires finally subsided. He found himself choking on the smoke from the burning rubber. The officer was quiet. Owen thought for sure the man would have protested or at least called out in anger. Nothing. This was not a good sign.

His brother was out of his truck shouting that they would never get his guns. He was prancing around with his chest puffed out and acting like himself. A complete and total maniac, with mental issues doctors were never quite able to pinpoint as to exactly what was wrong with him. If he got his prescriptions from his girlfriend, he surely must have not taken them today, because his brother was in rare form.

Owen struggled to get up. He had scraped his knee going over the rail and it was throbbing with pain. The officer was bleeding from the head. They had hit a sizable rock when they dove over the guardrail, the officer's head taking the brunt of it. The good thing was he was still alive, the bad thing was Owen had done this to the poor guy. He called to his brother.

"You idiot. I had a flat tire. He was helping me. Why did you try to run him over?' The question Owen already knew the answer to – those stupid guns his brother cherished.

He listened to his brother explain his side of the story, half-listening as he formed his plan.

"Help me get this guy back into his cruiser. I'm going to drive him to the hospital," Owen explained to his brother.

"No, we're not going to do that. We're going to get a new tire on for you and get the hell out of here." He rummaged through the junk in his truck bed and found a floor jack and a lug wrench. Todd worked like a pitman for a NASCAR pit crew. Within minutes, the new tire was on and they were ready to depart.

"Now help me with the officer, Todd."

"You did it to him, you help him. I'm out of here before another cop shows up and we're both arrested."

Owen watched his brother get into his truck and drive away leaving him to deal with the situation. Owen pondered what to do. He knew in his heart that he couldn't just leave the man on the side of the road. He climbed over the guardrail, grabbed the officer by the armpits, but struggled to get him over the rail. The officer slipped out of his hands and did a face plant on the roadside. This was all blocked out by his SUV, so a camera on the cruiser was unable to see what was going on. He dragged the officer between the SUV and the guardrail to the passenger side of the cruiser and opened the door. Owen struggled once again to get the man seated inside of the cruiser. He picked up the handset and pressed the call button.

"Officer down, officer down. Mile marker 120 near Frackville. Officer has sustained a head injury and needs assistance."

He put the handset down, walked to his SUV, and drove off. He wondered if he would make it to the state line before they arrested him. He had one thing on his mind at that moment. Get those damn guns out of his vehicle and let his brother deal with them. He knew for sure he wasn't going to let his brother keep them at his house. That is if his living arrangements weren't something the bad guys referred to as the Big House, then for sure, he would not have to deal with those guns. At least he thought he would be able to write his stories from the confines of his little living space they called a jail cell. His luck, his brother would be in the next cell over from him and once again he wouldn't be able to get anything accomplished.

CHAPTER 12

Ryan was off doing what he did when he wasn't assisting Karma on some important mission. He knew what today's mission was – make Lori appear irresistible to Owen when he returned. He knew he need not be there for that. Karma had that part down to a science. Making women do things with guys they never would do on their own was something she did well. A temptress was a main item that Karma used to get men in all sorts of trouble. Women were not immune to her ways as well. Often, they would find themselves in irredeemable situations that they were not able to overcome. It was a double-edged sword that Karma learned to wield with the best of them.

His mission that day was to keep Owen out of jail. He stood in the bushes until Owen pulled away and then got to work. First thing was to make the traffic cam on the cruiser so blurry that nothing was able to be seen on it. Next, he drove the officer to the hospital and crashed the cruiser right into the emergency room doors. The head injury the officer sustained might have been from that accident. The heart attack the man had might have been the reason for the crash. He would let the medical personnel sort all that out. He teleported out before the dust settled, the officer placed back in the driver's seat before he departed.

He thought the officer would live, but that was up to the powers above. His was to administer the karma that was due to them for something that they had done in the past. What that was with this guy, Ryan did not know. All he knew was that it was meant to be dealt out. He had done his job. Keep Owen safe and maybe save this man's life.

He had many other stops before he needed to be back in Richmond. There was a lot of karma that needed to be handed out, and a busy day was indeed par for the course today.

* * *

"Lori, wake up sleepy head. We have a busy day ahead," Karma nagged at her within her head.

Lori raised her head and peered at the clock. It wasn't even seven in the morning yet and Karma had kept her up half the night talking about all kinds of things that Lori could have cared less about. When a spirit is in your head, it's hard to turn them off or block them out. Now, running on just a few hours of sleep, Karma wanted to get up and going to accomplish something she had planned.

"I'm going to take a shower and wash my hair. Give me about an hour and I'll be ready."

"No need to wash your hair. That will be one of our stops today. I booked you for an appointment at this salon downtown. God knows you sure do need some touch-ups. Just get a look at yourself in the mirror. Letting yourself go, Lori. Not good. Way too young and single to be doing that already."

Karma was nagging her to the point where she wanted to scream. Just leave me the hell alone already, she thought to herself. If she didn't need to wash her hair, she felt she might be able to be ready in half an hour. Karma had her out the door in twenty minutes headed down Route 64 into Richmond.

The first stop was the salon, which didn't even open until nine o'clock in the morning. They were going to have to wait almost an hour before the damn place opened. Karma said they had an appointment, that time was now. She pushed Lori out of her Volkswagen Jetta.

Lori wanted to get back into the car, but the door's locked, and her keys were still in the ignition. Great! She thought to herself. Now some punk is going to come along and bust out her window and steal her car. Karma said not to worry about that. If that should happen, the person who did it would have to deal with her. Lori prayed that no one damaged her car. She didn't want anyone to get hurt; if they did, she would just blame herself. It was no use to fight Karma. She was much too powerful for her to overcome. She decided to just go along with her for now, fight her battles when they needed to be fought and hope for the best.

The door was locked but miraculously opened when Lori gave it a nudge. The frame was going to require some professional help before the day was through. Wood splinters fell to the floor as she entered the salon.

Bo was in the backroom getting ready for the day. She had heard him call out when she entered the shop. Karma told her he was the owner and lead stylist in the shop. He had pictures of what appeared to be Scarlett Davis with different hairstyles placed around the salon. Had to be at least ten pictures that Lori could see, probably more that she hadn't seen yet. She figured the guy must have some sort of obsession with the woman. Karma told her those were pictures of Scarlett's doppelganger. The woman's name was Maria. Bo had driven the poor woman insane with his secret obsession and Maria had gone to Hollywood to make things right. They ended up becoming close friends and now pretend to be each other. A series of events happened to cause a tremendous shift in the universe all because the two of them met up with each other. God was still trying to get the Earth back on course after what Bo had done. This is the reason Karma was here to visit the man today. Lori was going to be the beneficiary of the things that were going to happen today.

"Just you wait and see how beautiful he is going to make you before the day is through," she gushed. "He has an amazing talent few can hold a candle to. One of those few people is someone I'm after. Bo is going to give me an address where I can find my old friend, or he is going to suffer the consequences."

Bo came out of the backroom confused as to why and how Lori had gained entrance to his salon. He looked at the damaged door and immediately started for the phone. Lori beat him to it.

"I need a wash and style. I heard you do eyeliner. I want you to do my eyes as well. You do this for me and I'll keep it a secret from Maria that you purposefully had people in LA spy on Scarlett and tell you what her latest fashions and styles were right up to the minute. You have seen first-hand what you have done to Maria. When she went to LA, the world hasn't been the same since. Be a shame for everyone to know you were the cause for everything that has happened since then. Now be a good boy and take care of my needs."

Lori sat down at one of the stations. She looked at an astonished Bo. He seemed to be contemplating as to what to do. Lori needed one extra push to get him going. Karma gave it to her.

"Leon told me everything. Steven filled in the rest. Now get busy before I call Maria."

Lori had no idea what names Karma had just got her to use, but it had done the trick. Bo escorted her back to his station and began his magic on her. Karma asked her if she could find out where to find Leon now.

"Small talk him and get me a location or an address. That's all I need for you to do for me today." Lori did what she was asked, got the information that Karma wanted, and relaxed in her chair as Bo performed his magic on her. He offered her a cup of coffee that was laced with a sedative. Within minutes of finishing the cup of coffee, she was out like a light. It was time for Bo to get busy. First thing was to make a call.

"Leon. What the hell? I have this young lady come into my salon this morning saying all kinds of things about you and telling me you told her all about my Scarlett Davis obsession. She is threatening me by saying she will tell Maria everything I did. If Maria finds out what I did, she'll kill me herself," Bo said with obvious panic in his voice.

Leon let Bo get it all out of his system, listening carefully to everything he had said. Leon knew for a fact that he never told a soul about his brother in Richmond. He knew Steven hadn't had loose lips, or so he thought. He pondered as to whom this woman was and why now, was she saying all these things. The time for Maria to have known what her boss was doing had long ago passed. He thought that even if she did find out what Bo had done, that nothing would be done about it now. The two of them were like sisters now. It was hard to tell them apart except for a small tell that Maria had. He kept that secret to himself, as the girls liked to switch places a lot and pretend to be each other. All he knew for sure, was that since the two of them had met, life as he knew it hadn't been the same.

"I'm in Miami at this moment. I can be in Richmond by tomorrow morning. Find out what you can about this girl and write down the details for me. I'll take care of her when I get there. Now just be calm, do your magic, and let me take care of the rest."

Bo said he would do his best to stay calm and get the information that Leon required. Karma was nearly jumping up and down when she listened in on the phone conversation. Revenge is sweet; God never put Leon on her list of people to administer karma to. She had just moved him up and onto the list. He and Steven would pay for killing her so many years ago. Just because it was self-defense is no reason to kill somebody, she pouted to herself. She felt Lori stir and sang her a song. It was soft and sweet – "Beloved" by Say Lou Lou. She felt Lori drift back into a deep sleep.

Bo worked better around the eyes when his client was sedated. There was nothing nefarious about what he had done. It was just so he could do the delicate work around the eyelids. He outlined her eyelids with the eyeliner henna makeup, giving them a defined look. When he was done, he remembered that she said she wanted her eyes done. So, he went the extra mile and brought out all the henna makeup. He stained her eyelids and used colors that made her blue eyes stand out. He found a lip stain that went perfect with her hair and complexion. Once he had done all that, he went to work on her fingers. He had noticed that she kept her nails short and only used a clear polish on them. He gave her a complete manicure, and when he was done, the color of her nails matched her red-stained lips. He hoped he hadn't gone overboard with what he had done, and that she would like the outcome. The henna took twelve hours to permanently set before the color and the eyeliner were impossible to remove. It was better than a tattoo. Maria had come up with the formula to make the henna permanent if left on for more than half a day. If Lori didn't like it, all she had to do was use makeup remover and it would clear away the stain around her eyes if removed in a timely manner. He left her in the backroom where he had done his work, moved out to the main salon area, and began working on the clientele for that day.

Lori woke a few hours later. The sedative had long worn off. She had slept the extra time because she had been so tired from the night before. She glanced around the room trying to get her bearings, confused as to where she was at. After the cobwebs finally cleared, she remembered where she was.

Rising from the chair, she caught her reflection in a mirror and raised her hands to cover her face. She was slightly in shock as well as in awe. The woman staring back at her was something to marvel at. The work Bo had done brought out all her best features as well as the style he had given her hair. She gazed down at her hands and saw that he had polished her nails the same color as her lips. She hadn't worn any color on her nails since she was in high school. This was something she was going to have to get used to. Lori reached up and touched her lips. Nothing came off on her finger. This was not the regular lipstick that she was used to.

Lori stared at her reflection in the mirror, looking closely at her eyelids. The look he had achieved was nothing she would have ever dreamed of doing. Karma welcomed her back from her restful sleep and asked her if she liked what she saw.

Lori just gushed out that she loved it, and that's when Karma said, "Good, it won't come off all that easy. Don't worry about doing your eye makeup ever again. I had Bo use the good stuff. You can thank me later."

Lori didn't know if she wanted to be mad or happy with what Karma had done to her. One thing was for sure, she wasn't mad at Bo and quickly went to find him to thank him for the job he had done.

When he saw her coming, he quickly put the chair and customer he was working on between him and her, just to be cautious.

"I want to thank you. You do terrific work. Shall we say another appointment in two weeks?"

Bo wasn't sure if that was a good thing or a bad thing. Lori assured him it was a good thing when she pulled out her visa card and requested the bill.

"This one is on me. I have a friend who would like to meet you. He is out of town right now, but he assured me he would be back by tomorrow. Will you meet up with him?"

Karma was ecstatic and told Lori to tell him that she would be overjoyed to meet up with his friend. Before Lori could form the words, Karma was saying them for her. The meeting was set, and Lori was on her way home.

"What do you plan to do to this guy when I have my meeting with him? You going to kill him like you have done with so many of the others that we have visited, or is this guy going to get a pass?'

"Lori, let me tell you something about the guy we're going to meet. I was in love with him when I was a young teenager back in California. He treated me like I was his kid sister. He loved me, but that was as far as it was ever going to get with him. He likes batting from the other side if you get my drift."

Lori pretended not to know what she was talking about. So, Karma shouted out in her head that Leon was as queer as a three-dollar bill. So was Steven, but she was able to get into Steven's pants when they were just teens. They came calling on her when she had her place in Georgia. She had something they wanted, they had something she wanted. She wanted to make a trade. They were having none of it and stabbed her in the back, leaving her to die in her basement. Lori thought that was so cruel, but she knew that wasn't the whole story, just the spin Karma was putting on it.

Lori thought maybe she might be able to get Leon's side before anything happened to him. The thought did cross her mind that maybe Karma wasn't telling a big tall tale and that her life might possibly be in danger when she met this man. Time was going to tell.

When she got home, Ryan was there lying on the couch like he lived there or something. He had raided her refrigerator and taken the last of her sandwich meat. Funds were low, her refrigerator was already bare, and now there were slim pickings in there. She grabbed some pickles and made her way out to the parlor.

"I'm broke. I need to make some money so I can pay the rent that's due next week. You guys think that you can give me some time off so that I can go out and make a living?"

Ryan chuckled and reached into his pocket and came out with a wad of bills. Mostly twenties, but a few Benjamins mixed in. Lori counted the cash and gave out a small whistle. She had just counted up close to three grand in cash.

"I had a client who was accused of embezzling. I took the cash so that he would be discovered more easily. They dragged him away kicking and screaming, claiming he was innocent. The guy was guilty as sin, just not for what they caught him for. When I left him, he was pleading out a deal so that he would only have to do a few years in the pen. Enjoy the money, use it to buy some food, and pay your bills. I know that guy isn't going to be needing it any time soon."

Lori thought Ryan was as bad as Karma. Some of the things he did without remorse or conscience were as bad as Karma. She would like to know what her real name was. Apparently, she couldn't have been dead all that long if her killers were still out walking the streets. Tomorrow she would find out what her name was. Until that time, it was time to go shopping. Her clothes didn't match her face. She was going to need something that sang out, "Look at me, I'm damn sexy and I know it."

Karma called out to her.

"I'm going to take a nap. Don't be foolish and do anything stupid while I'm sleeping. When you go to pay the bills, forget about paying the rent. We are packing up and headed for greener pastures. The call should be coming in by tomorrow at the latest. Rent-free, baby! All you got to do is shake that sexy ass of yours and were home free," Karma said with confidence.

Lori wasn't all that sure about it. If she had to shake her ass, it meant more than just that. The oldest profession in the books – she was going to be selling herself. Is this why Karma got her all dolled up? To entice some rich guy with the promise of a piece of ass? Lori shook her head and shivered with the thought. Tomorrow was indeed going to be a big day. The one thing she feared was, would it be her last day?

CHAPTER 13

Owen was never so happy in his life to be driving down the road to his house. That was until he pulled into his driveway. He first looked to the other side of the street where his former neighbor once lived. The lot was now a big hole in the ground. Some bulldozers had come by and plowed down what remained of the place. Now it was just a big pile of debris waiting to be hauled away. He then glanced at the damage to the front of his house. All six windows were boarded up. His front door was boarded up. The guard at the gate had warned him that the repairs hadn't been started yet and be prepared for what he saw. He was seeing it all now and wondered if maybe he might want to stay in a hotel until the repairs were completed.

Fishing into his wallet, he found the number for Lori Stenville. The window treatments were going to be a priority. He would have her measure everything up and by the time the windows were put back in, the window treatments might not be that far behind. The last thing he wanted was for his neighbors to be staring into his house with his wild and crazy brother running around inside the place.

The phone rang twice, and a sweet voice answered.

"This is Lori Stenville. I'm not in the office right now, but if you leave your name and number, I'll get back to you as soon as I can." Owen waited for the beep and left his message. The last time he had seen this woman, he thought he was being chivalrous by throwing a rock into his neighbor's plans. The guy was a no-good, lying womanizer. Now he felt bad about what he had done now that his neighbor was dead. Still, he was sure he had saved her from that man by what he had done. The simple fact Lori was alive, and Ekhart was dead, proved it.

His brother had not arrived. He told the guard to keep a lookout for him and let his brother into the community when he arrived. He would be staying with him for a while, just for a short while Owen tried to emphasize. The guard gave him a knowing look while a Saturday Night Live skit bounced around in his head, "The Thing that Would Not Leave." He laughed out loud and wished Owen well.

Owen walked back to his house, went around the back, and let himself inside. He walked to the front of the house to check the damage within. For the most part, everything had survived. He would have to rehang most of the pictures back on the wall. The dining room table had taken the worst of it. He doubted it could be saved, a large gouge down the center of the table said that he might be right.

He began the task of hauling all the stuff from the SUV into the house the long way, all the way around to the back of the house, and back through the house to the stairway that led to the second floor. Each trip taking over five minutes to and fro. It took several trips to complete the task. All that was left in the SUV were the guns. He couldn't just leave them there, but he didn't want them in his house. Where was his damn brother? He hung out on the front steps and waited. An hour went by and still he hadn't arrived. Maybe the damn fool got arrested and that was why he was late. The truck might have broken down; many other scenarios that might have taken place began to rummage around in his head. Frustrated, he dialed his brother's number just to hear it go unanswered. No voice mail, just constant ringing with no answer. It was the fifth time he had called that number. He began to think he had the wrong one. He dialed his mother.

When she answered, she was anything but gracious, tearing into Owen like he was a naughty child that needed a good scolding. He tried to explain, but she hung up before he could even ask her any questions about Todd and his phone number. That was a dead end. For now, he would have to wait.

Just before dark, his brother came rolling down the street. He could see him searching for the number on his house. A wave got his attention and Todd pulled into the driveway.

"Man, I saw the cutest little thing I have ever set my eyes on in this diner in Maryland. She was all over me like flies on manure. I thought I was going to score for sure with this one. We checked into this hotel and she asks me for the money upfront. I say, what money? What you talking about? She says the loving don't come free. She got to feed a couple of small children at home. I thought she liked me. It just broke my heart. I thought for sure I had found me a girlfriend. A real one! Not a pretend one like back in New York."

Todd began to cry, and Owen felt he had to cradle him in his arms to calm him down. It was times like these he felt the most pity for his brother's condition. Whether it be a mental issue or a chemical imbalance somewhere in his system. God knew the doctors couldn't determine what was wrong inside that stupid little head of his. He felt he had to try his best to take care of his little brother. If that meant it was going to drive him insane, so be it. He was going to suck it up and do the best he could.

"I need you to find a place to store all these guns."

Todd picked up a few weapons and began to carry them inside.

"I don't want them inside the house," Owen called to his brother.

"Can't leave them outside all night. I'll find a spot for them in the morning. For now, they come inside."

Owen resigned himself to the fact that the guns were coming in and probably would never leave if he knew his brother like he thought he did.

He tried Lori's number once again, this time she answered. Once he talked to her, his whole world seemed to lighten up. Just listening to her soft sweet voice over the telephone had him stirring down below. He knew what she looked like and she was actually flirting with him over the phone. He felt something akin to love. He just couldn't wait to see her. He tried to set up an appointment for tomorrow. She said that she had a full schedule but might be able to drop by later in the day. Owen told her he would be home all day and whenever was convenient for her was fine with him. With that, he hung up.

A feeling of dread coursed through him. What if his brother acted up and ruined all his karma with this girl? What should he do about him? He thought about it for a while. He would sleep on it and hope something came to him by morning. He had to find something to keep his brother busy all day. Something would come to him, he just had to wait for it.

* * *

Lori drove into the city. When she woke this morning, she looked at herself in the mirror and marveled at how her eyes appeared without her putting on any makeup at all. The only thing she applied was some mascara. Everything else was perfect, even her lips.

She wondered how long she would have before she once again had to do her makeup, giggled, and thought about what she had said to Bo.

"I'll come by every two weeks for some touch-ups." It was a threat she thought, but maybe it wasn't.

She liked the look Bo had given her. Once she was ready, Karma had whisked her away for a quick mission on a cruise ship. Drowned in a sweet, aromatic perfume, all she had to do was mingle with the people on the ship. A couple rounds around the deck and grabbing some coffee along the way was all she had done. Then it was back to her room and a quick shower to relieve her from the smell of her perfume which was overpowering and making her slightly lightheaded. Once that was accomplished, it was time to head downtown.

She parked downtown just a few blocks from the salon where she had refined her appearance and walked over to the same picnic table where she had had her problems with the Snake gang members. Her stomach growled a few times and she realized that she hadn't eaten breakfast that morning. A cup of coffee was all she had for breakfast. She pulled out her meter to check her blood sugar. It remained steady at 95 mg/dl. Ever since Karma had entered her body, her blood sugar levels had remained normal. The last five days she hadn't even used any insulin, which in the past would have been a death sentence. She placed the meter back in her purse and looked around to see if she could see Leon. He was late, but that didn't mean anything. He might have got hung up in traffic or something. He did say he was coming from out of town. She remained patient, while Karma remained fidgety.

A woman with honey-blond hair sat down beside her. She had just come from the Hot Stuff. The smell of her hot chicken sandwich got the best of Lori and her stomach began to complain loudly. The blond lady laughed when she heard it and asked Lori if she would like half of her sandwich. Lori blushed, excused herself, and ran across the courtyard to grab a sandwich of her own. While in line, her meter began to go off. She checked it to find her blood sugar was dropping fast. The meter displayed an arrow pointing straight down. This was not good. The line was long because it was the start of the lunch hour, and everyone was trying to get something in the short amount of time they had for lunch.

Lori broke out in a cold sweat. She began to get anxious and irritable. When the meter went off again, she pushed by two people and put her order in. Those people must have thought she was rude or just a plain old bitch, either that or they saw she was in distress because nobody made a big stink about her cutting the line.

A few minutes later, she had her food in hand and was greedily stuffing her mouth with french fries, trying in vain to get her blood sugar back up. It was now down in the forties. If it went much lower, she was going to need some help. Confusion set in— she forgot what she was there for in the first place. She glanced around at her surroundings trying to get her bearings. When Lori looked up and saw the blond lady sitting at the picnic table with a large feminine-looking biker dude, she remembered what she was there for. The man had another guy standing behind him. That guy looked as girly as he did. They both had leather vests on with the letters surrounding a bee that read, "Queen Bees."

She heard Karma take in a breath, and mumble the names, Leon and Steven. These must be the gentlemen she was there to meet. Finally, she would learn who Karma was and what she wanted from them.

As she started across the courtyard, the one Karma had said was Leon pulled out a pistol and shot the blond lady right there in the middle of the town center in front of dozens of witnesses. Lori heard screams and people running to take cover. She just stood there watching in disbelief as Leon and Steven began walking straight toward her on their way back to the salon where they had parked their motorcycles.

Karma told her to take a back seat. She had it from here. Lori felt Karma take her entire body over. The feelings of low blood sugar were entirely gone. She felt like she could lift a couple of hundred pounds and toss it over her shoulder – which she did when she grabbed Steven and tossed him through the air! Leon was completely caught off guard and went down in a pile when he received a kick to his solar plexus and had the wind entirely knocked out of him. Steven had regained his feet just to receive a foot placed exactly on his chin. The kick was so hard he bit right through his lip. It was lights out for him. This is what Karma wanted as she looked forward to having a conversation with Leon.

"Killing me once wasn't enough for you, just had to try again I see. I would have left you alone if you had given me my Last Rites like I asked you to. I reached the pearly gates and instead of being welcomed in, they gave me this stupid job of being an angel of Karma. Lucky for you, I was instructed to leave you alone, let the others take care of you. I only set this meeting up so that I could warn you about an upcoming event. So, listen closely, my dear Leon."

Lori stood over Leon like a female gladiator about to drive the sword into her quarry for the final time. She screamed out to the heavens to let her finish him, but the answer must have come back in the negative. Leaning down within inches of Leon's ear, she whispered what the message was she was instructed to give him. Lori tried to hear what was said, but Karma had made it impossible. Leon turned pale, his complexion turning white even though he had more makeup on than Lori had.

"Let's go, Lori. We're finished here."

As they were walking away, Lori saw several other men dressed in the same vests as the two she had just assaulted come and collect their fellow gang members. A yell from Leon had her spin her head back to see what was going on. She turned just in time to see Leon helped back to his feet and while yelling her name, flipping her off.

He had yelled Bethany. Lori now knew who Karma was. It was time to do an internet search and find out exactly who this Bethany was.

She would have liked to have known what she told him, but Karma was holding that tight to the vest. She told Lori she would learn in good time. For now, enjoy what she had and go and visit Owen. Lori thought that was a nice idea. Her foot hurt from kicking the guy Steven in the face. She had a slight limp as she walked back to her car. She had questions that she needed answers to. First off was, why did they kill that nice lady in the town center and if she hadn't gone to get food, would that have been her with a bullet hole in the head?

Karma smiled for Lori even though Lori didn't feel like smiling. Her foot hurt and she was feeling dread. Karma still had some control, stopped, and rubbed her ankle. Within a minute, the pain was gone along with the swelling. Lori asked her if she could control her blood sugar in the same way. Karma responded that she could definitely do that and more. If she hadn't done it today, Lori would not be here now complaining about what she had done today. Lori felt her hand go to her forehead and examine it for bullet holes.

"Nope, none here. Guess I saved your life today. It's good to know who you're dealing with Lori. Those two I knew very well, ever since I was a teen growing up in California."

"The one you whispered to, he knew who you were and that you were inside of me. How can that be?" Lori asked inquisitively.

Karma became exasperated. "The information I gave him could have only come from me. No other would have known. I told him what was on the tapes he left at my house the day they killed me. It incriminates a powerful and influential person. Many have died over that tape already and many more will die in the future. I warned him what was coming and how to protect the most important of them. I can't save them all, it has gone too far, but we can save the ones that will make a difference. You happy now? You have the whole story."

Lori was perplexed. Karma had said she was given the whole story, but there were so many gaps in the story that she was more confused than when this had all begun. She wondered if she would become sickly again when Karma was finally out of her body, or would she be rewarded for putting up with her for so long and get her health back.

Her day had started out on a cruise ship this morning. Karma had made her wear this fragrant perfume and walk all about the ship mingling with as many people as she could. She was never told what it was all about, just do it, so she had. On the way to Owen's house, she discovered why Karma had her do what she had done.

While listening to the radio on her way to visit Owen, she found out the ship was quarantined out at sea for at least another week while they dealt with a severe stomach bug that had affected more than half the ship. Karma had struck once again. Lori had been used to spread the bug throughout the ship without her even knowing she had done it. This just had to stop, but what would the consequences be once she was able to excise Karma from her body? Would she become sick once again and die? She was in a quandary. She was going to have to decide. Would it be better to die than to put up with this invasion to her soul, or could she deal with it until Karma got tired of her and moved on? She took her hands off the steering wheel and folded them to pray while driving down the interstate at over seventy miles per hour.

She closed her eyes and put herself in God's hands. She heard Carrie Underwood singing, "Jesus Take the Wheel," and he did, or maybe it was Karma, for when she opened her eyes, she was outside of Owen's house. Amazed that she was still alive somehow, she opened the door and began her new life.

* * *

A police officer lay in bed recovering from a heart attack. The head injury he was dealing with was assumed to have happened when his cruiser smashed through the doors of the emergency room. He had vague memories of something else that had happened, but he was confused and disorientated. His memories were somewhere between reality and a dream. A fellow officer who was on duty the day it happened had been searching up and down the interstate looking for him. He had heard a call of officer down and a mile marker. Clearly, the call had been made by a civilian. When he questioned his friend, the man had no memory of even stopping someone. The tapes from the onboard camera were somehow corrupted, so no information was to be had from them. Both men knew something had taken place, but with no witnesses or memories, and no proof that something had taken place. They had no choice but to drop it and thank God that everyone had made it out alive.

* * *

Officer Delahunt was on his way back to his office to wrap his day up and call it a night when he got the call. A hunter had found something in the woods. His playtime with his new girlfriend was going to have to wait. The hunter would be waiting for him and take him to the location in question. Officer Delahunt was not in a good mood when he arrived on the scene.

A forensics truck had arrived minutes before him and the technician was just unloading his stuff. Delahunt knew this meant he wasn't going to get any tonight, probably be stuck in the woods getting gnawed on by mosquitos.

"What we got going on in the woods, Ralph? This better not be another one of those college pranks where they hide a foam skeleton in the woods to make somebody think they came across a body. I'm getting darn tired of spending my nights in the woods dealing with these college misfits."

The technician, whose name was Randell, but put up with the sheriff getting his name wrong constantly, mostly because he was tired of correcting the stupid idiot, just gave him an impersonal look. He never uttered a word to the sheriff, just kept gathering the items he thought he might need for the hike into the woods. Randell didn't know how far it was going to be, so he made sure to bring all the things he thought he might require.

Sheriff Delahunt brushed him off and went in search of the hunter that was supposed to meet him right here at this spot. He found the guy sitting on a rock about twenty yards into the woods. The hunter's name was Kyle. Delahunt knew the man well. He had arrested him on more than one occasion, mostly for hunting without a license or DUIs. Delahunt knew one thing for sure, the man had probably drunk at least a fifth of whisky before grabbing his shotgun and stumbling out into the woods. His trailer was about five miles down the road from where they were now standing.

"What you find in the woods, Kyle? It had better not be another waste of my precious time being out here tonight. I don't want to have to ask you if you're carrying your hunter's license. We both know you don't have one, because you're too damn cheap to go get one," he snarled at poor Kyle.

Kyle smiled up at the sheriff. Yes, he was feeling good at this moment. Maybe he had a few too many before he got the idea that he might want to fire off a few shots in the woods. He hadn't planned on finding what he did, but it was like it was gift-wrapped just for him to find. It was sitting on top of a rock like it was placed there – right on the path he always used to wander up to the old beaver dam and catch a deer coming for a drink of water. Some of the biggest bucks in the area came to that watering hole. He felt lucky today, but damn, what he found had shook him up and ruined his good day.

The fact that Andrew Dotson was a drinking buddy of his might have been the reason the skull had been left for him, a warning that he might be next. It was the damn tooth that had clued him in that it was his old missing buddy. He had cracked Andrew's front tooth in a fight a few years ago. Andrew had never bothered to have it repaired. The skull up on the hill, placed on that rock for him to find was smiling that cracked tooth smile as he hiked up the hill to his favorite spot. It scared the bejesus out of him. He ran as fast as he could down the hill to the road where they now sat. He had no phone of his own, so he flagged down a passing motorist and asked them to call the cops for him. That was the story he gave to Sheriff Delahunt.

"I don't know who killed him, Sheriff, but I'm begging you for protection. I'm sure I'm going to be next on the list. You got to believe me," Kyle pleaded with the sheriff.

Sheriff Delahunt brushed him off. He had his own ideas of what happened to Andrew Dotson, and those brothers had left town a couple of days ago. He had been keeping their mother safe and sound ever since that time. He wasn't sure what the retard was capable of doing, but the writer. Now that guy could be a bad influence on his brother. They might have worked together. Owen had told him that he realized that Dotson was the one that had killed his wife – Andrew's former high school sweetheart that Owen had swept off her feet and whisked away. Dotson hadn't been the same since that day, year after year falling into greater and deeper depression. The sheriff had it in mind that if, and when, he had found Dotson, that he was going to have a conversation with the man. If he was now dead, that changed things.

Deep in thought, the technician from the forensics squad called for him to accompany him to the spot where Kyle had found the skull. Delahunt said he would be right along. He had to make a phone call. He walked to the street and called his sweetheart. She had better be in the mood for answering questions about her children, for he had many that needed answers to, like if she thinks Owen was capable of getting his brother to commit murder for him.

Five minutes later, he caught up to Kyle and Rodney, or could it be Ralph? He struggled to remember the man's name, never quite recalling what it was. The reason might be because the guy was so aloof with barely any personality. Every time he dealt with the guy, it was the same thing, strictly business. He had tried to have a conversation with the guy, but it was useless. The guy was an empty shell.

They found the skull right where Kyle had said it would be. Delahunt had no doubts it had been placed there within the last day or so. That eliminated his theory that the brothers had done it. A bullet hole at the top of the skull was confirmation of how Andrew had died. His car burning up in flames was a coverup. All DNA had been lost.

Sheriff Delahunt knew he had a murder on his hands. He was way out of his league with this one, but did he want to call in the authorities from Albany? Those guys were such a pain in the ass. His quiet rural life would be turned upside down. Raul, or whatever his name was, would probably make the call for him, giving him no choice in the matter. He needed to have a talk with the guy, let him know he had it under control. He had suspects and there was no need to bring in the big guns.

"Thank you for your help, Kyle. We will handle it from here. You can go home now and sleep it off. Just remember what I said about hunting without a license. It isn't worth doing jail time. Spend some money on the license and not on the booze, it will be well worth the money, trust me."

Kyle nodded his head, waved goodbye, and headed back to his trailer, leaving his shotgun leaning against a rock. As soon as he got to his trailer, he packed up his few belongings and fired up his old Jeep Comanche. The truck was old, but it still ran well, and that was just what he planned on doing, running. He wasn't going to wait around for Andrew's killer to come and get him next, no way, he was out of there.

He made it several miles down the road when the deer came hunting for him. A sacrificial doe ran across the street from a blind spot in the road. Kyle saw the deer at the last moment. He swerved and ran off the road smack dead center into a tree. He wasn't wearing his seatbelt. His head launched up and forward upon impact with the tree. First his truck, then his head. He died moments later from a fractured skull. Sheriff Delahunt found him on his way to place the murder weapon where it would incriminate Kyle.

Reggie had a hunting accident out in the woods, Kyle had left his shotgun. The sheriff couldn't get the boy to listen to reason. Accidents happen out in the woods when no one is around to see them. He figured Kyle might not even remember being in the woods, and if he did, Delahunt was going to convict him for shooting the forensic tech. That plan was shot all to hell with this latest discovery. He just couldn't catch a break. He wiped the shotgun down, removing all his prints, and placed the gun on the front seat of the demolished pickup truck. When he pulled away from the accident, a new plan was beginning to form in his head. Nothing like a little sexual activity to get the brain functioning once again. Mrs. Canton was going to have a swell time tonight. He could feel his member swell just thinking about her.

He stepped on the gas pedal and made a beeline straight for her house. Now that her husband was out of the way, he didn't have to sneak in a quickie anymore. He could have her the whole night long. He thought it was genius of him to have her husband's death listed as a suicide. The insurance wouldn't pay off and she would be in need of him to take care of her. God knew the retarded boy wasn't going to be able to support her. When the kids acted up when they got together, what better thing to do than fuel her flames when she was at her maddest at her sons. He was standing right beside her to give her all the comfort she so did require when she tossed those boys out and made them go back to Virginia together. He ensured her that she had made the right decision. When he called her tonight, she was having second thoughts. He needed to make sure she knew she had made the right choice. Asking questions of her that made her feel that maybe her children might be possible suspects in a murder, reinforcing the fact she had made the right choice in sending them packing.

Sheriff Delahunt knew he would be unable to sleep tonight. His brain would never shut down. He had to come up with a foolproof plan. Maybe somehow he might be able to pin these deaths all on the Canton boys, or better yet, all on Owen. He worked the plan all night long. Mrs. Canton didn't get any sleep either. After the sheriff left, she used a tube of Bengay on her aching muscles and slept the entire day. She didn't know what had gotten into Delahunt, but she liked it. Her husband never satisfied her like the sheriff did. She slept deeply for more than ten hours.

When she woke, it was with a fright. Her dead husband had been in bed with her. He kept asking her questions. He wouldn't shut up. He had something to tell her, but she was unable to hear what he was saying, yet she knew he was talking to her. She chalked it up to a bad dream, tried to let it go. The memory was persistent, it would not fade. With a fresh cup of coffee in hand, she suddenly recalled what he had said. "Delahunt chased me onto the tracks with the help of Andrew

Dotson. They were shooting at me. I was running in fear for my life. Beware of Sheriff Delahunt, he is a cold-blooded killer and you could be next on his list. If I were you, I would pack my bags and head for Virginia. Owen will keep you safe."

Mrs. Canton got up and headed for her bedroom. She reached into the closet and grabbed an overnight bag. Also, in the closet was a box that she kept emergency funds in. It was enough for a bus ticket. She called her friend from the church and asked for a favor. She needed a ride and her friend's silence. Nobody must know where she went. Only her friend would know that she had left town.

"Promise me that you will not tell a soul. It could be a matter of life and death. Even if the sheriff asks you, you must not reveal that I have left." The two women agreed. They made a pact with each other, then used a pinky swear. Her friend asked where she was headed, Mrs. Canton told her it was best she did not know. Her friend thought it was for the best this way, that way if she were pressured, she would be unable to reveal the truth. Although her friend was disappointed about being kept out of the loop, they knew that it was the right thing to do.

The two women headed for Albany International Airport. Mrs. Canton's friend dropped her off at the departure gate and headed back home. Mrs. Canton headed straight for a taxi and a ride to the bus station. She hated to fly. She much preferred the ride over land than through the air. She found it more relaxing. It would also give her time to figure out what she was going to say to Owen when she showed up unexpectedly. This trip was totally unlike her. She never did anything spontaneously. Always did everything with a goal and a plan. Except for her friend that drove her here, everyone would think that something had befallen her, that her being missing was a bad omen, a work of something sinister. She felt guilty, but also like she was doing the right thing. She had just left town before something bad that was going to happen to her, happened. That was all it was. She smiled to herself and got comfortable in her seat. It was going to be a long ride and she knew she would have plenty of time to think. The first thing on the agenda was how she was going to apologize to her sons.

She never got a chance to begin her thought sequence. A man slightly older than she was sat down beside her. They struck up a conversation and never made it to Virginia. Hell, at least she tried to make the trip. She had just found a better place to shelter down for now. Time flies when you're having fun. A month later she was still having fun. Sometimes you miss out on all the excitement when you're having a great time like she was. It was for the best. If she knew what was going on, it would have upset her. Best not to know what was happening in her world that she had left behind, and that was exactly how Karma had arranged for it to happen. It would have been a disaster if Owen's mother had joined him in Virginia, Karma just couldn't let that happen at this point of the story. This was the time for Lori to shine. She needed to be Owen's focal point, his guiding light. The only woman in his life. His mother would only have gotten in the way. Karma figured she would give the lady the time of her life with memories to last her a lifetime, it was better than killing her, or so she thought.

Sometimes Karma had to deal with her own karma, the kind the big guy deals out when she misbehaves, like she did with Leon and Steven. A price to be paid for everything, Karma was not immune from being punished. Even in the afterlife, there were rules that needed to be adhered to. This she was to soon find out as her perfect plan dissolved into mayhem.

CHAPTER 14

Lori walked around the house checking out the damage the explosion across the street had rendered upon Owen's house. The windows in the front were all severely damaged and the front door had been blown in. Everything was now boarded up waiting to be repaired. The house had two stories and as she glanced to the second floor checking out the damage, she saw someone run across the roof. He was a tall muscular man about her age. Then she saw Owen peak his head out of a window and scream at the man, yelling at him to get his ass off the roof before he fell and hurt himself. Clearly, whoever it was running across the roof wasn't supposed to be up there. She determined it could not have been a repair man with the way Owen was acting.

She yelled to Owen, announcing her arrival. He was embarrassed and apologized and told her he would be right down after he took care of a small problem. She watched him climb out the window and carefully make his way out on the roof in pursuit of the man who was on the roof. She found this to be comical, as Owen was so careful and clearly afraid. The person he was pursuing seemed to be at home on the roof, not the slightest bit afraid of heights or falling.

What felt like ten minutes, maybe it might have been more, or it could have been less, Owen joined her in the back yard. Lori had found a three-seat porch swing and was relaxing on it, swinging gently as she awaited for Owen to join her. She sat on one side, he sat on the other. They had just begun to talk when they were joined by the rooftop runner. He sat his sweaty body between them, squeezing the two of them apart to get his large body between them.

"Hi, my name is Todd. You sure are pretty. Would you like to play a game with me? Owen doesn't like to play, he's afraid he might get hurt, but it sure is fun," Todd rambled on to his brother's discontent.

Lori could see right off that Todd was not a normal person, that he might have some slight issues. His speech was a bit slow. His manners were uncivil to the point of being rude, yet he had an air of innocence to him that Lori could see. He wasn't trying to be rude or obnoxious, it was just the way he was. Owen once again apologized for his brother, which his brother took offense to. They began to argue and before she knew it, they were on the ground wrestling with each other. Todd was much stronger than Owen and easily won the match, shouting out to the sky in victory. Todd regained his feet, walked over and kissed Lori's hand, and ran back into the house, yelling all the way that victory was his.

Lori looked over at a defeated Owen, lying on the ground with mud covering his face. His brother had shoved his head into a mud puddle while they wrestled. Owen struggled to get to his knees. It seemed to Lori that he might be crying, so she went over to see if she could offer some assistance. Owen waved her away, asked for her to just let him be and give him a minute or two to regain his composure.

"I tried to get him out of the house today, find him something to do, like find a job. My brother has a mental condition if you haven't already noticed," Owen tried to explain.

"I think his condition is quite obvious Owen, but your brother has a big heart and I can see he really loves you. Have the two of you been apart for some time? He seems to be acting like he has missed you."

Owen was exasperated and laughed, "He misses me, well he sure has a fine way of showing it. If I survive finding him somewhere to stay before one of us kills the other, I'll be amazed."

"I think the best place for him is right here with you. He needs his brother, you will see. The longer the two of you are together, the better it will become."

Owen looked at Lori like she had just betrayed everything he ever stood for and had just turned him over to the enemy. The words that were coming from her mouth must be from a nightmare that he was experiencing right at this moment. He shook his head to get himself to wake up, but no, he was wide awake. The girl of his dreams was turning out to be the girl from his nightmares. He stood up and invited her into the house, trying to hide the disappointment in his face at her betrayal. The mud had helped, so he left it on until he got to the kitchen sink and grabbed some paper towels.

"You seem upset. Did I say something that upset you?" Lori asked.

"Yes, you did, but I'm over it. You just might be right. I have spent the last week with my brother and it has been a week like no other that I have ever had. I'm sure one of us needs to be committed, just not sure which of us it's going to be."

Lori walked over to him and put her hand on his shoulder. She had grabbed a paper towel and rubbed his shoulder to get off some more of the mud that had smeared into his shirt. Talking sweetly to him and getting Owen calmed down, he had just begun to feel like things were turning a corner when Todd came bursting back into the kitchen.

"I need some chocolate milk. You need some? I see my dear brother never got you a drink yet. I'll pour some for you."

Lori had declined, but when Todd departed from the room once again, she was holding a large glass of chocolate milk. She looked over at Owen and they both laughed out loud.

"Maybe you might need to find him his own place after all." She laughed. Owen thought that was the first thing she had said all day that had made any sense to him. He had to agree.

They talked about business after that. Lori went to the front of the house, was able to measure out the windows and get an idea of what Owen was going to be needing, and gave him a price. He never tried to barter, just said, "Whatever you think is appropriate for those windows."

"My wife always used to take care of these things. I have no clue what looks nice and what looks tacky, so you have free rein, just make it look homey. I have confidence in your tastes," he told her.

Lori was writing down everything that she thought would bring out the room and make it look tasteful when her phone rang. She looked at the number and excused herself. This was a call she had to take. It was Ryan on the other end of the line, someone she called, not the other way around.

Walking out of the house and into the backyard, she redialed the number and got Ryan on the line. She could hear another woman giggling in the background. Ryan was trying to be discreet and not let the other woman hear him talking on the phone.

"I don't have much time. I have got to get back to work. I wanted to tell you that you're going to find out that your apartment has burned down and the Ryan you know went up in flames with your place. I was done with that body, so I let it go up in flames with the rest of your stuff."

Lori was incensed.

"You burned my fucking apartment to the ground?! Are you kidding me? Do you realize how many other people live in that place? You put dozens of people out of their homes. Not to mention I have nothing now, all my memories, my stuff, everything I owned was in that gosh darn apartment, you stupid son of a bitch!"

"I know, but Karma said it was the way it needed to be. The other folks in your building needed some karma in their lives, this is all just part of the big picture. I had to get rid of the body I no longer needed, and you need to get Owen to invite you to stay with him. If you don't like it, take it up with her, I'm just the messenger, that's all," the new Ryan yelled back softly so his guest wouldn't hear him.

Lori hung up in disgust. She began to cry big huge elephant tears. This was a complete disaster. She found she was having a hard time standing and returned to the porch swing. Todd was already there, watching her the whole time she had been on the phone. He had taken in the whole conversation.

He placed a soft hand on her shoulder and pulled Lori to him to comfort her. Todd could see she was clearly upset and let her have her moment. It felt good to have a woman cry on your shoulder and give comfort to them, he felt like he was needed. It was all completely innocent until Owen walked out and saw the two of them together on the swing. Todd could see his brother's face as he slammed the door and went back inside, never coming out to see why the girl he fawned over was so upset. Todd could see in his brother's face that all he was concerned about was that his dream girl was being held by his brother. Todd thought his brother could be so stupid and insensitive at times, always thinking just of himself and not of others. He held Lori tighter and vowed he would take care of her. She wasn't fighting to get away from him, so that was a start. Most girls he held were squirming and screaming and couldn't get away from him fast enough, but not Lori. She was holding on to him for comfort, and he liked that. Todd smiled to himself. He had finally found himself a girlfriend.

* * *

Sheriff Delahunt was having a bad day. The feds came looking for their man. He was missing. They found his truck at the bottom of the trailhead, and after a half-hour search found his half-eaten body just below a beaver dam high up on the trailhead. The skull was long gone. Delahunt had gotten rid of that. Thrown it in the pond that reformed after the beavers had repaired the damage Todd and Owen had done to it earlier in the week.

The feds could clearly see their man had died from a shotgun blast to the midsection. The animals had been hungry, but they needed another half day to eliminate the evidence. Delahunt hadn't been lucky enough to get that time. Kyle became the fall guy. Delahunt had lied and said that their guy had not shown up and the reported hunter was nowhere to be found. He thought it was another prank that the college kids liked to play on him, so he had gone home.

Later that night, one of his men had found a pickup truck with a local man DOS. That means Dead on Scene. He had a shotgun in the front seat with him and he seemed to be traveling at a high rate of speed. Toxicology reports had not come back, but he knew the man and he knew exactly what they would show. The man was driving while under the influence, he had no doubt. It wasn't hard to put two and two together. The hunter must have mistaken their man for a deer while drunk off his ass. When he saw what he had done, he ran, had the accident, and justice had been served. As far as Delahunt was concerned, it was case closed.

The damn feds had other ideas and kept their noses in his business for days to come. His story had holes in it, and the damn feds started looking at him as a suspect. Delahunt was indignant. The gall of these people. He was an elected official. He put up a stink, it was enough for the feds to back off and stay in the bushes watching him but staying out of sight. He was no fool, so he did what he always did, except for one thing. His damn girlfriend was missing, and nobody had a clue where she had gone to. The feds caught wind of this and they came back with all sorts of questions. This was not a good time for Delahunt. He began to have stomach problems and started to take medicine for IBS. He spent a lot of time on the toilet trying to figure things out. As long as he didn't do something stupid like confess, he would be okay, he told himself.

The evidence wasn't there to convict him at the moment – unless somebody had a damn game camera in the woods that had taped the whole event. He began to get paranoid just thinking about it. A hike in the woods was called for, he had to make sure. No stone could be left unturned, his survival was at stake. When a wild animal is cornered, that animal is at its most dangerous. Delahunt was beginning to feel the walls closing in on him. It was time to go on the offensive, take things into his own hands and make the outcome come out in his favor. He began to search for someone to take the fall for him. The sons of his girlfriend were the first to come to mind.

Their behavior was atrocious during the time Owen was back in town. He had a motive. This he knew after viewing what Dotson had done when he took his trip down to Virginia. It was clearly Dotson that had pulled the trigger, killing Owen's wife. Revenge for her abandoning him years ago and choosing Owen over him. The security camera video caught it all. He cringed when he viewed the evidence of the event as it unfolded all in vivid HD. It was obvious why Owen had not recognized Dotson when they had first shown him the video. It was hard enough watching your wife be assassinated, but to then be asked if you knew who the person was and being able to identify someone you had not seen in over ten years was nearly impossible, especially when they had changed as much as Dotson had over that time.

Delahunt was beginning to see a way he could frame the boys for all his troubles. They get together and kill Dotson. Then they blackmail Kyle and say they're going to pin the murder on him. Kyle is such a drunken fool. He falls for their threats when he finds Dotson's skull which was conveniently left for him to find and remind him of their plans. He panics and kills the federal guy. He then packs up some stuff and runs. Unfortunately, he crashes his vehicle because he is so drunk that he can barely drive. The accident claims his life ending the story. Game over.

Delahunt thought this might make for a good story that Owen might write someday from his jail cell. He smiled to himself but knew he needed to change his ways. If he hadn't coerced Dotson to help him get rid of his girlfriend's husband, things might have turned out different. He knew Dotson hated the Cantons and would do anything to cause them misery.

The elder Canton knew he was screwing his wife. The man had confronted him and told him he would have his revenge. Canton had told him that karma was a bitch and that he, Delahunt was going to get a large taste of it. Delahunt thought that was a personal threat and had set out to counter it. He and Dotson had chased the man onto the tracks about the time they knew a freight train was going to be passing through. The plan went flawlessly, and the elder Canton was smashed like a bug.

Now, just as the elder Canton had predicted, he was getting a large taste of karma. Delahunt was not going to let that stop him. He was going to turn the tables in his favor. His stomach made the same gurgling sound it had been making lately. He got up from his computer and made a mad dash for the bathroom. Delahunt knew he had to make this work for him. If he didn't, a lot of men that he put in the pen were going to be searching him out. Death was preferable to anything he could imagine in the pen. This was a life-or-death situation that he had gotten himself mixed up with. He stood up from the toilet and went to flush. The bowl was filled with more than his excrement. The amount of blood in the bowl made him a little dizzy and lightheaded. He staggered for the door and drove straight to the emergency room where he got to spend the rest of his night and the next day.

* * *

Karma smiled to herself as she made her way back to a dozing Lori. Now if she could only focus Lori on Owen and not on his stupid brother. The plan to get Lori to be part of the Canton household was almost too easy. When Owen found out why Todd was holding a weeping Lori, he had insisted that she stay with them. He had plenty of space. Todd was ecstatic, thinking he would have his girlfriend staying in the same house with him. Owen was thinking on the same lines, sort of. He just didn't realize his stupid brother had the hots for the girl that Owen thought was sent by God for him. The boys would get some more time outside wrestling in the mud, this Karma was sure of as she laughed to herself. Once she settled back into Lori, she woke her up.

"Playtime sweetheart, wakey, wakey my dear sweet Lori. We have much to do today."

Lori stirred in her new queen-sized canopy bed. She peered around in confusion for the first few minutes until she got her bearings and realized where she was. The room was ultra-feminine in color pattern and design. The bed was her first clue. The pink walls were her second clue. This is what she might call an indoor she shed; where guys had a man cave, this was the complete opposite. Owen's wife must have had this as her escape place, where she could go and do her thing while Owen typed away in his office ignoring her while he worked.

Lori opened the closet doors and marveled at all the outfits on their hangers just begging to be tried on. The opposite wall in the closet was lined with cubbies filled with various pairs of shoes. Lori counted over three dozen cubbies and all were filled with a pair of shoes. Boots and heels from various designers. Sandals and running shoes. Lori pulled a pair of heels out and tried them on. They fit her like a glove. Curious about what size Owen's wife was, she began to check out some of the outfits and a Sherri Hill evening gown caught her eye. It was a red strapless cocktail dress that looked like it might have been worn once. She stripped off her jeans and blouse and tried on the gown. It fit her like it was meant just for her. The closet also had a floor-to-ceiling mirror at the end of it and she marveled at how good she looked in this dress. Staring back at her was Karma. Lori found it easier to talk to her when she peered into a mirror. It was like they were separate, and it was easier for her to relate to the intruder that had invaded her body.

"I like it, Lori. You have some fine taste. I bet if you freshen up your makeup and go shake that cute butt of yours at Owen that you would have him eating out of your hand within a minute. Shall we try and see what happens?"

Lori knew that Karma was right. This dress screamed ravage me as soon as we get home. I'm hot and I know it. It would have any man looking for an excuse to leave a fancy function and take his woman home and make love to her all night long. She decided this might be a bad idea and removed the gown, causing Karma to frown.

"Chicken. Think it might stir his brother more than him? Well, you might be right. Owen does seem a little distracted. Maybe you should go and get to know him better and see what makes him tick."

Lori wanted Karma to shut up and leave her alone, but that was impossible. She searched for something a little more conventional, but this was a closet that had the good stuff. Owen's wife must have her everyday things in their bedroom. She spotted a black Kangma party dress and tried it on. The fit was perfect. She searched for a set of heels and found a pair of open-toed pumps with a three-inch heel. She exited the closet and sat down at the vanity. She didn't need much as the henna makeup still looked fresh. Everything she would need was at the vanity. Five minutes later, she strolled out of the room to find Owen and begin the seduction. To Karma's dissatisfaction, she found Todd first.

"You sure do look pretty, Lori," he gushed. Todd was practically groveling at her feet. Karma brushed him aside and continued her search to a surprised and disappointed Todd. He stood there in the hallway dumbfounded. He thought Lori liked him, and she had just treated him like he was a fly that was pestering her. He followed her as she searched out his brother.

"He's in his study working on a book, if you're looking for Owen," Todd called out to her.

"I need to see him right now. Take me to him, Todd. It is extremely important that he see me right now."

Todd led the way reluctantly. He knew his brother liked to steal other people's women like he did with Andrew Dotson. He stole his girlfriend and made her his wife. Andy vowed revenge, and he would have killed Owen if he hadn't been there to stop him. He wondered what he was going to do if his brother tried to steal his girlfriend. Lori was special to him. He didn't want his brother to have her, he had to make sure that didn't happen. Todd knew he could never hurt his brother, maybe shove his face in the mud and make him cry, but never more than that.

They reached the far end of the house and Todd warned Lori before she entered that Owen was trying to work on a project that he was far behind on and was struggling to complete.

"You sure you want to go in there? He's going to get mad you disturbed him, even looking as beautiful as you do." Todd grabbed her hand and raised it to his mouth. He kissed the back of her hand and asked her if she needed anything else. He told her he was an expert when it came to a good old-fashioned foot massage.

"Thank you, Todd. I'll keep that in mind. For now, let me talk to your brother in private. I have a few things I would like to discuss with him. I'll come and find you when I'm done, and then you can show me what you got." She playfully touched his shoulder and made him blush.

Todd left and she took a deep breath and entered Owen's private sanctuary. Owen was sitting behind his desk. His hair was disheveled from him running his hands through it many times in frustration. Lori could see he was fighting an inner demon, one that was keeping him from accomplishing a simple task that had once come so easy to him. Her presence had not helped him, in fact, it had distracted him even further than it already had. Just the fact that she was staying at his house was a major distraction that he regretted from the time he had offered her a place to stay. He knew it was only going to be until she could get back on her feet. His thoughts were centered around her and now here she was, looking like she had just stepped out of a fashion show, stunning people with her model-like face and body. He tried to figure out why she was here and why she was wearing his dead wife's clothes.

He had put Lori in his wife's private room. The place she stored all her favorite things. The place where she would retreat to work on the things that made her happy. That room cost him a small fortune with all the stuff his wife said she needed. Owen figured, just in clothes alone, that her closet contained over half a million dollars of stuff. That's what he could get for it now, not what she had paid for it. That figure was much higher. He found that it was no surprise that Lori was drawn to that closet and was now wearing an outfit that was contained within it. She wore it like it was made for her and this had Owen yearning to hug and embrace her.

Owen missed his wife and began to tear up. Lori took this as an opportunity to get close and give Owen some support, which to her surprise he rejected.

"Please, can you just leave me alone right now? I have so much work to get done and you are a major distraction. I'll be down for supper and then we can talk. I have this manuscript that needed to be out last week, and I've barely begun to work on it. I must get this done, please understand," he begged Lori to leave him so he could get his work completed.

Lori complied and left him to his work. She found Todd in the kitchen making himself a sandwich. He offered to make her one, but she declined. Lori wasn't very hungry at the moment. Her thoughts were how she could help Owen get his work completed so that he would have time for her. She broached the subject to Todd, who in turn came up with an idea.

"I have a story. Let's write it together and give it to Owen. Then he can take it and put his spin on it and the next thing you know he will be done with his project and not be such a party pooper. I think it would be fun. Can you write? Because I'm not good at putting my words to paper, or even getting my words out of my head. We could be a team and do it together. What do you say?"

Lori gave it a thought. It might be fun and what could it hurt. She excused herself and went out to her car and retrieved her laptop. When she came back in, Todd was pouring himself a large glass of chocolate milk. His sandwich was gone, devoured in the time it took her to go get her laptop from the car. The boy must have been hungry. They went and sat down in the parlor. With the laptop resting on her lap, she opened up a file and they began. It wasn't how she was expecting it to go. She thought Todd would speak and she would try to translate what he was saying and type it up. Karma had other ideas.

"Lori, I can read his mind. The whole story is right there for the taking. I'm going to have him relate it to me and I'll repeat what he is saying so that you can type it up."

"Todd, I want you to think of the story in your head. Start at the beginning and we'll make it all come out on the page. Do you think you can do that for me?"

"I don't have to talk. I only have got to think it. How will you know what I'm thinking? Maybe there are some things I don't want you to know I'm thinking."

"You mean like how you want to carry me up to your room and strip my clothes off and show me a good time?"

Todd stuttered out an answer. You didn't have to be a mind reader to know that was exactly what he was thinking, it was that obvious. Lori giggled because she was admiring his solid body and thinking about what he might be capable of doing with a body like he had. If his mind wasn't so discombobulated, he might be a fine catch. Karma gave her a mental smack in the head.

"Focus Lori, we have a task at hand. Now get to it," Karma said, frustrated with Lori's thoughts.

"Okay, Todd. Now focus and begin at the beginning."

He started with how the sheriff would stop by the house when his father was at work or out of town and his mother would go out with him. He knew that his mother was having relations with the sheriff because his father was sleeping on the couch more frequently now. That and the glow she had on her face when she would return from having coffee at some local motel downtown.

Todd told it all, and Lori wrote it all down. What happened in the woods with the bobcat, the shot that saved his brother's life and the shot that ended Andy's. Todd told it all in detail from beginning to end. Karma added a whole lot more that Todd hadn't had any idea about. She just filled in the blanks so that the story made sense. It was told like it was a story of fiction, but was in all actuality, a confession. It implicated all parties involved right down to the sheriff and what he had been up to since the boys had returned to Virginia.

"Now take this up to Owen and let him read what we've written. Instruct him to rewrite it so that it appears to be a story written as fiction. Tell him not to worry, that it will all work out for the best. The story needs to be told or he will be facing extensive jail time. I must warn you though, this is going to scare the crap out of him. Be ready for anything, I'll be there to protect you if things get out of hand."

Lori was nervous when she wrapped on the door to Owen's office. Between her and Todd, with Karma's help, they had put down over forty thousand words of text in just eight hours. It was getting late and Owen had never come down for dinner. She had sent Todd out to get some pizza while she went up to present her writing to Owen.

He didn't answer the door, so she opened it and peeked inside to find Owen fast asleep on his desk. She glanced at his computer and saw that Owen had written a grand total of fifty five hundred words all day. Karma insisted that she wake him up, but Lori resisted.

"We'll continue this in the morning. Let him be, Karma. He obviously needs some sleep. The man is clearly stressed out about something, and from what I just typed, I have a good feeling what he's stressed out about." Lori stormed out of the room to Karma's dissatisfaction.

Lori sat in the kitchen with Todd eating pizza and drinking some cold beer he had found on his way back from the pizza place. They were having a grand old time laughing and joking about all kinds of stupid things when it happened. Todd had spilled some beer on his shirt. Not even thinking about what he was doing, he removed his shirt to reveal a very muscular body and a tanned chest with minimal chest hair. His pecks were developed from all the hard labor he had done over the past few years. His shoulders and deltoid muscles were also well-defined. Lori began to get aroused, first just slightly, then with each slug of beer and each glance at Todd's naked chest, her arousal became more and more difficult for her to control. Karma almost screamed out in panic, but she kept her cool. If Lori were to give in to this desire, it would ruin the whole plan.

Karma had to do something drastic, so she decided to hurt Todd. He was leaning back in his chair with his legs in front, off the ground. She just kicked out the remaining two feet and sent him tumbling to the floor making sure he hit his head on the way down. Nothing like a good concussion to take the wind out of any sexual sails. Lori spent the remainder of the night at the hospital with Todd. It was well worth it to keep these two love birds from each other, Karma thought. It worked this time, but what about next time and the time after that.

She would have to up the timetable on her plan if it were ever going to work. She also had another problem on the horizon. Leon and Steven were meeting up with Pastor Ted. They had sought him out, found him, and were discussing their problem with him. It wouldn't be long before he was once again in the picture, throwing holy water at her trying to make her go away once again. Karma laughed at this for she wasn't a demon, just a spirit in need of making people pay for their sins. A thought crossed her mind, maybe she could get the good father to marry Lori and Owen. It was worth a try. Now all she had to do was get Todd out of the picture.

CHAPTER 15

Delahunt was released from the hospital after a minor surgery to repair some hemorrhoids. When he had first seen all the blood in the toilet, he thought for sure that something major had taken place and that karma had snuck up on him and bit him in the ass. She had, but he didn't know that. All he knew was that he had a problem, which was karma delaying his journey into the woods. Delahunt thought he was dying, and so he drove straight for the hospital where they took good care of him and delayed his search for the game camera.

Now, after a good night's rest, he ventured off to explore the trail that led up to the beaver dam and the place where he had lost his cool with the forensic agent. He walked slowly, searching all the places where a camera would most likely be positioned. The pain in his ass wouldn't let him walk much faster. The feds had already conducted this search, but Delahunt had no clue what they had done and what they had found.

At that very moment, they were inside Kyle's trailer looking at his computer. A trail camera had been missed. This they knew for certain because it would send back video whenever something moved in the woods that set off its sensor. They were watching a bobcat prowl the woods hunting for food at this very minute.

Delahunt was practically back to the spot where it all went down just a few short days ago when he heard a noise. A noise that had him pulling his service pistol from its holder and ducking behind a tree. He peaked around the tree and searched the woods for what had caused the noise. At first, he saw nothing, then the bobcat struck out of nowhere and attacked. The first thing that he lost was his firearm. The big cat had swatted it right out of his grip and left a bloody gouge on the back of his hand and lower forearm.

In a panic, he searched the ground for his firearm and found nothing but leaves. The trees were releasing them like rain from a cloud. A slight breeze made it feel like he was in a downpour. He brushed the leaves around, knowing his pistol had to be close by. He needed it before that damn cat came back at him once again.

The feds watched it all from the comfort of Kyle's small trailer. They were all packed in together watching the show. They conversed with each other on whether they should go help the man, but each one to a man shrugged it off. Delahunt had been such an asshole and uncooperative that this was just what the man deserved, so they watched the action unfold before them on the computer.

The big cat moved once again, this time taking a nip at him as it quickly passed by, driving Delahunt out into the clearing and open for a good shot. The camera was pointed right at this specific spot. The rock still stood in the middle of the clearing where Andy's skull had been found. The camera had caught everything that Delahunt had done that day. It was all on Kyle's computer. The feds just hadn't gotten to it yet, being distracted by what was going on at the moment.

An arrow came from high up in a tree. A hunter had been positioned in a tree stand overlooking this spot, crossbow in hand just waiting for a specific prey. That prey had arrived, causing the arrow to fly, finding its destination. Delahunt went down. An arrow sticking out of his chest slightly left of his heart and just below his shoulder. It had nipped the top of his lung making it difficult to breathe, and even harder to talk.

The hunter appeared on camera now, peering down at his quarry in disgust. The feds were confused, they began to gather their stuff but couldn't take their eyes off the computer screen as the drama unfolded before their unbelieving eyes. One of them cussed and said he wished they had sound to go with this video. The others agreed with him.

The hunter stood above Delahunt, never letting his face be seen on camera. He appeared to be a young man, maybe seventeen years old at best, the feds discussed among themselves. He was dressed in camouflage, no bright orange for this guy. The feds watched the two men converse. They could see that Delahunt was pleading for his life. The hunter had a few coarse words for Delahunt. The feds could clearly see the man was animated. He reached down and viciously pulled the arrow from Delahunt's chest, always making sure his back was facing the camera. The feds watched him wipe it off on Delahunt's uniform and walk away.

Delahunt had rolled over in extreme pain and never saw the man walk away, which might have been a good thing, for when he rolled over, the bobcat was there to finish the job. The bobcat had no problem facing the camera as it ripped out Delahunt's throat with a massive bite.

The feds cringed at the sight before them on the screen, each one of them blaming the other for their inaction. A couple of them ran out the door but were called back. It was too late to save the sheriff. The only thing left to watch was the bobcat making a meal out of him, so they had searched the computer some more and found the files they had been looking for. They watched as Delahunt raised the shotgun that Kyle had forgotten to take with him and blow a hole in their man's chest. They had found the killer of their agent. The search for Delahunt's killer would be conducted with little enthusiasm. That man had done them a favor. It's never good for business when you have got to arrest one of your own law enforcement agents, especially an elected one at that. They blamed the big cat and made a big stink out of hunting it down. A few days later, they exited the woods with the body of a large male bobcat.

* * *

Owen woke with a start. He practically fell out of his office chair. The lack of noise in the house was deafening. His biggest dread in the back of his head was that he would go in search of Lori and find her snuggled up in bed with his brother. While his brother had been nothing less than cordial and affectionate, he had been aloof and distracted. Even though Lori had seemed to have a crush on him, he felt his brother was winning the battle for her love.

In a panic, he fled his office and searched the house for them. Every room was searched, even outside. He noticed that his brother's truck was missing. They must have taken a ride to who-knows-where. Maybe a makeout spot where they could have privacy.

Owen walked back in the house to music. He could hear it clearly coming from the kitchen where he found an overturned chair, some blood on the floor, and a pizza box with a couple of slices of pepperoni left uneaten. He also found a few empty beer bottles and an open laptop. It wasn't one of his and he knew his brother didn't own one. The music was flowing from the laptop. It had a retro style to it that just begged you to come closer and give it a listen. The screen was flashing colors like a kaleidoscope, spinning and whirling. The words to the song said that it felt like he was dreaming but he wasn't. He reached down to touch the enter button and a flash of light and a shock struck him, knocking him out of his office chair. He looked around his office. The whole last few minutes had been a dream.

The only thing that was the same was the music. He got up and ran for the kitchen. He found everything like his dream had foretold. The pizza box, the blood on the floor next to the overturned chair, and the open laptop. He hit the enter button to view a screen which showed the album cover to the song he was listening to and the name of the group and song. He was listening to The Rising and the name of the song was, "Feels like I'm Dreaming But It's Real." The album cover was asking him if he was ready to fly. The song ended and all the music stopped, so he hit the enter button and a document came up.

What he read was unbelievable. He wanted to go back upstairs to his office chair and wake up once again. The story on screen was a detailed account of everything he and his brother had done while in

New York, only it was told like one was reading a story of fiction, which Owen knew was nothing but the truth told through his brother's eyes.

As he sat and read what was written in the file, an idea came to him. He was getting nowhere fast with his manuscript, but this stuff was gold. He knew he could spin this story into a masterpiece. He read every word that was written, over forty thousand words of text. Owen ran for his office forgetting all about the blood and the pizza and empty beer bottles littering his kitchen table. His focus was developing the story that would save his career. He sat down and typed throughout the remainder of the night and into the early morning. The open laptop next to him, to refresh his memory on what Lori had typed into her computer. It never occurred to him that he might be stealing someone else's idea. His deadline had come and gone, he needed this, and damn it, he was going to have it. These thoughts passed through his head, but Lori and his brother's whereabouts had not.

* * *

A doctor came into the waiting room and asked for a Miss Stenville. Lori stood prepared to take the bad news. The doctor had told her that Todd would spend the night. He had said Todd's behavior was erratic and his speech was slurred and slow at times. Lori laughed and told the doctor that was how Todd was all the time. Puzzled, the doctor said that just in case, they would like to keep him overnight and monitor his brain functions.

Lori looked at her watch and saw that it was nearly 3:00 a.m. She wasn't sure where she should go or what she should do. Jumping into Todd's truck, she decided to make a quick stop by her old apartment and see how extensive the damage was to her place. To her shock, her place was as she had left it. The story of her apartment burning down was just that, a story. She felt so deceived when she saw her apartment, to the point that she couldn't get herself to enter it and change out of the party dress she was wearing. It wasn't that the dress was uncomfortable, because it was – it was all the staring from judgmental eyes that made her uncomfortable.

She found herself driving around town when she noticed a sign that had been vandalized. It was a sign for a church. The Church of New Hope. The sign now read, The Church of No Hope. She knew this was Pastor Ted's church, so she parked in front of the church and watched the sun rise above the city. A knock on her window a while later woke her from a sound sleep. It was the good father smiling through the window getting a good look at her cleavage.

Startled, she jumped up, opened the door, and nearly fell to the ground, but thankfully Pastor Ted was there to catch her on her way down. He unintentionally had caught a handful of the cleavage he had been staring at just a moment before. Lori got her composure back and her dress straightened out.

"You look like you're ready for a big night out in town." He whistled as he stared at the outfit she was wearing. The permanent makeup made her look like she had just left the house.

"I sure hope your date didn't stand you up, because if he did, I feel sorry for the man."

Lori wanted to smack the pastor in the head, instead, she began to cry. Through her tears, she told the pastor that her friend had hit his head and was in the hospital. She begged him to come to the hospital and pray over him and maybe help heal the poor boy.

R.J. had a big day ahead of him with little free time. He thought if he took Lori with him and combined some of his meetings with her along in tow, he might be able to accomplish everything he had on the docket. He explained these minor details to her, and Lori readily agreed to them, never really knowing what she was getting herself in for.

A day with the good father was sometimes very eventful, combined with his meeting with Maria Gambella, and all bets were off. Anything was possible with that woman, especially if she brought Joey with her. Pastor Ted began to recall some of those times when Joey had been close by. He felt like a cat that had used eight of its nine lives. A shutter came over him, he sure hoped Maria hadn't brought that man with her this visit. One look at Joey Hopkins and a day full of mayhem and destruction was assured of. He knew this for a fact, for he had spent quite a few days with the man himself.

He brought Lori into his office, gathered a few items he was going to need for the day, and offered to drive her around town with him. The parking in the city was difficult and instead of her following him, she gladly accepted the ride. He told her he should have her back to the church no later than lunchtime. Lori felt refreshed from her nap in the truck. Feeling confident and safe with the pastor, they set out.

The first few stops were to deliver food to some rough neighborhoods. R.J.'s truck was filled with crates full of food items that he brought around to some folks that he was assisting, helping them get back on their feet.

He told Lori, "These folks need a helping hand to get over a hump, but if you keep giving to them, they become dependent. I give them a hand just until they can sustain themselves once again. Sometimes it's a loss of a job, or an illness. Other times it's something that they brought on themselves like an addiction. I help them get through it. Most of the people I help go on to live productive lives and in turn, they return the favor to the needy. You are going to meet one of those people this morning. My biggest success story ever. I want to warn you though, she can be a bit of a drama queen. Don't let her fool you. This woman is by far the smartest, most self-reliant person you'll ever meet."

Lori sat in the passenger seat and took it all in. Pastor Ted wouldn't let her get out of the truck. He was afraid for her safety if she did. As big as he was, he didn't want to have to deal with a bunch of horny guys trying to get a piece of Lori's flesh. Sometimes these guys could be animals, he had told her. Safer in the wilds of the jungle than in these neighborhoods, he said as he looked around.

After the food delivery was accomplished, they were right next to the city hospital so that was their next stop. Pastor Ted said he had one last stop after they picked up Todd, then he would take her back to the church.

Lori went inside and Pastor Ted hung out in the lobby, sharing some funny stories with the people he encountered there. When Lori returned with Todd, all she could hear was laughter coming from the lobby. Even Todd was laughing, but she didn't know why. No joke could be heard over the ruckus coming from the lobby.

A nurse grabbed Lori's arm and asked if the good father was with her, she nodded that he was.

"Can you please get him the hell out of here before he kills someone?" She laughed as she ran, holding her side to assist someone who was hyperventilating. The whole lobby was in tears, and Pastor Ted had a big smile on his face knowing he was the cause of it all.

"Laughter is good for the soul. These people needed something to uplift their spirits. I gave them something," he explained to Lori as they were ushered out and told never to come back.

"You just got thrown out of a hospital, how can you be happy about that?" Lori said exasperated.

"They love me here. I do a lot of work here at the hospital. They never throw me out until after I've been there for a few minutes. Once they lose control and I start to become a bother do they ask me to leave," he snickered, and then started to laugh out loud when he got a good look at Todd.

"This was your date last night?" Pastor Ted inquired.

"If you must know, yes, we were having a nice dinner together when he fell out of his chair and hit his head." She looked over lovingly at Todd as he drooled, and his eyes rolled around in their sockets.

Pastor Ted looked at him and mumbled that it must have been a hell of a hit to the head, turned to Lori, and smiled.

"One last stop. It's just down the street from here."

A few minutes later, they were parking just up the street from the salon where Karma had brought her to get her ridiculous makeover. It had been close to a week now and the makeup showed no signs of fading, but her nails had a few chips in the polish. She gazed down at the unfamiliar polished nails that she still hadn't gotten used to. She would find herself catching a glimpse of her nails as she did this or that and stare at them for a moment. Maybe she could get Bo to remove the makeup and polish and let her start feeling like her old self once again.

This is what was going through her mind as she entered the salon, guiding Todd along while trying to keep up with the pastor. They sat in the front while Pastor Ted went through the salon looking for Maria. Lori could hear him calling out for her among all the noise from the hair dryers and blow dryers that were doing their work on several heads throughout the shop.

Bo entered the shop and noticed Lori right away. He stopped and stared at her. At first, she thought the man was going to turn and run, but he didn't, he just peered down at her. He stepped in front of her and asked if it had been two weeks yet. Lori told him it had not, but she needed his assistance. She wanted him to remove the makeup. He laughed at her and told her she should have done that herself. Now it was too late. This made Lori just slightly mad as she knew karma had gotten one over on her.

Bo guided her over to his station and asked her about her friend.

"He looks like he's overdue for a haircut. Would you like for me to take care of that for you as well today?" Lori thought about it and told Bo she would get back to him. For now, let's get to work on her before she ran out of time as she was here with the pastor. Bo just shook his head and mumbled that he would have plenty of time then. He took out a brush and started to run it through her hair.

"Um, Bo, what about the makeup?" Lori asked impatiently.

Bo told her Maria enhanced henna makeup to the point of no return. If left on for a certain amount of time, it was like getting your makeup tattooed on. It was there to stay now. Her hair needed his time right now. He brushed and spritzed her hair with water, grabbed a pair of scissors, and got to work. A few minutes later, he had the blow dryer fired up and it mingled with the noise from the rest of the shop. Lori had her eyes closed and when she opened them, she was no longer staring at Bo. Somehow, Leon had traded places with him, and he was the one working on her.

Lori felt like she had been set up. She wanted to jump out of the seat and run for her life, but she remained calm. Karma had taken hold of the reigns, pushed her to the back of her head, and out of the way. Lori hated this when Karma took control. She felt so helpless yet so powerful.

"So good to see you once again. I must say you pack one hell of a kick. My ribs are still sore from that last kick to the gut. I digress. I wanted to ask you a few simple questions."

"Is it going to end with a bullet to my head like the last girl you questioned that you thought was me?" Lori had to ask the question.

"No, my dear, that woman was a doctor doing evil deeds in the community. She had something we required, and she had no intentions of turning it over to me. I did what I had to do. I will let you leave here alive and well. Your friend over there, well let's say what you tell me might seal his fate."

Leon was pulling no punches.

"The last time we met, you whispered in my ear things that only one person would know. I must know who gave you that information. Since that one person is dead, I'm sure you didn't get it from her."

"I wouldn't be so sure of that. There are things in this world that you have no clue about Leon. Take the fact that Bethany was in love with you but you would never give her the time of day, treated her like a kid sister, brushed her off, and let her sleep with your best friend."

Leon jumped back from this revelation. He took a deep breath and returned to stare into her face.

"I see that Bo has worked his magic on your eyes. He says that you want to remove the henna. I can't take care of that for you, but Maria might know a way. Give me a second and I'll be right back."

She watched Leon rush for the backroom. Lori kept her eyes on the door waiting for his return, instead, she saw Pastor Ted come out with the movie star Scarlett Davis. Lori thought she might be one of the ten prettiest women in the world, had seen most of her movies. In the latest couple of films, it seemed she had picked her game up and taken it to a new level. They were walking right toward her.

"So, this is the lovely young lady that you brought for me to see. You are correct in your assessment, she is gorgeous."

Maria walked around Lori, looking at her hair and poking at her face.

"My name is Maria. Leon asked me to come out and talk to you while he makes a phone call."

Lori had thought for sure she had misheard her. The resemblance was uncanny.

"Bo did your eyes." She smiled. "They look like a masterpiece that only he can create, but he taught me well. Did you notice Leon's eyes? I did his." Maria was proud of her work.

"I'm working on a makeup remover for the super henna. I haven't yet found anything once the makeup sets, but it's something on the back burner of things I'm meaning to get to. At this moment I have bigger fish to fry. I'm trying to save millions of people from a deadly disease that is about to be unleashed upon the world."

While Lori was trying to comprehend what Maria had just told her, Maria picked up Lori's hand and mumbled that these nails would just not do. She called over a manicurist and led Lori to her station. Then she grabbed Todd and led him to the chair Lori had just vacated. Lori was watching what Maria was doing to Todd. If she tried to put eyeliner on Todd, she knew she would jump out of her seat and save him. All Maria did was give him a haircut, carefully worked around the knot on his head. She watched as they talked. Todd kept calling her Scarlett, which she seemed to not mind. Lori couldn't tell the difference between the two of them. She thought to herself that people must confuse Maria for the movie star constantly.

She hadn't been paying attention to what was being done to her own nails. She was enthralled by the conversation between Todd and Maria and she concentrated all her focus on them. Maria was telling him she had a good idea of what was wrong with him and wanted to try something on him. The girl who was working on her nails escorted her over to the drying station to put her hands under the UV light, and Lori saw for the first time the change in her hands. The nails were a bit longer than when she came in, and a whole lot redder too. My god, she thought to herself. It's like I'm wearing ten stop signs on my hands. Before she could cause a fuss, Leon came back out and sat beside her.

"Very nice, you look good," he said while peering at her hands and then her eyes.

"Todd is going to be staying with us for a while. We need to sort out a few things. Maybe you can tell me what's on the tapes that you told me I left at your house? I took the ones that I thought were important. You say I left one that will have deadly consequences."

"It already has killed many, and many more are going to die because of that tape. I told you I feel responsible and want you to retrieve it. What is so god damn hard about that, Leon?"

"You sound just like a friend I once had who met a tragic end. Somehow when I talk to you, I feel like I'm talking to her," he said while he adjusted in his seat, trying to settle his emotions.

Lori stifled a giggle, took a deep breath, and told Leon what was on the tape. Leon took a deep breath and recapped what she had just told him.

"He confessed to killing his wife while you had him in your little torture chamber. People might say you coerced him into saying that, but you're right. If the whole tape is played, you see what took place and how he enjoyed what you had done to him. Bethany, this isn't right. How could you do such things and why?"

Lori sat and listened to Leon call her Bethany once again. She had done the research and knew that Bethany Devlin was found dead in her basement from a stab wound to the back. The news report said they had found many sex tapes involving many influential people in the area. Apparently, one of her clients found out they were being taped and killed her, removed the incriminating tape, and left the rest. That was as much as she could get. Now she was learning the truth of what had taken place.

"Leon, the money was an aphrodisiac. The amount of power I held over these powerful men was like a drug. I made the tapes in case one of these guys wanted to get the upper hand on me one day. If I had something to blackmail them with, then they would never be able to get the better of me. How was I to know the next President of the United States was going to confess to me he had a hand in the murder of his wife?"

Lori felt all the compassion flowing out of Karma through her and into the noisy salon. Thankfully, no one was paying any attention to them.

"I know a guy close to the President. I figure the President has already been threatened with blackmail from this. I'll find out who has the tape and destroy it for you. It comes with a price. You'll have to join our team in fighting evil whenever it rises its ugly head and administer justice where it needs to be dealt out. Are you agreeable to this?"

Lori let out a laugh that emanated from her diaphragm. It was so loud, the entire salon paused to see what was going on.

"I am so far ahead of you Leon. I think it would be the other way around. You will be joining me. I am the spirit Karma now, and what you propose of me, I already do on a regular basis."

Lori let out another laugh that raised the hairs on the back of Leon's neck. He thought to himself as he rushed for the backroom, "What have I gotten myself into?"

Maria had finished with Todd and brought him over to a table by the backroom and made him take a seat. She went to the room and returned with a glass in her hand which Lori at first thought was sweet tea. It was not. Todd picked it up and guzzled it all down before Lori could stop him.

"What have you given him?!" Lori asked in a panic.

Maria smiled at her and said. "He has a chemical imbalance in his brain. He's not retarded nor does he have autism or any of the other things the doctors have told you he might have. It's just a chemical imbalance. In the next day or so, as long as you don't let him consume chocolate milk, you will see a vast improvement in him. He will need to take this drink once a week. This is how we are going to ensure you stay in touch with us, unless you like him the way he is, then don't come back," Maria said nonchalantly and walked away.

Pastor Ted asked her if she was ready to depart. He had a busy afternoon and he wasn't feeling comfortable any longer being here. It was time to go. Lori agreed with him and they walked back to the truck to the screeching of tires, the sound of metal twisting and glass breaking. Funny thing how there were so many accidents on this stretch of road here in the city. It surely couldn't be from the clientele leaving the salon heading back to their vehicles. This is what Todd was saying to himself as the fog in his brain began to slowly dissipate. He was beginning to see the world in a new light, and he liked it. He liked it a whole lot.

CHAPTER 16

Owen had been typing like there was no tomorrow for about eight hours. The story had been written. He was just giving it life. It was what he did best. He wrote fiction. Just because the story was based on the truth was no reason he couldn't make it sound like it was a work of fiction. The last few months of his life had felt like something that was totally made up. The circumstances surrounding all the events were nothing short of unbelievable.

His thoughts were totally involved with his writing. Nothing else was distracting him from his work, and it flowed like water over a waterfall, the ideas just kept coming. He would stop now and again to check what Lori had written and then would dive right back into it. One of the times he stopped was to check what she had written when he was dealing with the bobcat. He had to read what she wrote several times, then he reread it. His brother had said they were not alone in the woods. They were being watched from above. At first, he thought his brother was talking about God, then he thought maybe his brother had seen his father like he had. He read it once more and began to feel ill.

His brother was clearly referring to someone else in the woods with them. A watcher from the trees that blended with the scenery. A man that remained silent and hidden but had seen all that had happened. Owen now knew how a deer felt when a hunter was positioned in a tree stand and decided if it was worthy of a shot, or would he let it pass by and wait for a better deer. Clueless. He had never known anybody was watching, but his brother did and never said a word to him. He felt his anger ebb inside, grabbed for some antacid. He felt slightly nauseous, his vision blurred. He needed air and he needed it now. He ran for the stairs and out the door as the sound of his cellphone ringing reached his ears.

Owen couldn't believe his bad luck. He paced around the yard. The sun had come up and still, his brother and Lori had not returned. Many scenarios began to rattle around in his head. The memory of the blood on the kitchen floor inspired a few more. A whole bunch of what-ifs started to play out in his mind. He ran back into the house and grabbed his cellphone. It wasn't Lori or his brother that had called, it was his friend Wade. He had left a short and sweet text message.

"Delahunt is dead, you need to call me immediately if not sooner, your pal Wade."

The news of Delahunt's passing was bitter and sweet. He disliked the man, yet he was taking care of his mother. The man had threatened him and encouraged his mother to run him and his brother out of town. He also was making his mother happy, and he hadn't seen her that way in some time. A sudden thought crossed his mind – what if his mother was hurt? Wade hadn't said how Delahunt had died. Maybe it was a car accident and his mother lay dying on her death bed. Wade would not have wanted to break that type of news in a text message. He quickly dialed Wade only to find himself playing phone tag. He screamed out in frustration and punched the wall. Now he needed an ice pack. His hand hurt so bad he thought he might have broken a bone or two.

He tried his mother's number not expecting her to answer his call. She didn't disappoint. No answer at the house. He wasn't sure if she had a cellphone; she and technology didn't get along too well. This would be something Todd might be able to answer for him if he could find his stupid brother. He tried to dial Lori's number only to hear her phone go off in the kitchen. He then dialed his brother's number only to hear it go straight to voice mail. Either his battery was dead, or his phone was shut off.

Owen grabbed some ice from the freezer and iced down his swollen knuckles while quickly cussing to himself. He begged God for some answers.

"Please God, don't do this to me, please!" he cried to no one in the room. Suddenly he heard music coming from his office upstairs. He quickly scrambled to his feet and attacked the stairs two at a time. Carolina Liar was playing, "Show Me What I'm Looking For," on Lori's laptop. Owen stood there in shock thinking this had to be some sort of joke that was being played on him. His cellphone rang. It was Wade.

* * *

"How could you set me up like that R.J.?" Lori asked the pastor.

The use of just his initials caught him by surprise, but the fact that she was so angry had not. When he received the phone call from Maria the previous evening, she had said that she was in town and wanted to have a meeting with him at Bo's place before noon the following day. That was all the information she would give him. He had not known Leon was going to be in attendance and he also did not know that Leon and Lori knew each other. He barely knew who Leon was, only that he was friends with Maria and that he ran a national biker club called the Queen Bees. He tried to explain this to Lori, but she was having none of it.

"I had this meeting set up before I even knew you were going to show up at the church this morning, so how could I have set you up?" he whined.

Lori pulled Todd along behind her. He seemed to be dragging his feet. She turned to see him gazing at a mural, enthralled with the design and detail in which it was created.

"Come on Todd, we have got to be getting home. Your brother must be worried sick."

"Why don't you use my phone and call him?" Pastor Ted said holding out his cell for her.

"I don't know his number, it's in my phone, which in my rush to get Todd to the hospital, I forgot at his house."

"What about his phone?" Pastor Ted pointed at Todd.

"It's got a dead battery in his truck. He forgets to charge it. His mind wanders off in all directions sometimes and he quickly loses focus, like right now."

Todd was once again stopped. He was looking at a window and drooling. The drink Maria gave Todd seemed to just have made him a bit more retarded than he acted before.

"Pizza, I love pizza. Can we get some?" Todd was acting like a little kid in a candy store.

Lori explained to him she didn't have any money on her. R.J. saved the day and bought them a large pizza to go. He ate most of it, but even so, when they got back to Todd's truck, she fished through her purse and gave him enough to cover the pizza and a small donation for the church.

R.J. thanked her, took the money, and pocketed it.

"I want to tell you about Maria before you go. I told you that you would meet my biggest success story, and you have. Maria is that story."

"I find it hard to believe that a woman that looks like her could ever be down in the dumps, but if you insist in telling me stories, then go on." She said this while getting Todd buckled up in the passenger seat. His eyes were glassy, and he seemed to be bobbing his head, like he was listening to a tune that only he could hear.

"A few years ago, more like five or six, the time flies by so fast, Maria married this man who was working for her father. Her father was a rich mobster from New York, and she was a spoiled little college brat living here in Richmond. I met her doing some dinner theater shows at some of the local hotels here in Richmond. We became friends and when I heard of her husband's demise, I reached out to her. She turned in all the evidence her husband had gathered on her father. Turns out her husband was an undercover ATF agent. When she did this, her father cut off all her finances and then she discovered she was pregnant with twins. She used her degree in chemistry to get a job at this pharmaceutical company but was fired when some drugs came up missing. She swears it wasn't her, but got fired anyway."

"Her savings were quickly depleted when the boys were born, then she was evicted from her apartment in the city. I came to her rescue, set her up in one of my places, and got her over the hump. Along came Joey Hopkins and all her problems were solved, but that was when they all began as well. Joey claims that her former husband is haunting him. Maria claims her former husband is whispering things in her ear. She writes them down and low and behold, they come true. This has gotten her into a whole lot of trouble that I've been dragged into more than a few times. If it wasn't for the good Lord looking out for me, surely, I would be dead by now. If I could only get him to keep Joey away from me, I might even live to a ripe old age."

Lori laughed at his story. Clearly, he was making this all up for her entertainment.

"This Joey Hopkins you're referring to, is that the Hollywood actor who won an Oscar for his very first film? I think he went on to do some voice work on animated films after that, didn't he?" Lori inquired.

"That would be the one and only I'm referring to. If you see him, run – run like the wind and don't even think about turning your head back to look at him. I would hate to see you turn out like Lot's wife, a pillar of salt," R.J. said so sincerely that Lori speculated if he was playing with her or if he was dead serious.

"I'll do my best Pastor Ted. I have one question for you though."

"Yes, my child, what is it?"

"Do I turn you on?" Lori asked him playfully.

A huge smile crossed R.J.'s face when she asked him that. Then he blushed bright red. He stuttered out an answer, one that made Lori blush. She threw him a kiss and started up the truck, waved goodbye, and headed back to the house. When they arrived, they found a note from Owen. He had an emergency. A trip back to New York was required, no time to explain. She found herself alone once again with Todd and he had a huge glass of chocolate milk he was getting ready to devour. For some reason, she found herself knocking the glass from his hand and splashing it all over the wall. Maria had said to not let him drink any more chocolate milk, but it was his favorite drink. He whined when she explained to him why she had done what she had done. They cleaned the mess up together, laughing and joking with one another.

Lori was very tired. Todd's eyes were looking heavy with dark circles below his eyes. When she suggested they should go to bed, Todd was more than happy to oblige, nearly dragging her to his room. When she explained that she meant in separate beds, he pouted, but then he lay his head down on his pillow and was fast asleep before she had left the room. She stopped by Owen's office and found her laptop open on his desk. Owen must have found what she and Todd had written. She wondered out loud what could have possibly spooked Owen into returning to New York after the trip he had just experienced.

Opening her file, she peered at where he had left off and read that page. It hit her then. She had written that Owen and Todd were not alone in the forest. A thought crossed her mind – Owen was going to go look for the man in the forest. This would not be a good thing for that man, but how was she going to get Owen to turn around and come back before he did more damage than necessary? She had added that to the story, something that Karma had told her to do. Todd never even knew she had added that to the story.

Lori tried to remember where she had left her cellphone. She must warn Owen before he did something stupid. All she heard was Karma laughing as she ran in search of her phone. Karma can be such a bitch.

* * *

Owen had brought his SUV to the autobody shop and now had a nice new rental. It was a Nissan Altima that was twice as good on gas as his vehicle. He almost made the whole trip on one tank. Impressed with the ride and the fuel economy, he thought he might even trade his car in for one of these. Unlike his last trip north, this one was uneventful.

Wade had told Owen his mother had gone missing over a week ago. Delahunt had been asking everyone if they knew of her whereabouts, but he was getting nowhere. When he was murdered in the woods, the news had mentioned Owen's name as a person of interest. That was when Owen had decided he had to make this trip. He had already read what Lori had typed into her laptop. This information only confirmed that he was not alone in the woods. The feds knew something they were keeping close to the vest, and his future hung on that information.

His first stop was at his mother's house where he found the mailbox overflowing with last week's mail. He didn't have a key, but he knew there was a fake rock in the rock garden. After examining over ten rocks, he finally found the one with the key within it, opened the door, and replaced the key. If his mother were still alive, she would have his ass if the spare key wasn't where it was supposed to be.

A search of the house gave no clues as to where she might have gone, so he decided to make a trip up to the trailhead and have a look around. Upon arriving there, he noticed that the place had been marked with yellow police tape, but it had been cut down with some pieces still visibly left behind. A sort of warning to others that might want to venture this way that a tragedy had taken place on this trail.

He hiked the mile or so up the trail and found the clearing where it had all begun. He searched the trees above and noticed where the tree stand had been mounted. The marks on the tree gave away where it had been positioned. The feds must have removed it as evidence. The game camera was still in place, which Owen found to be strange. Why would they take the tree stand and not the camera? Puzzled, he sat down close to where the bobcat den had been. The little bobcat kittens were gone, hopefully, the mother had just relocated them and they were still alive and well, he thought to himself.

Owen jumped to his feet when he heard a noise behind him. A noise only an animal could have made. Wade had told him that the bobcat had torn out the sheriff's throat and had consumed some of his flesh. Goosebumps rose on Owen's neck as he searched the forest for the killer animal. He had no weapon to defend himself. It was hard to believe that the mother bobcat had allowed him to remove the shard of glass from her paw. The animal seemed to him to almost be domesticated. She did not appear to him to be a ruthless killer.

Owen sat back down, pondered his predicament and what his next course of action was going to be. He even pondered going into the police station and confessing just to relieve all the stress he was under. Owen tried to get a handle on how this could have all happened to him, the choices he had made, and the actions he had taken. He smacked himself in the head for his stupidity. The bobcat smacked him in the head as well. If her claws had been extended, Owen's head would have been a mass of blood, but she wasn't there to hurt him, just get his attention.

The bobcat snuggled up against him and began to purr. Owen found himself scratching behind her ears like she was just an ordinary house cat. The camera was catching it all, and the feds were at the edge of their seats watching the scene unfold before their unbelieving eyes.

One of them concluded that Owen had trained this animal to attack and kill. He had returned to the scene of the crime to check up on his prized animal. The guy was some sort of a cat whisperer or something like that. This got the other agents thinking on the same level. The only problem was that this was not the man who shot the arrow from the tree. The body size and the way Owen moved about were all wrong for the hunter they had on tape. Owen must be working with an accomplice. They were sure if they kept monitoring him, that he would lead them right straight to the other man. As much as they wanted to go arrest Owen on the spot, they remained vigilant in their watch. The time would come, they just had to be patient.

Owen spent about five minutes or so with the bobcat before she decided it was time to move on. She had even let him examine her paw, her own way of thanking him for helping her. Owen was sad when the cat bounded off back into the depths of the woods. He lost sight of her within a few seconds. He had come to see if the story was true that he was not alone that day, got his confirmation, and departed.

When he reached his rental car, he decided to go and visit the bar he and his brother had gotten so smashed at just before the funeral. Nothing like a few good stiff drinks to take your mind off your burdens. His burdens were weighing heavily on him now, he needed to numb his mind of all his problems. He thought he would get shitfaced, sleep it off, and then decide what to do next.

The trip to the bar flew by, maybe because he was driving erratically and at a high rate of speed. The feds thought he was driving that way trying to lose their tale. He slid into a spot out in front of the bar and hurried inside. He was immediately recognized by the bartender and informed that he had left the bar the last time without paying his bill. Owen had no idea if he had or not, so asked the barkeep what the previous damage was, paid him, and gave him a handsome tip for his troubles.

Owen didn't want to mix drinks like the last time, so he just ordered up a Jack and coke, told the bartender to go heavy on the Jack. If Owen was going to give him another healthy tip like he had just done, the bartender had no problem going heavy-handed on his drinks. He just made sure he got his payment upfront this time, no sense in taking chances.

Owen was on his second heavy-handed Jack Daniels and coke when the man came inside the bar and sat beside him.

"You're Owen Canton, the writer?" he asked.

Owen stared at him to see if he might know who this intruder to the watering of his sorrows was. The guy rang no bells to him, but he did buy him a drink. One that maybe Owen should not have had. They talked for a few minutes about some minor town gossip, which Owen had no clue as to what he was talking about. The man was just talking to make it look like they were talking about nothing. When the barkeep was out of earshot, the man passed him a zip drive and slid it under his hand.

"The game camera caught everything on tape. I removed the file and put it on this zip drive. You now have the only copy. I was in the tree stand when it all took place, saw and heard it all."

Owen now knew it was true, they had not been alone in the forest that day.

"I was impressed with how Tessie befriended you. I raised her from a kitten. Her mother was struck and killed by a car. She never would have survived if I hadn't found her and saved her. I trained and worked with her for the last couple of years. She is a very smart and lethal cat. I had to pay the sheriff back for framing my father for murder, I got payback for you as well. I bet you didn't know that Andy wasn't the only one chasing your father the day he died."

This last comment got Owen's attention and brought him out of his alcoholic haze.

"What did you say about the death of my father?"

"Andy liked to come over to my father's trailer and drink with him. They both were drunks as far as I'm concerned. Andy liked to brag about the things he had done. He bragged about killing your wife, then he bragged about how he and the sheriff had run your father out on the tracks and watched him get spattered by the train. He laughed about it and was proud of himself. My father punched him right in the face, breaking one of Andy's front teeth. When I found the skull, I had placed it on top of the rock in the clearing while I was checking up on Tessie and the kittens. It was clear to me who it belonged to, with the broken front tooth. My stupid father strolled up and found it, rushed off before I could stop him. The man was so drunk he never even knew I was there at the time."

Owen felt sympathy for the boy. He knew it could be tough growing up in that kind of environment. He thought about asking about the whereabouts of the boy's mother, thought better of it, and let the boy continue.

"The feds got involved, I knew why you had shot Andy. The man was inciting you to do it. I know because I was in the tree listening to it all go down. I would have shot the bastard in the head long before you had done it." The boy was getting all worked up, ordered them another round. He wasn't old enough to drink, so he was drinking soda while Owen was getting sloshed.

"I was in my tree stand the day Delahunt came looking for the game camera. I knew he would. The bastard had already told the feds it was my father and had planted the evidence on him. He had killed a federal agent while trying to dissuade him from doing his job. The agent wasn't going along with him, so he blasted the guy with the shotgun my dad left behind. I left it all on my computer for the feds to find. They were in my dad's trailer investigating when the sheriff showed up. I put an arrow in his chest and let Tessie have a bit of fun with him. I might have gone a little too far by letting the feds watch it all while it was happening, so I'm leaving town and giving you the last thing that could possibly implicate you in any of this. Just keep your mouth shut and all will turn out in your favor."

It was a good story the boy had spun. Owen wanted to compliment him on his imagination, but the boy had somehow left him behind. He looked up at the barkeep to ask him a question when he noticed something on the back wall. The damn things were everywhere, intruding on a person's privacy, no place was safe anymore. A damn camera was filming everything that he and the boy had just discussed.

Owen tried to stand on wobbly legs. He knew he had to leave and destroy the zip drive. His legs weren't cooperating with him. He was in desperate need of a pot of coffee to sober himself up. The thought that maybe he should have eaten something before consuming all that alcohol crossed his mind. Unsteadily, he made his way for the door. Two nice men in suits helped him to a car, one that didn't belong to him, and got him seated in the back seat. They took the zip drive from him and thanked him for his help in their investigation. He noticed the boy was in the backseat of the car that was parked beside them. The poor child was crying. Owen thought they must have done something mean to the boy. His vision blurred as he thought about what was going down. He had a bad feeling about all of this. These thoughts passed through his mind as the world got darker and darker until they faded to nothing.

* * *

Lori was beside herself. Karma had hidden her phone. She couldn't get Todd's phone to hold a charge so she could get Owen's number from it. Frantically, she raced around the house searching for a bill or anything that would give her a hint to what his cellphone number might be. She even tried to call information, but his number was unlisted, and they weren't allowed to give out that information on a famous person such as Owen Canton.

Karma laughed at her the whole time, saying that this was how it was all going to play out, nothing she was going to be able to do about it. Frustrated with her inner intruder, she thought that she would pay back Karma for making her life a living hell. She walked to Todd's room, opened the door, and entered inside. Todd was peacefully snoozing when she slid her naked body under the covers beside him. Karma was pitching a fit the whole time. This made Lori smile. She said in her mind that she could be a bitch just as well as Karma could be. She reached over and gently woke Todd from his slumber. She smiled at him and asked him if he would make love to her. She knew she wouldn't have to ask him twice.

Karma let out a scream.

"What have you done Lori?! You stupid bitch, this is all wrong!"

Lori smiled to herself and then gave herself to Todd, anticipating a night of passionate lovemaking. The sky grumbled with thunder and lightning flashed across the sky. The clouds released their moisture and the rains came down in buckets, like the tears that Karma now shed. This was a complication she had not anticipated. Lori had betrayed her and gone against her wishes. She was just trying to do her job and implement the plan God had laid out. Now as she listened to God show his displeasure in the outcome she had forged, she thought about resigning and taking another position in the realm. Maybe she could be a guardian angel. It was a demotion from the position she now held, but she thought it might be more than she was able to handle. Her failure tonight was not going to shine a bright light upon her.

Suddenly music started playing from Lori's laptop. A song from Jonathan David Helser and Melisa Helser called, "Abba"(Arms of A Father) began its wholesome tune. Karma immediately began to feel better about herself and her mission. She began to sing along with the music, of course, it was Lori's voice singing, causing Todd to pause at what he was about to do, and Lori to become distressed. She felt Todd's hardness fade away knowing that Karma had once again gotten her way. No matter what Todd did after that, he was unable to perform.

"It's okay, Todd. We'll just snuggle and enjoy each other's company," Lori said soothingly as she kept the anger that was stewing within her from ebbing forth.

The following morning, she awoke to an empty house. Todd was gone. No note, no nothing. Lori was beside herself. Karma reassured her that he would be back. She then made some wisecrack about Todd needing a whole lot of Viagra if he couldn't get it up with a girl that was as beautiful as Lori. They argued back and forth for a few minutes until Lori finally gave up and went to take a shower.

Lori sat at Owen's wife's vanity and used her cold cream to remove all traces of the makeup Maria had applied the day before that would come off. Her lips remained redder than normal and she couldn't get the eyelashes off. Frustrated, she removed the bright red nail polish. She then reached for some nail clippers to cut her nails back but kept dropping them. Without a doubt, she knew Karma was responsible for this. A closer look in the mirror slightly upset her. The lashes must be glued on with something she didn't have at her disposal to use to remove them. Without any foundation or blush, she looked foolish. Damn Karma was going to make sure she looked good or she would look the fool.

After her shower, she searched Owen's room and found some of his wife's everyday clothes. His wife was into fashion and she didn't have much stuff that didn't make her look like she had just stepped out of a glamour magazine. She took a seat at the vanity once again and began to apply what she felt was a light amount of makeup. Once she was done, her nails were once again coated in polish, but this time a soft pink. She decided that her look was not going to stop traffic or cause any car accidents, at least that was what she hoped.

Satisfied that she didn't look like a floozy now, she grabbed her purse and keys and went to her car. She needed to go to church, it was a Sunday and Pastor Ted had a service at nine and eleven. She would be able to make the eleven o'clock service if she hurried. It was time to get saved, and she sure as hell knew she needed saving. The car started as well as the music on the radio. A message was being sent, she was sure of it. The song on the radio was by Chris Tomlin called "Nobody Loves Me Like You." Was God trying to tell her to be strong and stay the course? Lori wasn't sure, but as she was backing out of the driveway her cellphone went off. She stopped the car and found her phone under her front seat. She now knew where Karma had hidden it. A glance at who was calling revealed that it was Owen.

What he had to tell her was not the news she was hoping to get. He was locked up in jail and was being charged with murder. He wanted her to take care of his brother until he could get things sorted out up there in New York. He asked her not to come up, but just wait and be vigilant. He needed her to be strong for him and his brother. She never got a chance to get a word in before he hung up. She quickly hit redial only to get his voicemail. His cellphone had been turned off. Unsure of what to do, she headed for the Church of New Hope. Then she thought about the vandalized sign that read Church of No Hope and began to wonder exactly which one it might be. The first tear of the day made its way down her cheek. It wouldn't be long before it was joined by many more.

When she arrived at the church, the parking lot was overflowing with cars. A man with a high visibility vest told her she could find a spot just about a block down the street. This turned out to take just a bit longer than she had anticipated as that lot had enough room for one more vehicle, and it wasn't in a location that was easy to navigate her car into. With just a slight scratch on the fender of the car she parked beside and a quickly written note placed on the windshield, she hurried to the church. She was wearing heels, which made running difficult. The skirt she had chosen had a slit up the side that showed a whole lot of leg when she made larger steps. Her pace slowed when she realized this.

When she opened the door to the church, she found that the service had begun. She glanced down at the watch she had borrowed from Owen's wife's jewelry box. It was 11:15 – she was late. A seat was open a few rows from the back that she quickly made her way to. Feeling the tears begin to cascade down her cheek, she reached into her purse to find a tissue. Not one could be found. More tears made their way from the corners of her eyes. An elderly lady who was sitting beside her took pity on her and gave Lori some tissues. Grateful for her kindness, Lori began to cry more and a whole lot louder. She just couldn't help herself. Pastor Ted was trying to give his best performance, but was now being distracted by Lori, which was causing the rest of the church to become distracted and begin to turn their heads to see what all the commotion was all about.

Pastor Ted motioned to his office assistant, Desiree, to go over and try to handle the situation. They began to argue with hand motions, no words, which was making the congregation laugh. The faces Pastor Ted was making as his frustration with his office assistant mounted was even funnier. Finally, Desiree stood up and announced to everyone that she would go and take care of another woman that the pastor might have impregnated, which caused Pastor Ted to announce that he hadn't gotten anyone pregnant, now or before. This made the congregation laugh even harder until Lori stood up and announced that she was a virgin and was not in any kind of a relationship with the pastor. Lori apologized through her tears that she was sorry that she had made a scene, asked the good people to pray for her, and walked out of the church to a stunned crowd.

Pastor Ted motioned to his intern minister to finish up, which nearly gave the poor fellow a heart attack, as he was not prepared to lead a service. Pastor Ted quickly exited the church a couple of minutes later in search of Lori, listening to his intern stuttering that he wasn't prepared and forgive him as he tried to pick up where Pastor Ted left off.

As he ran into the parking lot, the man with the high visibility vest pointed him in the right direction. Lori was half a block ahead of him. He ran as fast as his big body could run. He thought she might be walking faster than he was running. Each step she took flashed a very shapely leg and then hidden just as fast. He reached the parking lot to the sound of her car scraping the vehicle parked beside her, making a line down the length of her car. He blocked her exit and prayed that she would stop and not run him over. He wasn't sure what she would do, so he put his faith in God and stood his ground. He closed his eyes just in case and braced for the pain. It never came, she had stopped.

He opened his eyes and gazed through the windshield. Her mascara had run all down her face causing her to look like Alice Cooper on a bad makeup day. He knew she was upset about something, had come to the church for his support, and been embarrassed right out of the church and into the street. He had to do something for her, so he opened the door and sat beside her.

"Want to tell me about it? Take your time. The church is in good hands with Ricky, my assistant. He doesn't have much experience, but he does have some big cajones to jump in for me like he did as I ran out of the church to help you, my dear."

He wanted to say more, but he let her sit there with the car idling and her eyes closed tight. He wasn't sure if she was angry or sad. What he did know was that she was upset, and he sure hoped it wasn't something he had done, which was very little for her. She had asked for his help and he hadn't come through for her. The spirit inside of her had scared the living crap out of him the last time they had been together. The damn thing knew a lot about his personal misgivings, the things in his life he was trying to put behind him and begin anew.

The radio was on and the DJ announced the next song, Needtobreathe, "Forever on Your Side." The song began to play, and R.J. found himself staring out the window and toward the sky. He also found Lori hugging him and crying on his shoulder. The car was still in drive and they were easing out into the street, out into traffic. In a panic, R.J. grabbed the wheel and turned them away from danger and into the side of another parked car. They were still alive and R.J.'s heart was beating a mile a minute. It wasn't from the close call with death. It was from Lori's body pressed firmly into his as she cried on his shoulder. He had eased off the alcohol altogether as he had rehabbed himself, rarely falling off the wagon lately. When he had done this, his sexual urges had waned, and he found himself wanting a steady girlfriend. He had been dating Sofia from the hospital for a few months now and was strongly thinking of asking for her hand in marriage. Now with Lori so close to him, he questioned everything he had planned. He needed to get out of the car now and get away before it was too late.

"What's the matter R.J.? Your little weeny growing with excitement?"

It was Lori talking, but he knew the spirit inside of her was controlling what was being said.

"If you must know the truth, yes, it is. She is beautiful and sexy, and you are not. I want to help her rid you from her body."

Lori laughed, it almost sounded like a cackle.

"If I leave her, she dies. I'm the only thing keeping her alive. She was on her deathbed when I took control. I thought she had passed, but she fooled me. When I finish with her, she will revert to when I entered her. Do you really want her to die? Or do you want to learn how to control me so that she may continue to live a healthy life? Can't have it both ways, so tell me, which is it going to be?"

Karma had spoken the truth to Pastor Ted. When she's bored of Lori and decided to transfer to another body, Lori might last a day or two before succumbing to the deadly and destructive diabetes. Lori had been brought back from the depths of a diabetic coma. Her body was shutting down and she was moments from death. Karma was the only reason she was still living and breathing.

Pastor Ted wanted to talk to Lori, so he asked the question that needed to be asked talking to Lori, not Karma.

"What do you need me to do for you? Is death preferable to living the way you are now? I need to know so that I can help you."

Lori looked at him, wiped a tear from her eye, causing her mascara to darken her face even more.

"I want you to help me get Owen out of jail. He was arrested for murder. He needs our help. I didn't know who else to turn to. I'm begging you to help me." The tears began once again.

It was clear to Pastor Ted. This wasn't about Karma. This was about Owen. He made the determination that Lori had decided to live with her demon, or spirit, whatever they wanted to call themselves. He reached for his cellphone, realized it was still in the church. He hadn't memorized Joey Hopkins' phone number. That number he never wanted to remember, in fact, he barely ever wanted to be around the man anymore. If anybody could help Owen, it was him.

He had Lori drive him back to the church. He instructed her to park out back next to his truck where they had plenty of parking spaces. Lori was invited back inside with him while he made some phone calls. She excused herself to use the restrooms while he went to his office and grabbed his phone. The few seconds of hesitation was enough for someone to notice.

"You sure you want to call him? This isn't no game R.J. The man is like a bull in a china shop. We both have seen the incredible things he can do, but at what price. Don't do it unless you're sure and prepared to pay that price. I'm just warning you," Desiree said as she took a seat at his desk.

R.J. held the phone in his hands with his finger close to the call button. He wasn't sure if he wanted to pay that price. His leg had healed with minimal damage from the two bullet wounds he sustained the last time he was anywhere near the man. His memory was full of all those adventures and near-death experiences he had survived doing things for and with the man. Those days had occurred when he was drinking. He wondered if he would be able to handle them sober. Lori answered the question for him.

"You can do anything you want if you ask God to help you do it. Call him, you know you want to. I'll tell you a story of a man that went body surfing at the beach while you're deciding."

Desiree and R.J. just looked at her in utter silence. This was not the girl who had been balling her eyes out inside the church just a few moments ago. This girl was strong and confident. This girl was in control and knew what she wanted and what she wanted was for him to call Joey. This he knew from the story she began to tell.

"A man went to the beach to relax and sunbathe. A storm was brewing off the coast and caused the surf to be rough. The waves were tall and violently breaking upon the shore. He looked at them with a longing, thinking it would be fun to ride a few waves like he did when he was a younger man and had a surfboard. He decided that he could ride a couple of waves using his body and body surf a couple of them. When he got to the edge of the surf, he began to change his mind. The water was not inviting him in, it was warning him away. It said that there was great danger within its waves and only a fool would venture within. He heeded that warning and began to walk away thinking about all the fun he was walking away from."

"Just then while he wasn't looking, a rogue wave broke the surface and engulfed him, dragging him under and into its depths. It dragged him back out to the sea and the only way to get back was to ride a wave back in, which he did. It was so much fun, that instead of walking away he ventured back into the water to ride some more waves. God had let the fool ride one so that he would not miss out on the adventure he so clearly wanted. When the man went back out into the surf, he ended up drowning. The moral of the story is, take what is given to you, but know your limits and don't try to take more than you can handle. The man had made the right decision in walking away and the wrong one when he made it back to shore and decided to go back in for more. Now call him, I'm the wave that is dragging you into the surf. Just know when you reach the shore to get the hell out of the water."

Lori laughed to a stunned R.J. and Desiree as they both stared at her with their mouths open, not knowing what to say.

Pastor Ted hit the call button on his phone, and everything changed in a flash. Joey answered his call and said he would be right there. A few moments later, Lori was staring at a man in his thirties with a wild look in his eyes. He introduced himself to her as Joey Hopkins. She asked him if he had been in the next room listening in on their conversation. He said, something like that.

This had her baffled. She looked to R.J. for an answer. He just shrugged.

"You told me to call him. Here he is, how he got here I don't want to know. The sooner he leaves the safer we'll all be."

He smiled down at Joey and gave him a hug. Lori thought she might have heard one of Joey's ribs crack.

"Good to see you, old buddy. I have a friend here in need of your assistance. Take a seat and let's talk." He motioned for Joey to take a seat opposite Desiree. When he was seated, R.J. began his pitch.

'It seems she has a similar problem you have, only it shares her body with her. I thought maybe you could help her with that and one other problem. Owen Canton has been arrested for murder. I know you have connections and I thought if you were to use them, that maybe you could have Owen write your story that you say you've always wanted to have told. Maria just writes about the future. Owen can write about how you handled one crisis after another that Maria wrote you would have and how you dealt with them. He already has written more than one bestseller. This could be your chance to get your story out and tell the people of the world how God works in strange and mysterious ways."

Joey stood up and thanked him for inviting him over, but that he had to go. He turned to leave and found himself face to face with Lori and her pleading blue eyes. One look into her eyes was all it took.

"You either know Maria or have met her. I can see her handy work around your eyes."

"I have met her, and it was Bo that defined my eyes, not her."

"Same difference, he taught her everything she knows. How did you meet Maria and live to talk about it? Every time I'm anywhere near her, I have a life-defining moment. Seems she is always around the action and I get dragged into it. Sometimes I save her life, but sometimes she saves mine."

"I had a small problem with some Queen Bees. We had a talk at the salon Bo owns. She came out of the backroom and we discussed a few things. A friend of mine has a mental problem. She seems to think she has a cure for it, gave him a drink, and asked us to return on a weekly basis to get more. My friend didn't show any sign of getting better after drinking it. I'm thinking she was full of it."

"I can tell you firsthand, be careful drinking anything she gives you. Take a good look at me. Do I look like I'm in my sixties to you?"

Lori gasped. Joey looked to be mid-thirties at best. No way he was in his sixties. R.J. reached into his drawer and pulled out a scrapbook. It was of his first super bash. He showed her a picture of Joey taken several years before. A man with gray hair, balding, and clearly in his mid-fifties smiling into the camera.

"I age well as you can see. It's all because I drank something Maria made for me. It didn't happen right away. It took a few hours before the drink took effect. I could go on for weeks about some of the things she has created, but we don't have that much time. Hopefully, your friend will be okay."

Lori began to have a bad feeling. Todd had disappeared this morning. She had tried to seduce him into making love to her last night and he couldn't keep an erection. She knew without a doubt that Todd wanted to ravage her but was unable to do it. Could it be the drink Maria gave him was the cause of his body not being able to perform? She would have to see what else had happened to him since she had last seen him.

"I'll look into what I can do for Owen and be in touch with you in a few weeks or so."

Joey pulled out his phone and asked her for her number. He entered it and bid them farewell. As fast as he had shown up, he was gone. Lori looked for him after he left, but nobody had noticed him leave the building or had remembered even seeing him. She found this to be a strange thing. Everyone knew who Joey was in Richmond, yet no one had claimed to have seen him today.

She thanked Pastor Ted for his help and headed home. Todd's truck was back in the driveway and Lori grew excited in anticipation of seeing Todd and if any changes had taken place in him since she had last seen him. When she walked into the house, she got her answer. He had changed alright. He had not gotten younger to her relief, but he had gotten smarter. An intellectual in the making. He had gone from a slow-talking idiot to a smart and charming young man. So charming that he had brought home two women and was in the middle of showing them things that they would never have imagined. She stood in the doorway to his room with the three of them totally unaware that she was observing what was going on. They were so engrossed with each other that she could have screamed, and if she had, she thought that they still might not have noticed that she was there.

She got in her car and headed straight back to her apartment that she had been told had burnt to the ground but in all actuality had never even had a smoke detector go off. Feeling better being back in her comfort zone, she decided to relax and luxuriate with a bubble bath. The water was hot and inviting as she eased herself down into the bubbles. She closed her eyes and wondered what the next few weeks would bring. Her mind was at ease and as she slowly drifted off into a light slumber that was interrupted by the screech of the smoke alarm. The smell of smoke and the sounds of screams found her rushing to escape from her burning building. Dressed only in a towel, she felt she had only herself to blame for her neighbors being burnt out or their homes. One way or another, Karma was going to get exactly what she wanted.

CHAPTER 17

Owen lay in the holding cell pondering his future. When the feds had swooped in at the bar, they got the zip drive before he even had a chance to view what was on the damn thing. This might just be a setup to get him to confess. He had no idea who the young man was that gave him the zip drive, only that he said that everything he had done was on it.

Owen wondered if the feds could have put together a possible scenario where they had figured out a few things and then get him to confess to it all. He decided he would keep his mouth shut and ask for a lawyer. Until he saw the evidence against him, he was going to retain his innocence, no matter how guilty he was.

He was so drunk yesterday, that they read him his rights and stowed him away in this holding cell. When he woke, he talked the guard into letting him use his cellphone, told the guard he could listen in on the conversation. He wanted to call his girlfriend and his lawyer, let them know what was happening. To his surprise, the guard passed him his phone, stood beside him, and monitored the whole conversations. He wanted to say more to Lori, but with the guard standing right by his side listening to his every word, Owen found it impossible to tell Lori how he really felt about her and that he was jealous of his brother. He also wanted to thank her for putting the story in writing, and how it had inspired him to weave his latest tale of fiction that was embedded in the truth.

With the calls made, he thanked the guard and laid back on his uncomfortable cot. His back hurt just looking at the thing. Lying on it made it hurt even worse. He suffered through the pain and worked out in his mind how the rest of his novel was going to play out. The thought that he was going to rot in jail for the remainder of his life had made frequent appearances that he erased several times. The ending had to be better than that, he thought. Now all he had to do was think of what the perfect ending was going to be. His writer's block kicked in, there was nothing he could foresee that didn't end up with him in a jail cell. That was until the commotion from down the hall made him sit up and take notice.

Kyle Parker Jr., the son of a murdered drunk that had taken revenge on the sheriff and filmed everything on a game camera was missing. He was in his cell one minute, the next he was gone. The search was on for the missing boy. Owen thought that this was just too damn convenient. The feds were planning to set him up without a doubt in his mind. They had faked an escape of one of the key culprits. Now all they had was his testimony and he wasn't going to give them a single thing. He sat back on the floor Indian-style and tried to stretch out his aching back. The shouts of panic in the voices of the guards made him smile. They were putting on a good show just for him. Well, he wasn't buying it. They had nothing. His story began to unfold in his head. The ending was looking a whole lot brighter now.

* * *

Kyle was sitting in his cell thinking about Tessie and her kittens. He sure hoped they would be alright without him. It looked like his life was now going to be behind bars unless they decided to give him a lethal injection for killing the sheriff. Then his life was going to be a whole lot shorter. He figured they would reinstate the death penalty just for him and after he was dead, abolish it once again. That was how his whole life had been. If it hadn't been for the animals, he thought he might have committed suicide years ago. His father was just a useless drunk that had never done a damn thing in his life. His mother was even worse than his father, that was why he had chosen to spend the last few years with him in that tiny piece of shit trailer on the side of the mountain.

At least his father wasn't having a different man in the house several times a week having sex for drugs and a few bucks. What his father did was have friends like Andy Dotson come over and drink until they passed out with his creep friend bragging about how he had killed his former girlfriend for leaving him and marrying some loser. Then, he bragged about how he and the sheriff had run the father of that loser out onto the railroad tracks and laughed about how the train had squashed him and cut him up into unrecognizable pieces.

Kyle thought about how he had seen it all play out below him as he hid in the tree stand. He heard how Andy had taunted Owen into pulling the trigger. He also saw other things he could not explain. Owen was talking to someone who was not there with him as he stripped off all of Andy's clothes. Kyle was thinking maybe the guy was a pervert or something. The brother comes back with an ax and shovel. Instead of cutting Andy up, they leave him and go bury the clothes. With nowhere to go, Kyle watched in horror as the next few minutes unfolded. The first thing that arrived was a bald eagle. It took the first few bites out of Andy. Tessie and the kittens joined the eagle and before Kyle knew it, they were joined by an opossum and a fox. The eagle flew away, and then buzzards arrived to take a place at the table. The animals all worked together and made short work of their dinner. Andy was gone without a trace. That was until Kyle found the skull a few days later while checking up on the bobcat kittens. And then the rest of the story unfolded.

Who was Owen talking to before his brother showed back up? That was a question Kyle was struggling with. He hadn't seen a Bluetooth in Owen's ear. It just felt strange and all wrong to him.

"I can tell you who he was talking to."

A voice startled Kyle out of his reverie. He looked up to see who was talking to him. It was a slightly older man dressed in a pink housecoat with slippers on his feet.

"I'm sorry about the way I'm dressed. I only have a few minutes before she wakes up. The woman is an animal and keeps me busy day and night. You would think at her age that she would get tired, but you would be wrong. Anyhow, we have got to go. Now get up and let's be going."

The man was talking a mile a minute about nonsense and things that made no sense to Kyle at all. He remained where he was.

"I'm sorry, I didn't introduce myself. My name is Ryan and I'm an angel that works with Karma. I'm on a mission right now, but I was interrupted and told I must take you to a safe place. If you don't get out of here today, you won't see tomorrow. Seems some of the sheriff's friends and family have got this vendetta. You are the target and don't have much time left. Grab my hand and I'll get you out. Stay and you die. Your choice, pick wisely."

Kyle thought the man was slightly crazy. He never saw or heard the guards put this strange man in his cell. That didn't mean they hadn't done it. He could have missed it. He sat up and put his hand out, the man named Ryan told him he had made a wise choice. He tried to pull his hand back when he realized what he had done, but it was too late. A large flash appeared before his eyes and then they were in the desert sitting on the side of a sandstone ledge. Kyle jumped to his feet. His mind had suddenly shifted to overload. This was all wrong, he must be having a vivid dream. This just couldn't be happening to him.

"I have got to go. A little Latino boy riding a horse will pass by here in a few moments. Go with him and he will keep you safe. Kyle watched the crazy man named Ryan push a button on the side of his cellphone and disappear. One second, he was here with him, the next gone like the wind.

Kyle sat back down on the ledge and put his head into his hands. He prayed to God, a god he did not believe in. One that answers the prayers of even unbelievers like him. With his eyes closed deep in prayer, he heard the horse whinny. Opening his eyes, he saw a young Latino boy sitting on a horse holding the reins of another horse saddled up and ready to go.

"I had just saddled her up to go for a ride when something startled her, and she took off running. This was very unlike her, so I saddled up Drake here, and we came out looking for her. Funny we find somebody out here in the middle of nowhere. I bet you have no idea how you got here. Would I be right?"

Kyle lifted his head out of his hands and nodded.

"Kind of freaks you out the first time you do it. I know it did me. Hop up and we'll take a ride. I have a feeling you're going to be staying with us for a while. Are you good with animals? I need someone to take care of my chores while I'm away. I have a tour coming up in a couple of weeks and have got to leave and start rehearsing for our shows. Can you believe I'm going to be playing for the President of the United States? It sure has me jacked up."

Kyle listened as the boy spoke without listening to what the boy was saying. His thoughts were how he got here and what he was going to do next. The crazy guy had said he was an angel and had somehow transported him to some distant land. Kyle began to wonder if he was even still alive and maybe the flash of light was an explosive that had blown him all the way to this place. He wanted to ask the boy some questions, but he was afraid of the answers.

"I bet you are wondering where you are and who I am. I know I would be wondering those things. Would you like me to fill you in, or are you just going to sit on the horse and ride begging to know in your mind but afraid to ask?"

It was like the kid was a mind reader or something, Kyle was flabbergasted. Was the kid clairvoyant? Was that how he knew he would be out in the desert and he made up the story about the other saddled horse? Things were strange and getting stranger by the moment. The kid was waiting for an answer. Kyle gave him one.

"Kid, what is your name and how and where am I? Are you satisfied? I'm scared shitless, nothing makes sense to me. Am I dead or alive? I sure as hell have no clue," Kyle rambled out questions in quick succession. He didn't expect any answers.

"Okay, my name is Jesus, but everyone calls me Beats. I play the drums, so that is how I got the nickname. We are in Eastern California, east of LA. You are quite alive and well. Your prayers were answered, and God sent you here for a reason, I don't know what that reason is, but I'm sure we'll find out soon. Do you have any more questions?"

"You didn't answer how I got here, that is the one question I need an answer to."

"Yes, I did. I told you God sent you here. Didn't you listen to what I said?"

"I don't believe in God. I guess that might be why I missed your answer."

Beats let out a large belly laugh. He almost fell off his horse. Once he regained his composure, he told Kyle the truth.

"I was once like you. One day when I was in a stall with a horse back in Virginia, I was trying to will its broken leg to heal before the vet came back with the stuff to put the horse down. I was joined in that stall by Jesus himself and he showed me something. Together we healed that horse and some truly great things happened after that. You might have heard, her name is Truly, the horse that won the Kentucky Derby a few years ago."

Kyle had remembered that race well. The horse that won the race was disqualified and the second-place horse was awarded the victory. He also remembered what happened after the race and the tent going up for the injured horse. The jockey running from the tent and then the horse walking out alive and well. It had brought tears to his eyes. First thinking they were going to put the horse down and then when the horse walked out of the tent, he felt jubilation and cried his eyes out.

"I can see in your eyes you remember the race. I remember it as well. I ended up with a broken leg and some painful surgeries. When you're new at the healing game, sometimes you can mess things up, like I did that day."

"You can heal?"

Beats looked over to him and gave him a look that said, "Aren't you listening to a damn thing I'm saying?"

"I heard you, I'm just finding it all hard to believe. Your stories all sound like they're made up."

"Something like how you got here. Your accent reminds me of the time I was in New York. It was my first time here at the ranch. I was staring down the barrel of the gun that was going to end my short life when it happened. A flash of light and here I am in California. One minute I'm in New York waiting to die, the next I'm safe and sound right here on this wonderful ranch. Were you in a similar situation, waiting for someone to take your life and then whisked away to safety like I was?"

"A male angel came to me in my jail cell dressed in a female's pink robe wearing slippers. He told me I had to get out because my life was in danger and I would not survive the day if I stayed."

Beats laughed, "Boy could I tell you some stories about Angels. They crack me up sometimes. I know this one angel in particular, he is a guardian angel to a friend of mine. That angel is so jealous of my friend that he does all kinds of things to get him in trouble. Then he pretends to come in and save the day. That angel has so many issues, but in the end, he gets the job done. My friend is still alive, he carries plenty of scars, but he's still alive." Beats said it nonchalantly, like that was a normal thing for angels to have issues.

They arrived back at the ranch. Kyle marveled at the size and scope of the place. He also noticed plenty of bullet holes that had yet been repaired. Kyle made a point to show Beats he had seen them.

"We occasionally have to defend ourselves here. For the most part, it's safe. Do you know how to use a gun? If you don't, I can teach you before I leave." Beats was trying to make Kyle feel safe and comfortable here but was having a hard time achieving that with each word that came out of his mouth.

"I prefer a crossbow, but I can handle a shotgun with the best of them."

"Ever killed a man? It's not as easy as you think."

"It's why I was in jail. I shot a corrupt sheriff with my crossbow and let my cat finish him off. So technically, I've never killed anyone."

"You must have one hell of a mean cat," Beats said.

"She's a bobcat I raised from a kitten. I trained her."

"So, what you're telling me, is you're good with animals. Is that right?"

Kyle looked at Beats and responded that he was one of the best when it came to animals. His father said he was born wild like the animals he associated with. Kyle just thought it came naturally. He preferred animals to humans.

They dismounted and tied the horses up. Beats said he would take care of them.

"Go on inside and meet Samantha. She's a young pretty thing in her early twenties. The first person I ever brought back from the dead. In fact, the only person I ever brought back."

Kyle thought the kid had a wild imagination. What he was saying was impossible. All his stories were impossible. Then he thought about how he arrived at this place and the hair on the back of his neck began to rise. What would he find inside when he met this woman that Beats claimed he brought back from the grave? He pictured a zombie from the movies he had seen and thought better of going inside.

"Go on inside, she won't bite." Beats laughed as he pictured what might be going on inside of Kyle's mind.

Reluctantly, Kyle opened the door and entered. What he saw shocked the living daylights out of him.

* * *

Joey Hopkins found himself in the heart of Nebraska. Jacob had dumped him off and went to be with his wife, who was now causing all kinds of mischief in Richmond, Virginia. The first time his guardian angel had teleported him anywhere was to escape from a railcar that was on fire with him locked inside of it. Jacob had screwed up. In his haste to get them to safety, he had accidentally sent the gangbanger that was locked in the railcar with them back to the room where they had all started the day. The rest of his party went straight to hell where Lucifer greeted them and entertained them until Beats arrived.

Joey, Deke, and Jacob were all tortured until Beats came to save the day. The little child prodigy could do things that no other could possibly do. Like retrieve them from the grasp of the devil himself and whisk them away to safety.

After that day, Joey was reluctant to let Jacob teleport him anywhere. Circumstances had changed. The ability to travel had become extremely difficult. The commercial airlines were afraid to let him board any of their aircraft. The people flying would recognize him and deplane as fast as they could. Joey couldn't understand why. Very few people had died in all the incidents that had occurred while he was flying. He tried using a charter service. Two more plane crashes later, his pilot was now hiding at the ranch pretending to be dead. The last crash had contained millions of dollars of heroin destined for the East Coast. His pilot thought he was flying cargo for a pharmaceutical company, it turned out he was flying for a cartel.

Then Joey tried the railroad. That turned out to be worse than flying. He tried driving, but that took a large amount of time and ended up just like all his other forms of travel. Something always happened along the way, there was no avoiding it.

He found himself standing beside an old airport that advertised flying lessons. Joey thought that maybe if he got his own pilot's license, maybe he could just fly himself around and put fewer people in jeopardy, or so he thought.

Walking into the hangar, he found an elderly gentleman and inquired about flying lessons. The man laughed out loud, recognizing Joey almost immediately.

"I loved that last movie you made. It sure did hit home with that latest plane crash you were in. You going to follow in O.J. Simpsons' footsteps and write a book that says, 'If I did it.'" The man laughed at him some more, then surprised him.

"I'll tell you what I'm going to do. My normal price is two hundred per lesson. For you, I'll give you a discount and make it three hundred and fifty. It takes ten lessons to get your license. If you don't kill my brother, I'll refund you half of the cost. If you do kill him, well I'll be a rich man and can finally get my ass out of here and retire. What do you say, we got a deal?" The man said it like he was sure his brother was going to die at the hands of poor Joey.

"Yeah, we got a deal. When can I begin and where can I stay while I'm knocking out all these lessons?" Joey inquired of the man.

"My name is Lescott, but you can call me Les. My brother is a pain in the ass, but you can call him Ned. He works three days a week now. He will be in tomorrow by ten, be here by 10:15 sharp." He motioned over to a young lady that was dressed in coveralls and covered in grease.

"This is my granddaughter. She will find you accommodations for the duration of your stay. I figure you might make it through the first lesson and give it up, but if you should last the entire time, you will be in good hands with her."

Joey reached out to shake her hand and was given a greasy handshake. Looking around to find a rag, Les giggled to himself and handed Joey a greasy one that made Joey's hands even dirtier than when he had first shaken the lady's hand.

"If you touch her in some places that she doesn't want you to, you'll find that your tool will be greasier than your hands. Make sure you behave while you stay with us. If you do, you'll have a pleasant stay, if not, well all I can say is, those damn pigs will eat anything."

It had been given as a warning. Joey would be staying at the man's granddaughter's house without supervision. He had best behave himself, or he might find that the pigs did indeed eat anything that you threw into them. Bodies had been known to disappear that way. Joey felt a little uneasy, knowing that Jacob was back in Richmond and not here watching over him like he was supposed to be doing. Like any good guardian angel, Jacob did his job, but he was so easily distracted at times. Those were usually the times Joey got himself in hot water and Jacob would eventually make it to save him in a nick of time.

The girl cleaned up and when he next saw her, he gave out a silent whistle. He now knew why Les had given him the warning to keep his hands off. The girl not only cleaned up well, but she smelled terrific. Whatever she had put on was giving Joey some mental pictures of some bedroom time with a whole lot of hugging and kissing and other things that Joey was trying so hard to keep his mind from picturing.

It all started when Maria had slipped him a potion she was experimenting on with some homeless folks. It took several hours for it to kick in, but when it had, it had shocked Joey. He thought he just wasn't feeling well, but then after the initial nausea, he began to feel much better and much more energetic. A look in the mirror found him looking at an image of himself from twenty years prior. Damn Maria had discovered the fountain of youth formula and had used it on him and a few other people. Now there were three people still alive to give their testimony that the stuff worked. It was him, the President of the United States, and the Director of the ATF. All the others had been hunted down and killed. Joey had many close calls, but when the President had been forced to take it, all things had changed for him. He now had protection and a powerful friend that was keeping him alive. Now he had to keep the President alive and in power, or he might once again be running for his life. The discovery of a certain tape that might ruin the President had not surprised him. His friend in the Whitehouse had a whole lot of issues. The formula made it worse. It gave you virility and the overwhelming desire to procreate. This was what Joey was fighting right at this moment. He wanted to rip her clothes off and have her right here in the middle of this dirt road they were bumping along on at a slow and steady speed in the middle of a cornfield.

He fought his desire all the way to the farmhouse. Relieved that he had controlled his desires, he quickly exited the car. She sauntered up to the door and went inside, leaving him to take some deep breaths and smell the freshly plowed fields. The smell of manure permeated his nostrils and made him slightly lightheaded. He decided it might be time to go inside and check out his accommodations.

The girl was heating up a kettle on the stove when he entered. She had removed the sweater she had been wearing and was now showing a halter top that exposed a firm midriff. Joey found he was having trouble concentrating on what he was about to say when she gave him his out.

"I see the way you look at me. The yearning in your eyes. I bet my grandfather warned you to keep your hands to yourself. Am I right about that?" she spoke these words coquettishly.

Joey stumbled over any words that could make their way to his mouth. The words that did make it made no sense and she began to laugh.

"He knows I only have one bedroom in this house. Unless you decide to sleep on the couch, you'll be spending some nights in my bed. Does that make you uncomfortable? I could set you up in the barn. I have hay and an empty stall." She giggled at what she was proposing. Who in their right mind would opt for the barn and turn down a pretty young woman like this? Joey thought seriously of taking the barn option. He was opting for the safe course, but she had made his decision for him before he could give her his.

"Then it's settled. You will spend the night with me in my bed. I will make you quite comfortable, you will see."

Her mind was made up, that was until she told Joey what her name was, then it changed everything. Joey had been married to his wife Honey for many years. She was the love of his life. One day she had been taken from him when a soldier determined to kill his own wife blew them all to smithereens with one press of a button. Joey's wife had been caught up in it all and lost her life. Now, this sweet young thing had just told him her name was Honey and Joey's sexual desire was shot all to hell. Joey spent the night in the barn to the disappointment of the girl inside the house. Joey could not make love to another woman by the same name as his former life mate, it just wasn't going to happen.

The ride back to the airfield was done in complete silence. Joey tried to explain his side, but she was having none of it. When Les saw the look on his granddaughter's face, he fell to his knees in laughter.

"You are a strong man, Joey Hopkins. I got to hand it to you. Not many men would have passed the test you were given last night. I thought for sure you would be on your way to the hog farm by now. Congratulations. Now let's get you some flying lessons. Ned, your student has arrived."

He called out to a backroom in the hangar.

The man Joey saw shuffling out was even older than Les. This guy had to be in his seventies at least. He was pushing a portable oxygen tank alongside of him as he came out with a toothless smile and greeted his new student.

"Ned, you forgot to put your teeth in again. Go back inside and put them in. I'll get Joey situated while we wait."

Joey wasn't sure about all of this.

"You sure he can teach me to fly? He doesn't have dementia or anything like that, does he? I want to live to tell my children about this experience. I must say I'm not feeling so good about all of this."

"You're having second thoughts. I forgot to tell you about our no refund policy. You chicken out, you're out of the money, not me. I suggest you get out there and take that plane up. Ned was a fighter pilot in the Vietnam war. He fought for this country, been flying his whole life. He doesn't even need to think about it anymore, just does it. You're in the best hands around these here parts. Now go out there and make me a rich man."

Joey thought about it. To make Les a rich man he would need his brother to die. His brother Ned didn't appear to have the cognitive skills left to be flying. Joey thought about walking away, but then Ned shuffled out and got into the plane calling for Joey to join him. Reluctantly he did, searching for his guardian angel the whole while and not seeing him anywhere.

Ned began to explain all the gauges and controls Joey would be needing to know. He said that he would get them in the air and then he would let Joey get familiar with the controls once they were airborne. Joey began to feel more at ease when he saw how smooth and comfortable Ned seemed to be behind the controls. Once they were in the air, Ned told Joey to take over and get a feel for it, which Joey did. Nice and easy. Ned showed him how to turn the plane, ascend and descend.

Ned had Joey take the plane over to a field and fly low over it. He pushed a button and a cloud of something began to trail behind them. Ned told Joey not to worry. They were just doing a little crop dusting while they were up in the air. He had Joey turn the plane and make several more passes. Nothing like killing two birds with one stone. Ned was getting paid twice for this lesson.

Ned had Joey take them back to the airfield and demonstrated to Joey how to land the plane.

"Next time out, I'm going to have you try it for yourself. I'll guide you so we shouldn't have too much to worry about. That is if you don't panic and crash us into the ground and blow us to bits, roasting us in a flaming ball of fire." Ned started to laugh, then choke. His face turned bright red and he made quite a few pulls on his oxygen. A few minutes later, he was as good as new.

Joey saw Les watching them get out of the plane and saw the man throw his hat into the dirt and stomp around like he was having a temper tantrum. Joey guessed he wasn't happy that his brother had returned in one piece.

Les pulled him over to the side before Honey gave him a ride back to the farmhouse.

"I guess all the stories of you being a catastrophe waiting to happen are all just that, stories. I have a lot riding on this deal. I have the buyer banging at my door ready with the cash in hand, but that stubborn old fool won't sell. I sure hope you don't disappoint me again tomorrow like you have today. Get some sleep, you have two lessons tomorrow, one in the morning and one in the afternoon." He slapped Joey on the back hard enough to knock the wind out of him.

Once he was able to get his breath back, Joey stepped into the truck with Honey and they silently sped back to her house where she dropped him off and went back to work. As Joey watched her leave, Jacob returned and filled him in on a few things.

Jacob had found out who had the zip drive with the incriminating confession from the President. That was the easy part, Jacob said. Now the hard part was going in to retrieve it. Jacob asked Joey if he was doing anything except sitting around enjoying the sunshine. When Joey said he had the afternoon free, Jacob grabbed his hand and off they went, to Joey's dismay.

He only had to take one look around and Joey knew he was back in California. He also knew they were in Santa Clara by the road sign that was staring him right in the face. This was the twentieth district for the house of representatives and that meant Ivan was the person who had the tape. He had posed as Urstin Trenvosky's right-hand man for years while working undercover for the CIA. Joey thought he had been undercover for way too long and had moved his loyalty to the other side. Once his mission had been fulfilled and Urstin was behind bars, Ivan ran for and won the twentieth district here in California.

Jacob got them inside only the way Jacob could, they teleported in. They found Ivan and the zip drive in his hand. A big smile on his face.

"Looking for something, Joey?"

He held up the zip drive in one hand and a weapon in the other. It looked like a Smith and Wesson handgun, maybe an M&P 9 Shield by the look of it. By the look on Ivan's face, he certainly appeared ready to use it on an intruder that had entered his house uninvited.

"I only came for one thing. Give it to me and no one has got to know you had it. Better yet, destroy it right now and I'll be on my way. Too many people who have viewed that tape have already died."

"You talk like you're a person speaking from a position of authority, yet here I am with the gun on you and plenty of legal reasons to use it. I could kill you right now and no one would raise an eyebrow as to why I did it."

Joey thought he did raise a good point, but he didn't come here to leave empty-handed. Sometimes he felt invincible with Jacob by his side. The things they had gone through over the past few years would have killed a normal person many times over, yet he was still alive and breathing except for some additional scars added to the many he already had.

Ivan stood up and walked out from behind his desk.

"Say I should throw this down and stomp on it right in front of you. How would you know it was the right one and what if I had copies? I could be playing you for the fool that you are Joey. I know about your supernatural helper and some of the things he enables you to be able to do, like get into my highly secure home. So, tell me, what are you not telling me by being here when you must have known I would be waiting for you?"

Joey thought that could be a very good question that he had every intention of asking Jacob, if he could find the stupid idiot at the moment. He looked around but Jacob was nowhere to be found. He figured he had to stall, make something up, find a loophole or an excuse for his stupidity.

"I was giving you a chance to come clean, prove you were working for the people of this country and not the Russians. If you willfully gave it to me, and we destroyed it together, then I would be able to tell the President you were on our side and not a spy for the Russians. I guess I'll have to inform him you are a Russian spy and that will be the end of you and your network. Helen is gone, Urstin is behind bars, and you will soon be joining him. I'll be going now, good luck with that."

Joey spun to leave, but a clearing of a throat got his attention in a hurry.

"Where did you say I was, Joey? Behind bars is what I thought you had said."

Urstin revealed himself from behind one of the heavy curtains by the window. All Joey could think as he saw him was that this day had gone to shit in a hurry.

Urstin grabbed the zip drive from Ivan and crushed it with his boot. Joey could hear it crumble below his heel. This was not good, he thought to himself. It must be a duplicate. No way would they give away all their leverage on the man in the Whitehouse. Unless that is, they had already shown it to him, and he had dismissed it as just a bunch of homemade bullshit that didn't add up to a bowl of squat. The President hadn't been acting right, it was like he didn't care about his place in Washington or his legacy. His re-election would be determined in less than a year. If this tape were to get out, real or not, it just might end any hope of his re-election.

"We showed it to him. You want to know what he told us? I'll tell you what he said." Urstin was almost foaming at the mouth, his anger was so fervent.

"The bastard told us to shove it up our asses and to stop wasting his time! Then he tells Ivan he's going to give me a pardon and that will be the end of it. I was told to go away and stop pestering him. He treated me like I was a fly, nothing but an insignificant bug that he could squash any time he felt the inclination to do so. Well, let me tell you something Joey Hopkins. He has not seen the last of me. You tell him he's going to regret the day he ever laid eyes on me. Now get the hell out of here and never come back!" he fumed as he pointed to the door.

"One last thing before you leave Joey. Do you like music? Well if you do, I have a treat for you. Take a listen to this song you already have your friends playing and listening to. Tell me what you think it's foretelling you."

Urstin pressed play and let Joey listen to a song. It was by the Sidewalk Prophets called "Smile." Urstin had said to do it while he still could because the storm was coming, and it was going to be savage. He then laughed and threw Joey out onto the street, leaving Joey wondering what that was all about. The song was still playing in his head half an hour later, as Joey struggled to wrestle the message out of the song.

He had to get back to Nebraska soon or he would lose all his money for the flying lessons. Jacob found him a short while later, standing outside a store and sipping on a cold soda.

"Smile Joey, it can't be that bad. I wish I could have been there to see the look on your face when you saw Urstin was out of jail. I had business elsewhere, so I had to watch it all on my phone. Not as good as being there in person and seeing it all unfold."

"What could have been so important that you couldn't have stayed and watched me almost soil myself?"

"I delivered the tape to Lori. Left it plugged into her computer back in Richmond. You want to stick around and watch those two assholes when they discover we stole the damn thing right from under their noses. I bet you it will make you smile, just like Urstin wants you to do."

Joey thought Jacob could be alright on some days and others he was just a pain in the ass. Today he was an angel sent from heaven and they watched and laughed until their bellies hurt as Ivan and Urstin searched the whole house for the real zip drive. The last thing that Jacob let Joey watch on the phone was Urstin scream out: Hopkins, Fucking Hopkins! I'm going to kill the son of a bitch.

"I think you've seen enough for one day Joey. Let's get you back to your flying lessons." They both had a hard time knocking the smiles off their faces.

In a flash, they were back in the barn and the sun was rising in the morning sky. Joey thought it was sunset until Honey came in and got him a few minutes after he had laid down. Sometimes time moves at a different rate of speed when you teleport, one of the reasons Joey hates to travel that way. He was exhausted and it would be hours before he would be able to get any sleep. He took advantage of the ride to the airfield and slept soundly all the way there. Then his day began, and that was when he wished that he could smile, because a storm was coming, and he had no idea how he was going to get out of the way of this one. He sure hoped Ned knew. If he could wake the old man up, he would ask him.

Ned was snoring softly, so Joey knew he was still alive. He shook him several times to no avail. Panic began to show its ugly face. Joey wiped sweat from his brow and tried to remember the lessons from yesterday. Reduce speed, nose up, flaps down. He went through the checklist and put the plane on the ground like he had done it his whole life. The initial bounce off the runway woke Ned and he smiled.

"Nice job Joey, you're a natural at this. I'll have you flying by yourself before the week is over."

Joey already felt like he was flying by himself. He just didn't voice his opinion to poor old Ned. Les was right. The chances of him surviving these lessons with his brother weren't very good, yet he still went up in the plane with him. Joey began to question his sanity. Was it so important that he be able to fly himself that he would risk it all to get his license to do so?

Joey thought it was worth the risk, so he meandered his way to the hangar where he searched for Honey to give him a lift back to her home where he could grab a few winks and be prepared for the afternoon's lesson. He found the plane she had been working on, but she was nowhere to be found. His search did reveal an air mattress off to the side in a storage room. He blew it up, laid it down, and was asleep before he knew it. His dreams were full of big locomotives rushing by as he stood and watched them pass. One after another they flew by, making Joey yearn for the good old days when he would run one of those awesome machines down the track, trying to stay awake but failing miserably, like he was doing now.

CHAPTER 18

Lori was invited inside a neighbor's house while the fire department extinguished the fire that had engulfed her apartment building. A lonely elderly lady by the name of Agnes had seen her plight and had taken pity on the poor girl. Agnes had told her that her daughter had moved out recently and had left a closet full of clothes. Agnes offered some to Lori as she saw that Lori had only made it out of the burning building with a towel to cover her nakedness. Thanking Agnes, Lori peered into the closet of her daughter and realized that Agnes's daughter must have been a slut or at the minimum, a stripper.

With an open mouth, Lori fished through the clothes searching for something that wouldn't get her confused with a streetwalker. It was more than a little difficult. Realizing it was something in this wardrobe or the towel, she picked a leather mini skirt that hugged her hips. Then she found a pink crop top that barely contained her ample breasts that were being held up by a pushup bra she had found on the floor of the closet. For shoes, she found a set of heels that kept her balancing on her toes.

The trickiest part of her new wardrobe was panties. She had decided long before she picked anything out, that there was no way in hell she was wearing anything underneath her outfit that this girl had worn. The length of the skirt strongly suggested she wear something. Agnes told her she had an idea, ran into her room, and returned with a pair of incontinence underwear. They were red and brand new, never been worn. It was hard to tell they were an adult diaper.

"It's better than nothing," she laughed.

Lori looked at them and broke out in laughter. She never thought she would ever wear a pair of adult diapers before she turned thirty. Like Agnes had said, it was better than going commando and flaunting her stuff to a bunch of horny men trying to get a peek under her short skirt. Lori thanked Agnes and slid them on.

Lori left for the Canton home hoping that Todd had forgiven her and that he still wasn't entertaining those two women he was in bed with the last time she had seen him. It would be awkward chastising him with the way she was dressed.

When she reached the front gate, she had more problems to deal with, like the guard.

"I'm sorry Miss Stenville, but unless you're here to do work, I can't let you in unescorted without the permission of the owner. It's HOA policy. They came down hard on me about letting you stay the night when it was obvious Owen is out of town. Now his brother is acting up and causing a few feathers to be ruffled. You know how these rich people are. All they care about is their appearance and property values. Owen informed me his brother is living with him now, so I have got to let him in, but he never mentioned what your status is or that you would be living at the premises. Unless he tells me otherwise, I can't let you in," the guard tried to explain as he was staring at her chest instead of her eyes.

Karma told Lori that she could get her in, but Lori wasn't going to take the guard behind the shack and do that, she had her standards. Karma laughed and told her that was not what she meant, but that was an idea as well.

"Let me take the reins and show you the power that lies within you," Karma pleaded. Lori knew the spirit could take over in a flash and she would not be able to stop her, but Karma was treating her like an equal now, so maybe she might see what she had in mind.

"Okay, but you best not embarrass me."

Karma strolled over to the guard strutting her stuff and practically shoved her partially covered breasts into his face. She ran a painted fingernail down the side of his face and puckered her lips. She even let out a little tantalizing exhalation of her breath.

The guard was like butter in her hands on a hot summer's day. He just melted right before her.

"You let me inside and I promise you, I'll give you something you'll never forget for the rest of your life. Are you game, or are you afraid of what I'm going to say and do?"

Karma was using sex to create an atmosphere the guard thought was going to be a night of pure joy and fun. When he agreed to play her game, he lost.

"I know about you and your sister. She told me what you did to her. How you fondled her and played with her while you were supposed to be watching over her. You were her big brother. That is not what brotherly love is supposed to mean. Your sister and I, well, we have had many long talks about you. I told her she should turn you in and expose you for the dirty rat that you are, but she says she loves you, and can't do it, but I can. You let me in these gates each and every time I show up, and I'll keep my mouth shut. If not, I go straight to the cops tonight and tell them everything."

The guard was so scared that Lori knew all these intimate details about his affair with his sister that he bought the whole story that Karma had made up about being friends with his sister. It was what Karma does. She comes up and bites you in the ass when you least expect it. Lori was on her way into the gated community without another problem from the guard. He assured her he would pass on the information to the other guards that she was cleared to come and go as she pleased.

Satisfied with her performance, Lori pulled into the driveway to find Todd's truck had blocked half of it with his front tires clearly in the flower bed. She had to drive over the lawn to get all the way into the driveway. She thought to herself that he must be drunk to have parked that way. Taking a deep breath, she entered to find Todd passed out on the floor of the kitchen. A gallon of chocolate milk nearly emptied on the kitchen table. A glass in his right hand that contained the one thing he was told to avoid.

Lori helped him to his feet. Tears filled Todd's eyes as he wept and told Lori that he didn't want to be smart anymore. He liked the way he was and when he was smart, he hadn't liked the person he had become. Todd explained that person was mean and self-centered. A nasty bad man that does things to hurt people. He said he was sorry at least a dozen times, to the point that Lori began to become uncomfortable. She needed to know what Todd had done. Lori shook Todd and asked him to explain. Karma shook him even harder and knew beyond a shadow of a doubt this stupid idiot had done something that was going to come full circle and bite her in the ass.

Todd led her upstairs to Owen's office. Lori saw her laptop sitting at Owen's desk. It was easy to determine that Owen had read the manuscript that Todd had recited to her the last night she had spent here waiting on Owen to come out of his office.

Todd pointed out to her that Owen had stolen his story and rewrote it as his own manuscript. It was all right there on his computer. He told Lori how he was infuriated when he had first seen what his brother had done to the wonderful story he and Lori had written. Owen had taken the story and spun it into one of his works of art and was going to submit Todd's story as his own.

"I was mad. I wanted to smash something. As I paced around the office, I saw the zip drive in your laptop. I opened it up and found what it contained."

It was at this point Karma screamed out some very nasty obscenities and smacked Todd so hard to the side of the head that he went down for the count. Lori was confused, as she had no idea what was on the zip drive. She had never seen it before, but Karma had. This was the tape that they had asked Leon to get them. The one that they had called on Joey to retrieve for them. It looked like he had come through and left it here for them to find.

Lori looked at Owen's computer and saw that the file had been uploaded to a YouTube site. The video had gone viral in the short time it had been posted. Downloaded so many times it would be out on the net forever. Karma had wanted to protect the man that was on the tape, now he was doomed. His confession of the involvement of the murder of his wife was out there for all to see. The feds would trace the video back to this IP address and to Owen's computer and that would spell the end of Owen. Her plans had all backfired and the devil had won again. Karma could see no way out of this mess. Todd had realized his mistake shortly after loading the video, that was why he had drowned himself in the chocolate milk that would make the chemical imbalance inside his head return.

Lori pulled Todd to his feet and rubbed the side of his head. He had a huge knot where Lori's palm had made contact to his temple. She needed to get some ice on it and make sure that he hadn't suffered another concussion. It had only been a couple of days since he sustained the last one and she knew it didn't take much to sustain another one.

She tried to soothe Todd and tell him it was going to be alright, and it might have been if they could have been left alone for the night. Todd had set in motion many things that were coming to a head. A huge wave was coming right at them at this moment. Karma had said she was the wave, now Lori knew this to be true. Lori's one concern – would they survive this wave, or would they be swept away by it?

They arrived at the kitchen the same time their visitor did. One that wasn't too very happy to be visiting at this time of the day. At the same time, he was happy just to be alive, although he knew he would have to pay a high price for that fact. He wanted one thing, the zip drive. When Lori explained to him what had taken place, he disappeared right before her eyes, like he was a ghost or something. Lori fainted, but it wasn't her, it was Karma. The day had finally taken its toll on her.

* * *

When Kyle opened the door and called out, he expected to find a zombie-like woman prancing around the house. When he saw the young lady, he was infatuated immediately. That was until she pulled a gun and drew down on him. He heard another person from the other side of the room call to him. When he looked in that direction, he was staring down the barrel of a double-barreled shotgun.

He was warned not to move, or he would lose his head. Kyle nearly pissed his pants in fright, that was until Jesus came in the other door and saved him. The little boy known as Beats told everyone to calm down, that he would explain.

Beats introduced Samantha and Billy to Kyle. Told them that Kyle was the new guy that would be caring for the animals while he was away. He then whisked Kyle away out the same door he had entered and out to the stables.

"Sorry about that. I realized my mistake a couple minutes too late. I rushed in as fast as I could. Things are a little tense around here. They're going to get a whole lot worse in the days and weeks to come. Let me show you my setup."

Beats walked Kyle around the stable, introducing him to each of the horses. The last one he showed him was Truly, the Kentucky Derby winner a few years back.

"I rode her to victory. We got caught after the fact, but they let her keep her victory as long as we never mentioned a word to anyone. It was better that way. I guess you might remember that we came in second, but that we were awarded the victory after the winner was disqualified. It would have been a fiasco if Truly was disqualified as well, with all the money that was bet on the race."

Kyle listened to the boy ramble on about all these things as Beats showed him all the locations of the sniper nests hidden around the stable. He even crawled into one of the spaces and checked it out for himself. The rifles were all located in strategic locations, fully armed and cleaned, and ready for use.

"Would you like to try one out? We could use this spot over here. I have a target set up on the hill. We can take some practice shots."

Kyle was game, slid into the nest, located the target, and squeezed off a shot that just nicked the target. Beats laughed and said that it was a nice effort by a rookie.

"Now let me show you how it's done."

Kyle thought that the kid was just trying to show off. No way he was going to even hit the thing from this distance. A couple minutes later, he was looking at a destroyed target. The kid had hit it three times completely breaking it up into a million pieces. He had only taken three shots, hit it every single time. Kyle was beyond amazed.

He began to believe the story that the kid might have ridden Truly in the derby. Then they came upon a drum set. Beats sat down behind it and that was when Kyle knew the kid was the real deal. He also knew that this new world that he had been thrust into was a dangerous one. The bullet holes that riddled the house and barn foretold of what was to come. Kyle was no stranger to surviving. He had done it his whole life, but this place was a whole other story. One that captivated his imagination, but also scared the bejesus out of him.

He listened to Beats play until they heard the beat of rotor blades cutting the wind and heading toward their location. Beats told him that he had to go now, be careful, and he would see him soon. The helicopter landed and Beats ran out to it with a small suitcase and drumsticks in hand. He waved goodbye as he took off, leaving Kyle to wonder if he would ever see the boy again.

* * *

Honey found Joey in the only building that was still standing. The tornados had ripped through the airfield, taking everything in its wake. Thankfully, she and her co-workers were all in the storm shelter. The only one that was missing was Joey. Les had sent her out to find his dead body while he tended to his brother. After his last flying lesson with Joey, Ned had announced that he was all done flying. Joey had done his job, but instead of ending his brother's life, he ended Ned's career as an aviator. Ned no longer wanted to fly and told his brother he was ready to sell. This was all happening as the tornados ripped the once prestigious facility to shreds.

Les was on his cellphone to his buyers and informed them of the slight damage, but they really wanted the airfield badly, and told him they could rebuild. They did lower their offer, but it was a small price to pay as far as Les was concerned. He was free and on his way to retirement.

Honey searched the hangar and found Joey fast asleep on her air mattress that she had stored in case she had some big project that would require her to work late into the night on. Some projects required time-specific deadlines and she found she would often work late nights to accomplish them. The only plane that survived the storm and wasn't damaged was in the hangar, and it was one she had just spent a great deal of time refurbishing. This was her own private project. Her baby. To see it had survived had given her great joy. Then, seeing Joey fast asleep, well she couldn't resist and snuggled up next to him. She was overwhelmed with happiness, even after listening to Ned and Les talk about selling the airfield as they hid in the shelter fearing for their lives. A new job was on the horizon, a new life. Maybe Joey here was her ticket out. It was worth a shot. She reached around and hugged him tight, grabbed him in a place she should have thought might not have been a good idea, but she wasn't thinking clearly at the moment.

To her delight, Joey responded to her touch. He began to moan and grow in her hand. She rubbed a little tighter and harder, Joey moaned a little louder. He began to thrust in her grasp and suddenly, he exploded.

Joey jumped up and began to verbally assault poor Honey, while tucking his junk back into his pants.

"What's wrong with you?!" he shouted. "Don't you know, NO means NO!"

"If Les catches us, he's going to send me on a one-way trip to the hog farm to be fodder for those damn pigs. I told you I don't want to rock the boat while I'm here. I just want to get my damn pilot's license and be out of here. What don't you understand? Damn it, you made a mess out of my boxers!"

Joey stormed off looking for the bathroom, leaving Honey crying in the storage room. Her anger was escalating by the minute. How could Joey keep denying her like he did? She knew he was attracted to her, yet he wouldn't let her have any fun with him. Frustrated, she pulled her cellphone out of her back pocket and made a call. The buyer had been by a few times and hit on her. He was an older Russian guy with a scar on one side of his face. He was repulsive and smelled of vodka. The kind of person that her mother had warned her to avoid. An offer had been made the last time he was here. An offer that would make her a rich woman. All she had to do was eliminate Joey Hopkins from the face of the earth. She had originally found this appalling, but now after this latest rejection, the money sure was looking good. A plan was formed in the back of her head.

Walking to where the sky diving supplies were stored, she packed a parachute. She could have done this blindfolded. She had done it so many times. Once it was packed, she loaded it onto her plane. The only one left that Joey could fly, and of course, she was the only one left that could give him the rest of his lessons. One last lesson was in store for Joey. That one was going to be jumping out of a perfectly good airplane with a chute she had packed, guaranteed not to open until he hit the ground. The son of a bitch should have given her some loving while he had the chance. Now, he was going to pay for his rejections of her love, this she was going to make sure of.

Honey found Joey outside looking at the damage. The tornado had come across the airfield and tore everything to pieces. Planes were all flipped over and piled high. Buildings leveled. Joey could see where the funnel cloud had turned just before reaching the hangar where he was sleeping. The dreams of the trains had to be the storm passing over. He wondered if this was the work of Jacob, or if this was God's will he be saved. If it were Jacob, he thought he would be safe stuck underneath a pile of rubble waiting to be rescued.

Joey peered to the sky and praised his Lord. The song by Casting Crowns, "Praise you in this Storm" began to play inside his head. He raised his hands and slowly danced while the song played. Honey watched all of this, wondering what the hell he was doing. She had no idea what was going on in that head of his, one that would soon be smashed to pieces by his sudden impact with the ground.

"I'm going to give you your next lesson. Ned retired and decided to sell the place. Les has already made the call to his buyer. We have a couple of days left to get you your qualifying time in. That is if you still want to get your license to fly."

"All the planes are damaged beyond repair. How am I going to get any airtime?" Joey questioned.

"I have finished the work on my plane. It is in the hangar undamaged, like you. Help me get it outside and we'll take it up and check out what the storm did to the area. Maybe we can help get medical supplies to people in need. We have got to do something Joey, for God's sake!"

She had thrown in the God part to convince Joey that this was going to be a combination of flying lesson and mission to help people that might not have been as fortunate as them who survived the storm unscathed.

Joey jumped at the opportunity to help people like she knew he would and soon after that they were in the air flying around. She had instructed Joey how to take off and he had handled the takeoff without incident. Honey realized he was a good student and had the potential to be a good pilot. Too bad he wasn't going to live long enough to find this out. Her payday was coming, and this bastard was her meal ticket. Honey did have second thoughts after she had Joey take the plane up to ten thousand feet. Those thoughts were eroded when she went in for a kiss and he backed off like she was a leper.

Exasperated by Joey, she hit the kill switch she had installed by her seat causing the plane to stall in midflight. This was a lesson to see if the student would panic or try to work out how to get the engine fired back up in flight. Of course, she made it out to be catastrophic to get Joey to panic, which he wasn't doing. He remained calm and collected, like he knew that there had to be a way to restart the engine. There was, but it wasn't going to start until he put on his parachute and jumped to his death.

He fought her when she tried to get him to dawn the chute. She grabbed the good one and put it on. Made like she was going to jump while they still had enough altitude to do so safely. This got Joey to reluctantly put on the provided parachute.

"You ever jumped out of an airplane, Joey?" Honey asked him as she was opening the door.

"Whatever you do, when you land, don't lock your legs. They'll snap like twigs if you do."

"I've jumped a couple of times. It seems I've taken off more than I've landed. Planes don't seem to like me," Joey said with concern on his face.

Honey laughed at him and his predicament. She looked down and saw they were over a massive field of winter rye. It might not be until the spring before they found his dead body. The perfect place for him to exit her plane.

"You go now, I'm going to try one last time before I give up on her. I put a lot of work into this plane and it would be a shame to lose her." She gave him a kiss for good luck. He accepted it from her and then she pushed him out the door. Not wanting to look, she got back into the pilot's seat and went to start the plane. Nothing was happening.

Frantically, she tried every trick in the book to get the plane restarted. All her efforts went for nothing. The plane was not going to restart. She had wasted too much time trying to get it restarted and now she had used up the chance to jump. Her only chance now was to glide it down into the field and hope for the best.

She kept telling herself all the way to the ground that she could do this. If you repeat something enough times, sometimes it comes true. It was all she had. Karma thought if Honey had tried to pray, it might have helped her, but Honey was not the praying type. She had sold her soul for a few bucks and the devil was coming to collect his due. Karma rode the plane all the way to the ground with her laughing about how much fun this was, watching an assassin pleading for her life until the end.

Joey on the other hand was the praying type and when he pulled his ripcord and the chute flew out and into the wind, he began to pray. He pulled his reserve chute and that went the way of the first chute. The ground was fast approaching, and his options had run their course. The last thing left was the landing. He must remember to not lock his legs. The bitch had set him up.

Jacob appeared before him, probably to give him a hard time for the couple of minutes he had left in his life. Jacob kept trying to get him to flap his arms and fly like a bird. He even demonstrated it for him. Jacob could fly, but Joey knew that that option wasn't in his future.

"I can get you out of this Joey, but it will come with a price. All you have got to do is grab my hand and we'll teleport out of here and to a safe place. Take my hand Joey," Jacob pleaded with him.

Joey knew about the price that would have to be paid. The last time he paid he lost his wife. Blown to a million pieces by a crazed army sergeant that was enraged that his wife had left him and was staying with Joey's sweet and wonderful wife. She had been caught up in the frenzy and became collateral damage. Joey knew it was the price he had to pay for Jacob saving him from certain death, like he was offering now. If he were to take Jacob's hand, someone he loved was going to take the fall. Joey felt that this time, it should be him, but Jacob was frantic. It couldn't be Joey because he was the key to saving numerous lives in the future. There was so much for Joey left to do, and without him many would perish.

Joey closed his eyes and waited for the end to come. His life was flashing before his eyes and when he got to the part when he was transporting Jacob's twins back to his condo, the music that was playing on the radio came back to him. Messages from God, Joey had called them. He remembered how upset the boys had become when the song "Free Falling" by Tom Petty had come on. They had screamed until he turned the station and heard the next song which calmed the twins and brought a vision to Joey just before he almost crashed into another car. When he braked hard to avoid the collision, it knocked the vision away. He saw it now with clarity. His destiny, his future. Just before they were about to meet the ground, Joey reached out and took Jacob's hand. In a flash they were gone and in the kitchen of Owen Canton, staring at Lori and Owen's brother Todd. Joey asked for the zip drive and found another fire that needed putting out, another problem that required Joey's full attention.

He dreaded finding out who would pay the price for his being able to live another day. This bothered him more than finding out the tape had been broadcasted to the world. He had so much to do and so little time to do it. Joey looked over to Jacob and asked him to get them out of there. He needed to think and he wanted to be alone to do that. Jacob obliged and they were gone in a blink of an eye. Jacob didn't even try to hide Joey's exit. He just teleported them off to another location.

* * *

Owen was escorted out of his cell and down to an interview room. His lawyer had advised him not to talk, that he would do all the talking for him. When he arrived, he found he was sharing the room with his lawyer and two other agents. One agent was an older man with graying hair around the temples; the other was a young black woman that was slightly on the heavy side, but she had a sweet disposition and a huge smile, unlike her counterpart who didn't seem to be enjoying himself at all.

His lawyer had a nervous twitch today, unlike the previous day when they met when the man was full of confidence and vigor. His leg was bouncing around under the table a mile a minute. His hands were shaking, and Owen noticed he kept wiping sweat from his brow. All signs of his impending doom, Owen had assumed.

They began with the video of Andrew Dotson which was followed by the video Owen had seen of his father. His lawyer asked what his father's suicide had to do with anything. The elder of the agents told him they would get to that. Next, Owen had to watch himself put a bullet in Dotson's head. If there had been audio, they could have heard Andy Dotson confess to both murders on the previous two films.

The next video was the sheriff and his murder of the federal agent, followed by the sheriff getting killed. Owen felt sick to his stomach when they let it play out so long and he got to see what the bobcat did, the same one that sat calmly by his side and let him remove the glass from its paw. He could have quite easily ended up lunch like the sheriff.

Trying to recover from that one, they showed the bar scene and Kyle passing the zip drive to Owen. The same Kyle that had disappeared out of his cell and was yet to be found. Then they played something he wasn't ready for, this one had sound. He heard the President of The United States confess to participating in the murder of his wife. He was bound and clearly had been beaten. The red welts covered his mostly naked body. The feds informed him that this video was sent to the web from his house the previous night from his personal computer. They found the zip drive still in the computer. They wanted to know where he had gotten it from and what were his intentions. The conversation heated up from that point. His lawyer was barking out accusations of being set up and what kind of bullshit were they trying to play with his client. After a few minutes of that, his lawyer was led out in cuffs and had his own cell to cool off in. He didn't go quietly, kicking and screaming all the way. He was yelling instructions to Owen to keep his mouth shut and not say a word as they dragged him away.

Owen was confused. He had never seen that tape, nor had he had anything to do with it getting on the web. He wondered if it was his brother or Lori that had sent it out. He didn't think his brother even knew how to operate a computer, never mind post something to the web. It had to be Lori, he told himself.

They were trying to blame him for additional charges that might keep Owen behind bars for the rest of his life. It was irrefutable he had pulled the trigger and shot Dotson in the head execution-style. If he had audio, he might be able to prove justifiable homicide. Supposedly Kyle was hiding in a tree and heard everything that was said. Owen didn't know if he was a fed, or if he wasn't, where the hell was he now, and how did he escape. These things were going through his mind when the two agents returned and began to grill him. The sweet black lady turned out not to be so sweet, as she was in his face accusing him of all sorts of things that he had nothing to do with. He took his lawyer's advice and just sat there, not saying a word. The more they accused, the harder it was not to defend his honor and his pride. They even accused him of murdering his mother and hiding her body.

He endured, and when they realized they were not going to be able to get him to talk, he was roughly returned to his cell. Owen was not pleased with this turn of events. He had planned that he would confess to what he had done. He figured when he saw his brother had not been in the view of the camera that he would keep his involvement a secret. He had planned to throw Kyle under the bus and say that he had taken the shot. They already had figured it was him in the video even if they didn't have a shot of his face. These were the woods where he lived and hunted. His trail cameras sent video straight to the computer inside the trailer where he and his father resided.

Now they were trying to accuse him of things that he had nothing to do with. The fact they were trying to accuse him of killing his mother hurt him. He loved her so much and he was concerned for her safety. He began to wonder if the sheriff might have had something to do with her disappearance and whether she was indeed alive or if her dead body was hidden somewhere decaying in a shallow grave.

The pressure was so great, his head felt like it was about to explode. He began to have heart palpitations. His breathing became difficult and the room began to get dark. Small white orbs began to circle his head. Owen felt like he was about to keel over and die, instead, he laid down on his bunk and squeezed his eyes shut. He began to pray for the first time in a long time. He begged God to help him, pleaded with him. The tears were flowing down the side of his face dampening his pillowcase. Still, he prayed and prayed some more asking for God's forgiveness.

This became a daily ritual in which Owen prayed to a God that he thought wasn't listening to him. Each day things became worse for Owen. Instead of turning away from God, he reached out more. His life was completely torn down and dismantled. His good name was dragged through the mud and then stomped on. The jury took no pity on him and sent him away for life.

The President was able to say the video was fake and released to disgrace him before another big election, and the media backed him up. The fact that the President appeared to be so much older in the video than he did at this moment helped somewhat. At least the fountain of youth formula Maria had come up with had been put to good use for something.

Owen was transferred to Adirondack Correctional Facility where he would get to spend a great deal of the rest of his life. His house in Virginia had to be sold to pay for all his legal expenses and everything he owned was auctioned off. All his savings had been blown through and even if for some reason he were to be released, he was now destitute.

To think that Owen would be depressed and suicidal would have been expected, but he walked the halls with purpose in his steps. He petitioned and was then allowed to form a writer's class that helped other prisoners write their stories. The weeks passed by and Owen slowly became accustomed to his surroundings. He found a niche in this hell and worked it the best he could. His prayers never ceased, as he daily praised God even when he was at his lowest.

The words to the song "Rock Bottom" had come to his mind quite often, and one night he had a dream of a teenager with a guitar playing in his jail cell and singing the UFO song to him. The kid kept singing, "Where do we go from here…"

That's what Owen had been asking God. Just where did he go from here? He found out one night, just after lights out. He thought it was a spirit, but it wasn't. He had seen this man on television, in a movie and on the news. He was always saving people from one disaster or another, and now he was here in his cell, talking to him, of all people.

"Are you ready to begin a new life, Owen?" the man asked him.

"Is it better than the one I'm living now? This place here isn't exactly the Taj Mahal. I'll take just about anything better than this," Owen said sarcastically thinking he was talking to a mirage, one that had saved many people and was now here to save him. He began to laugh like a crazy man. He had only been here maybe six weeks and already was losing his mind, or so he thought.

"I need someone to write my story. I know you know how to do that. I'm offering you a chance to get out of here and begin a new life as my storyteller. You don't have to embellish. The stories are more than unbelievable already. Just take my hand and we'll be gone. Say you'll do it Owen, just say the word."

"Can I think about it? I'm really tired right now and I need to get some sleep. Come back in the morning and I'll give you my answer."

Owen turned over and fluffed his pillow, lay his head down, and closed his eyes.

Joey stood over him in disbelief. Jacob just laughed at him.

"Losing your touch, Joey. I bet you were sure he would jump at the chance to work with you. Well, let me tell you something – you're no picnic to be around. I don't blame the guy for wanting to choose jail over spending any time with the likes of you."

"Knock it off, Jacob. You would be lost without me, and you know it. We've had some good times together, you and I."

"Yeah, I just love taking a bullet for you. My gut still hurts from doing it from time to time. The stress you put me under protecting your dumb ass. I had to go to rehab because of you. Do you have any idea what angel rehab is like? Well, do you?"

"No, not really. I never knew you had to go."

"It sucks big time, let me tell you. Especially when the big guy comes in and talks to the class. I felt about this small," Jacob held his fingers close together, indicating a small size.

"Angels shouldn't drink. You had a problem. Hell, you were drunk half the time you were supposed to be protecting me. You deserved to have to go to rehab. Serves you right. I always wondered where all my liquor was disappearing to, now I know. Thanks for letting me know. I was always blaming someone else."

"Are you going to run your mouth all night, or are you going to leave me so I can get some rest?" Owen mumbled from his bunk.

"I'm trying to have a conversation with an irritating guardian angel who thinks he's the best at what he does, but in all reality, he's just average at best. He has a lot of issues that he carried with him from the real world and now he has to deal with them after he's dead."

Joey began to have a heated argument and before Owen knew it, he had Joey struggling with an invisible enemy laying on top of him. Owen realized he wasn't going to get any sleep until this spirit departed. He always thought Joey was more mature. This version of Joey seemed to be childish, not exactly what Owen was expecting.

"If I say yes, will you let me get some sleep? I told you I was tired," Owen whined.

"Well if you say yes, then we have got to go. That will require us to travel, so you won't be getting much sleep, but you will be gaining your freedom. I feel that you would be getting a win out of that deal. Sacrifice a little sleep for your freedom. I know I would take that deal."

Owen stared up at Joey. His face was red from struggling with something. His hair was disheveled, and he was breathing hard. He wondered if he really wanted to go with this entity, or whatever it was that looked like Joey Hopkins.

Owen stood up from his bunk, put his loafers on, and held out his hand. Owen never felt or saw anything except for a flash of light, which was blinding. When he was finally able to see once again, he noticed they were outside of the prison. They were at an airfield that was about a mile down the road from the prison. Owen was trying to comprehend exactly how he had gotten there when Joey pulled him toward an airplane. When he asked him if he was ready to fly, Owen suddenly felt sick. The last time he had seen or heard those words is when it had all begun. They were on Lori's laptop when he had heard the song in his dream. "Feels like I'm dreaming but it's real…" That had been a dream, until it wasn't. Could he now be dreaming? Is that what this all was? Just a dream that quickly turned into a nightmare.

No way was he getting in a plane with Joey Hopkins, whether he was real or not. He had read the stories of all his past flights and the mayhem that followed.

"Come on, Owen. I have my pilot's license now. We'll fly and get there so much faster. It will be fun," Joey tried to coax Owen to get on the plane with him.

Owen was having none of it and told him so. Reluctantly, Joey retrieved a 4x4 SUV from a stand of trees and drove over to where Owen was standing. Owen opened the door and slid in.

"Where did this come from and where are we going?

"Don't ask any questions and I won't have to tell you any lies." Joey smiled at Owen and put the SUV in drive.

"You sure you don't want to fly? It's not too late to change your mind. It's a long drive to California."

Owen looked at him with disdain. This dream was getting better and better by the minute. Owen had no desire to go anywhere near California. He had not enjoyed himself the last time he was on the West Coast. Owen had been mugged and pistol-whipped by a gangbanger who was desperate for money to buy drugs that were in high demand. A shortage caused by some federal agent that had made a huge drug bust was making what little supply expensive for the addicts. Owen voiced this discontentment to Joey and listened to him apologize for that one, like Joey may have had something to do with the shortage. The look on his face told the story, the man did have something to do with it.

"Lead the way. I'm going to get some shut-eye. Let me know when you get tired and I'll drive some for you." With that, Owen reclined the seat and shut his eyes. He was convinced that when he opened them, he would once again be in his jail cell and ready to start another day behind bars.

CHAPTER 19

Lori and Todd found themselves homeless when they returned from getting some food shopping done. The guard refused to let them inside the gate. He told them that the estate and everything within it was seized to pay for Owen's legal bills. The guard apologized to them, but said it was out of his hands. They were left with the clothes on their backs and the food in the truck. Lori pleaded with them to at least let her get her car. The guard made a call and took her keys from her. He told her to come back tomorrow and she would be able to retrieve her car. They would park it out by the front gate. Lori thanked him and inquired about the other guard that had been compromised by Karma.

"He had an unfortunate accident. Don't you watch the news? His sister stabbed him to death. She claims it was in self-defense. They had a big fight about something. I believe the sister. Just seeing her doing the interview with her eye swollen shut was enough to convince me he had been beating her. I think he deserved what he got."

Lori turned away, knowing Karma had been the cause of the fight. He was told his sister had been blabbing about what he had done to her, but she never said a word. The guard must have confronted her, and the fight ensued. Lori never figured it would end with a fatal knife wound. She asked the question of her inner spirit.

"Karma, you knew this would happen when you said those things to that poor man. Didn't you?"

Lori heard a small giggle inside herself.

"Alright, I admit I might have known what the outcome was going to be, but he had it coming. He could have gone to his sister and apologized, but he went looking to beat her for opening her mouth. I'm Karma, it's what I do Lori. Get over it."

Lori was fuming. She had thought the guard was a nice guy. She didn't feel he deserved what had happened to him. His co-workers seemed to have felt differently. Maybe Karma was right, the guy did deserve what he got in the end. The world was so full of surprises. Lori always tried to see the good in people, but Karma could see the bad, and that made her mad. The things they did to people to upset their lives. She felt these were good people, when in fact, they were being punished for something they had done.

Karma kept taking her on missions, using her good looks to get to some nasty people. Sometimes they would be gone for an hour, other times it took almost a day. Ryan had been gone for several weeks now, she missed him. He was able to keep Karma in check and make the damage she wrought upon people a little less severe.

She told Todd to drive back into town and go find Pastor Ted. She felt he would be able to help them. The gallon of chocolate milk he had drunk had made his chemical imbalance return and the old Todd was back. His words slurred and his thinking had slowed, but his hyperactivity had increased as well as the speed he drove. They were at the church within ten minutes. Lori had been holding on to the door handle so tightly that her knuckles were still white and in pain.

She thought another trip to see Maria was needed. Get the boy back in balance. This might get her to live a little longer if they were going to be together supporting each other. When they entered the church, they realized a trip to see Maria was not required, because she was already there and expecting them. She had the drink for Todd in her hands, like she had known they would be coming. To her, this was strange. To

Pastor Ted, this was normal. He called her over to have a conversation outside in the hallway.

"Can you go to the mall with me and help with a purchase I need to make? Todd will be fine here with Maria. I figured since you're a woman, that you would know what kind of ring women like. I want to propose to my girlfriend at the show we're doing on Friday night. Please help me. I have no idea what I'm doing," R.J. begged using puppy dog eyes.

Lori looked up at his eyes and could not find an excuse why she would not be able to do that. Women's taste in jewelry varied immensely. She inquired who the lucky girl was, and when he said it was Sophia, Karma had something to say about that. Lori tried to stifle her, but she couldn't keep the words from leaving her mouth.

"That bitch is not good enough for you. She's nothing but trouble. You'd be better off with a dog!" Lori bent at the waist and covered her mouth. Once she was able to get back control, she apologized for her outburst and asked him when he wanted to go. She put on her best happy face, which Karma was trying hard to wipe off. She excused herself and went to the ladies' restroom where she confronted herself in the mirror.

"What the hell was all that bullshit out in the hallway?" Lori gazed at herself in anger.

Karma gazed right back, pointing a finger at herself.

"He has no idea she has been compromised. The show he's doing on Friday just might be the last one he ever does. It will be up to her what the outcome is going to be. That's all I know. I've tried to look and see what's coming, but the future is all foggy beyond the show. What happens at that show will determine all our futures and it's in her hands."

Lori now knew why Karma had gotten so upset. If only Karma would let her in on some of the stuff she was privy to, maybe she would be able to help.

Lori went with Pastor Ted and they found a jewelry store that sold expensive diamonds. She saw the prices and knew that on his salary, he would be going into some serious debt to make this purchase. She tapped him on the shoulder and walked him away from the eager salesman.

"Let's go to another place where you can get a better bargain and you won't break the bank."

Lori had him drive them to a pawn shop.

"Are you sure about this? I want her to have the best. I don't want a tarnished diamond ring that's about ready to fall apart."

"Trust me on this. You're going to be surprised at what we find inside."

Lori led him in, and the Pastor was indeed surprised at what he found and was able to purchase. What would have cost him nearly ten thousand, he purchased for twenty-five hundred bucks. A happy man indeed when they left the pawnshop. He wanted to celebrate and make a toast. R.J. was on the wagon, so he got a soda, but Lori needed a stiff drink, so she purchased a drink called Sex on the Beach. A drink that got R.J.'s attention as soon as she asked for it.

"I don't come up with the names of the drinks," she flirtatiously said to him.

"I could have easily ordered a Slippery Nipple or even a Blow Job. Now wouldn't that have gotten your attention?" she said while laying her hand on top of his.

R.J. immediately pulled his hand back and wiped his forehead.

"Is it hot in here? I wish they would put some AC on in here." He grabbed his soda and downed it in one quick swallow, and ordered another.

Karma smiled at the effect Lori was having on the poor fellow. Maybe she could make him cheat on his future fiancé before he even proposed.

They had their drinks and headed back to the church. A group of people had arrived while they had been out. R.J. explained that it was Church Band and another group called Savage Storm. They were all here to go over the final rehearsal. He told her to take a seat and enjoy the show.

Lori noticed a small Latino boy behind the drum set. One of the members of the band must have brought their child with them. He began to warm up, and that was when Lori realized that this was no ordinary child. The kid was one of the best she had ever heard play the drums, and he was just warming up. Another man joined him. He had an electric guitar that he was making sing, like Frampton would do way back in the day. She could have sworn it was Joey Hopkins, but this guy had more gray hair and looked to be a little older. Maybe he was his brother, she thought to herself. She heard Karma laugh but didn't know the reason why.

A woman named Jenna Alston took the stage with the first group and they played half a dozen songs. She sang with this guy that appeared to be a choir boy. He had a baby face, but his singing voice was deep and wonderful. They seemed to be meant for each other the way they worked the stage and melded together to bring out perfect harmonies. Karma laughed some more and told her to check out the guy she thought was Joey. She told her that his name was Peter. He had a pissed-off look on his face as he watched the two of them on stage. Lori thought maybe this was a love triangle. Karma burst out laughing.

"That man on stage is Peter's karma. He hates everything about him. Jenna can't seem to resist him. He has tried and failed to resist her. They can't, because they are soul mates, reunited once again. Try as they might, they come together again and again. Problem is, God's plan has Peter and Jenna raising three young children. These children are the key to the world's salvation. So, you see, they have a complicated road ahead of themselves. You didn't think the devil was going to make it easy for the Lord? The Lord is going to have to work hard to achieve his goals. I bet you're wondering where you come into all of this?"

"You're going to be Jenna's karma, sort of a balancing act for the two of them. Make sure you catch Peter's eye, because I assure you, Jenna has noticed you already." Karma laughed some more. Lori didn't like being a pawn in any game that was being played. Then Karma brought to her attention the importance of the pawn towards the end of the game. Reach the other side and the pawn can become a queen or whatever it wants to be.

"I told you that you were very important to this whole story. Now stop fighting it and do your job."

Lori wasn't sure about all of this. It felt like she was being led around like she was a dog on a leash. She watched R.J. fawning over Sophia, acting like he was the happiest person on earth. She liked him and knew if she had a chance, that she would bed him down in a heartbeat. She peered over at Todd. He was sitting beside Maria; she was whispering things in his ear that she could not hear or possibly imagine.

Savage Storm wrapped up and R.J. took the stage. He went through some material that had everyone in stitches. It seemed he had saved some of his best stuff just for this show. Then Church Band took over. The boy that had played the drums for the first band stayed in place to play with the next band. The only other person was Jenna, where she jumped on the keyboards and sang some songs with Peter. Lori could see that the chemistry between them was not even close to what she had seen from the previous pair. She thought about what Karma had said to her, that these two were destined to raise three children that were essentially going to save the world.

Her job would be to provide a reason for Jenna to become closer to Peter, or worse, break them up. It was going to be a fine line she would have to walk. Make Jenna jealous without splitting the two of them up. Then she thought to herself, why did it have to be Peter she was trying to catch the eye of, why couldn't it be the soulmate? A plan was formed in her head. Karma loved every minute of it. It was like leading a horse to water.

"Drink up my little pretty, you're doing a terrific job," Karma squealed in delight. Lori heard her, but still went about her plan.

Church Band finished up with what was going to be their finale. It was a Red Rocks Worship song called "Nobody Like You." Once they finished the song, she had goosebumps. The President was in for a real treat if they performed like they had in rehearsal. She wanted to go see the soul mate, but she was so moved by the performance that she went straight for Peter.

Lori was glowing and heaping praise onto Peter when Jenna quickly came and swept Peter away from her. A dirty look was directed toward Lori as he was whisked away.

Now to find the choir boy, where had he gone to? Karma directed her outside of the building where she found R.J. and the man, which she soon found out was referred to as Deke, but his real name was John Deacon, or at least it was now. She was told it was a long story best saved for another time.

"Should I call you Deke or John? She began to flirt and touch like only she knew how. This got R.J. to take notice, which Lori sort of liked, making him jealous. She put on a full-court press and before she knew it, R.J. couldn't take it anymore and pulled her inside away from Deke.

Once inside, he was about to kiss her when Sophia walked by on her way out to her car. She had a shift at the hospital that she was late for. After Sophia gave R.J. a departing kiss, Lori received another dirty look. Lori was beginning to feel like a slut, so she shut down all the flirtatious behavior.

Deke came inside and said he had to go, that it was nice meeting her. Once again she was alone in the hallway with an embarrassed pastor. He tried to explain himself but was cut off when Peter and Jenna were on their way out. The babysitter was waiting for them; they had to be going. They waved goodbye and were about to depart when Pastor Ted called out to them.

"You still have that spare room in that big house of yours?"

They acknowledged that they still did have a spare room.

"I have a couple that is in desperate need of housing until I can find them a place to stay. It shouldn't be more than a week. It sure would be Christian of you to put them up until I can set up a place for them. Good people, they can help you with the children."

The fact that R.J. held back who it was until they agreed was not lost on Karma. The look on Jenna's face when he revealed who it would be that would be staying with them was priceless. She noticed Peter had a huge smile on his face. This was turning out perfect. Karma was ecstatic. The next few days were going to be so much fun.

Ryan showed up about that time. He arrived about the same time they got to the house in Jarratt. He had bad news for Karma. They were being relieved of their missions and instructed to return. Karma knew if she left Lori's body that she would die. The body of the man that Ryan was using was lying dead as a doornail beside Mrs. Canton in the bed they were sharing. She wouldn't realize this until the morning when she woke up.

Karma felt sorry for Lori. They had been through so much together. Ryan said it was urgent, they must go now. The end was fast approaching. God had instructed Jesus to begin gathering the flock. The world was about to lose ten percent of its population in a mere few days. It would be longer than that, but Ryan was trying to get Karma to understand the urgency. It was the only way she was going to leave Lori to die.

Lori felt Karma exit her body as she was climbing the stairs on her way to the room she was about to share with a horny Todd. The drink had done its job and his chemical imbalance was once again straightened out. She had been looking for alternative resting places in the house to avoid a conflict. The Latino boy was occupying the couch, all the other rooms were full. The children shared one room on the ground floor. There were three bedrooms upstairs: one for Todd and her, another for Peter, and one for Jenna. She found it strange they didn't share a bed. The thought had passed her mind to go in and snuggle up with Peter, but she dismissed it as being rude and much too forward. If she asked Jenna, she might get punched in the face. Running out of options, she had been returning to the room with Todd when Karma left her.

The diabetes quickly came back, and she felt her blood sugar fall like a rock. Her legs became weak as she tried to catch herself, but she wasn't strong enough to keep herself from tumbling down the steps and out into the middle of the floor, almost at the little drummer boy's feet. Beats was not a normal boy, as anyone in the house could attest to. Lori wasn't privy to this information and was sure her time had come. She stared up into the little boy's eyes as he tried to help her.

"You play a great set of drums. I think you're marvelous. I would love to hear you play again. I guess I'll have to wait 'til you get to heaven."

She grabbed his hand and said goodbye, closed her eyes, and thought she would die any moment.

She woke many hours later in her bed, by herself. How could she still be alive? She asked herself. She knew that Karma had left her unexpectedly and the results would be fatal, yet she lived. Rising from the bed, she ventured out to explore the house. Two twin boys running down the hallway practically knocked her over. They were like looking at mirror images. Impossible to tell them apart.

"Glad you're feeling better. Good thing Beats was here to save you. He saved me once. I was shot and bleeding out. Now you can't even see where the bullet hit me." The boy pulled his shirt up to show her that he was scar-free. Lori wasn't even sure if he might have been making up a story, but she was here, so maybe there was some validity to what he had said.

"I'm Joey and this is my brother Jacob. My sister is here somewhere. Her name is Maria and she's a great big pain in the butt, but we love her."

The two boys giggled and ran off. Lori guessed they were about six years old. A little girl came strolling down the hallway with a doll in both her hands. The body in one hand, the head in the other.

"They pulled her head off. Can you believe them? I loved this doll, now it's junk."

Lori asked to see it, saw she would be able to repair it for her. She asked if she knew where her mother kept the sewing kit. Little Maria led her right to it and within a few minutes, Lori had it looking as good as new.

"You have a talent just like Beats. He brings the injured back to new, sometimes even the dead. I'm so glad God brought you to us so that Beats could save you when you were about to die last night. You are a lucky woman he was here."

Little Maria merrily danced off to find her brothers and show them the miracle Lori had performed on her doll. Lori figured her to be about a year younger than the boys. It must have been quite an interesting household when all three of them were still in diapers.

Lori walked down the stairs to find Peter sitting on the couch reading a Bible story to Beats. It was the one about Jonah and the whale. They were getting in depth on the meaning of the story when she walked down the steps. Lori wished they would have finished their lesson as she was interested in what they had to say on the subject. Especially when it came to defying God's wishes.

She knew beyond a doubt that she had been sent here, that Beats' presence here was also preplanned. The exit from her body of a spirit that she had so wanted removed had been a gift, but when it left her, she knew that she would die.

If Beats did indeed have the gift to heal, then this was what God wanted and she was given a mission. That mission was to make Jenna jealous and be closer to Peter. The fact they slept in separate bedrooms was not a good beginning to her plan to bring them together.

She sat down beside Peter and got to work. She begged them to continue. Beats laughed that Lori would want to hear a children's story. Peter was understanding, for he knew that this wasn't just a children's story. It was told so that children would begin to understand God's love for his people but wasn't exclusively told just for kids. Parents could learn a lot from a children's story.

Lori sat with them and absorbed the lesson like a sponge. It was a great day. No longer burdened with Karma constantly making her do things she dreaded, she spread her arms and called the Lord to guide her from this day forth. She hadn't realized she had been talking out loud. Peter said she had made the right decision. That God was indeed needed in our daily lives. They gazed into each other's eyes and a connection was made. Lori felt she had passed step one, so excused herself and went to make something to eat. She wondered if the diabetes was still present in her body or had Beats completely healed her. She would have to find a test kit and check her blood. It was the only way she was going to be sure.

* * *

Joey was becoming tired. A bad accident had left them in traffic for hours. Joey decided to divert from the route he had chosen, head down Route 81 and pick up Route 80 and begin his westward travel from there. He must have fallen asleep and Jacob picked up the wheel. He missed Route 80 and now they were closing in on Harrisburg, Pennsylvania.

"Don't blame me, I just took the wheel because you decided to play sleeping beauty. You can thank me later," Jacob said with a huff. He didn't like Joey criticizing his driving. While they were barking at each other, a familiar pothole had made its presence known once again. The front wheel found it and seconds later they were riding on the rim as the air in the tire blew out.

Owen woke expecting to find himself in his cell and was disoriented for a minute or two as he gathered his faculties. Owen checked out his surroundings and immediately knew exactly where he was. The same mile marker as before.

"You hit the pothole, didn't you?" he asked Joey.

"You call that a pothole, I call it a trench! We could have been killed. Damn state won't keep their roads up! Look at this tire. It's shot, rim as well."

Joey was venting and stomping around, so Owen went to the back of the truck and began to pull the spare off its holder. He found the spare was also in desperate need of air. They were stuck for the time being.

"You got AAA or any kind of road service? Your spare is flat."

This caused Joey to rant, cuss, and stomp around with a small tantrum.

"If the prison realizes you're gone, we're screwed. Hide in the damn woods until we can get the hell out of here."

Owen watched Joey make a call as he stepped over the guardrail. The cops were there before he was able to conceal himself.

"Hey mister, come out from there. What are you doing? Taking a leak?" the officer called to him.

Owen tried to conceal his face, hopefully the cop wouldn't know he was an escaped convict. Joey had given him a set of clothes when they were getting onto the airplane. It was a good thing, because his orange jumpsuit would have been a dead giveaway.

The cop looked him over. Owen could see he recognized him. The shit was about to hit the fan. Owen could feel it. Well, it was nice to be free while it lasted. It wasn't like they could add anything to his life sentence.

"I've seen you before son, haven't I? In fact, right here in this very spot. You want me to show you the rock you bounced my head off of? I bet you the bloodstains are still on it."

The cop walked over to the guardrail and shone his light on the very spot where Owen had tossed his body over. The rock was still in the same place. The blood had washed away.

"I wanted to say how grateful I was that you saved my life several times that night, but you disappeared into the wind." The cop walked back toward the road to shake Owen's hand. Joey grabbed them both and threw them over the guardrail, missing the big rock by inches.

"What in the world are you trying to prove, you idiot?!"

Joey laid on top of them as they struggled to get up.

"Keep your head low and wait for it. Trust me, you're going to want to keep your head down," Joey explained frantically.

They waited what seemed like an eternity but was more like half a minute. When you have two men that you've just thrown over a guardrail squirming beneath you, it can feel that way.

A truck passed by, hitting the pothole. One of its tires exploded, sending parts of the tire flying over the location that they once occupied. If they had had their heads up or had still been standing where they were, it wouldn't have turned out so well for the bunch of them. Jacob had saved them all, but his timing was just a little off, making it nondramatic, which was unlike him. He usually liked to wait a split second before the tragedy was to happen. It was more exciting that way, he had told Joey one time too many.

The grateful cop rose to his feet and brushed his clothes off. He looked closely at Joey and began to laugh.

"I've just been saved by the great Joey Hopkins! I'd never figured that I would ever get to meet you in person," he gushed as he gave Joey a hug that practically knocked the wind out of him.

"I was just about to tell your boy here that I was grateful for what he had done when he hit that pothole. My head still hurts but he saved my life that day. Between the truck that was out of control and his fast thinking of getting me to the hospital when he saw I was having a coronary, I could have died several times that day. I never got to thank him."

The service truck arrived and shortly thereafter, they were once again underway. Owen had a confession to make.

"I never drove him to the hospital. I left him there to die. Made a call on the radio and drove away. I have no idea how he got to the hospital or that he was having a heart attack. I wanted to tell him I was sorry, but I felt so much shame I was unable to do it."

Joey patted him on the arm and told him he understood. It had happened to him more times than he could count.

"You wait until I start to tell you my story. I can't wait to read your rendition of the story. I know you will probably put a wild spin on it. Don't try to embellish it too much. I want this story to be believable even if sometimes I don't believe it myself. We're going to need a new name for you. Your days of writing under Owen Canton are long over. I got it, how about we use –"

The sound of a siren followed by flashing lights told the whole story. Owen was recognized and now he was being hunted. Joey had no choice but to travel the only way he hated to these days. He put his hand out and asked Owen to take it.

"Hold on, we're getting out of here."

In a flash, they both disappeared leaving the cops to believe they had been chasing a self-driving car.

Joey made sure he appeared in public so that he could disprove the cops' account that he was the one helping Owen Canton escape custody.

"As you can clearly see, I've been here in California working on my latest film." His producer Adam Bennett verified it for him and gave him an airtight alibi.

Owen was reunited with Kyle. The kid was happy to see him and had his own stories he was dying to tell Owen. If he wrote up all the material that they had provided for him, he would have his next ten books without having to think up a single thing. His writer's block was gone forever, for now, he was reborn again. The song by Third Day, "Born Again" rattled around in his head. He felt like he was finally at home here on this ranch in the middle of nowhere. Kyle told him not to get comfortable, things were about to get interesting and dangerous. Just the way Owen thought they might get as he typed away on his new laptop.

His first story, the attempt to take over the government and assassinate the President. It all started with a violin case and a Russian with an ax to grind. They had been working on a virus for several years. The trick was to have the vaccine before they released the virus on Congress and the President. The concert was a go. They had their operative that was to deliver the virus. All she had to do was open the case and let it out. Nobody was going to be the wiser. It was invisible and they had people in place to make sure the violin got inside undetected. The vaccine was administered to most of their people with a slight hitch. The Queen Bees had killed their doctor before she could fully inoculate all their people, gunned down in front of many witnesses on the streets of Richmond.

They shrugged it off and continued with their plan. A few more casualties were a small price to pay to be able to take over the government. At least they had the power brokers they had paid off to be able to step in and complete their mission. The virus was fast-acting and those that were not vaccinated would be dead within hours of being exposed. It had a twenty percent kill rate. If it didn't kill you, then you would struggle to breathe and be incapacitated for several days. It was a nasty one this one was.

As plans go, this one was as well-planned as you could get it. It had a small glitch. The first one was Joey Hopkins. The second was R.J. Ted. The third was Lori Stenville.

Owen stopped his writing and listened to what was being said. He was the only one in the room. The voice had said her name – why? Confused, he began to type once again.

Lori had caused a fuss not only between Jenna and Peter, but between R.J. and Sophia. She also had gotten inside of Deke's head and this made Jenna furious with her. Lori was forced to attend the show with them. She would keep an eye on the children backstage while they performed. Jenna wanted to keep a close eye on Lori.

Jenna was not what you would call the jealous type, that was until Lori had entered the picture. Her beauty matched Jenna's right down to the sexy clothes they wore. It pissed her off that Lori was so beautiful and had mastered the look around her eyes that Bo and Maria were so good at applying to the eyelids. If Jenna only knew that Lori was stuck with this look, she might not have been so jealous.

All the men in Jenna's life had a thing for Lori. Jenna could accept her trying to get R.J., but her Peter was off-limits and Deke was forbidden to be around her. She had to remain in control, or she was going to lose it all. Best to keep your friends close and your enemies closer, she told herself.

While Jenna was out performing with Savage Storm, the plan was implemented. Two agents went into the dressing room and forcefully grabbed the twins. Their job was to dispose of their dead bodies once they got them away from DC. Lori was tied up with little Maria. The boys were dragged kicking and screaming to the parking lot outside where they met Joey Hopkins. He was the only thing standing in their way of escaping with their quarry.

As he argued with the agents, he was joined by a bunch of gangbangers. They were out causing destruction and mayhem while stealing items from cars parked out in the lot with smashed-in windows.

"Let them go. They are not as important as the Russians would have you believe. Take me, I'm far more a threat to them than they are."

"Back off, Joey. We're taking the kids, and that is it, you're not going to stop us."

The sounds of smashing glass and loud obnoxious voices approached them. The gangbangers had made an appearance and wanted to be seen front and center. This was their turf. Outsiders were not welcome.

"That's a nice gun you have mister. How about you give it to me, and nobody will get hurt."

The agent laughed at the idiot that was trying to get his gun. He had it firmly placed against the back of little Joey's head, ready to pull the trigger.

"We can do this the easy way, or the hard way. Your choice buddy, I suggest you give me the gun before somebody gets hurt."

The other agent was getting nervous when the gang members began to surround them and cut them off from getting to their SUV. He began to whine to his partner that it wasn't worth it. They argued with each other as the circle tightened like a rope around a condemned man's neck.

"Last chance, your partner is getting nervous with good reason. Somebody is about to die," Joey pleaded.

"It's not going to be me, his partner said as he threw little Jacob to the ground and began to fire his weapon. The noose closed and little Joey found himself on the ground beside his brother, crawling away from the ruckus. The boys made their way to Joey's waiting arms and safety, at least for the moment.

The gangbangers were finished with the two federal agents. They had lost a couple of their own people, which made them highly emotional. They focused their anger on Joey and the boys.

"You got money. These men we lost have families, bills to pay. How are they supposed to pay their bills when they're dead? I blame you. We need payment for what we have done for you! I'll take the boys and you go get us some cash. A hundred thousand sounds fair, for each of the children."

The gangbanger went to reach for one of the boys when little Jacob kicked him in the shin.

"You have no idea who you're messing with! This here is our uncle Joey Hopkins. Nobody messes with our uncle and lives to tell about it."

Joey was trying hard to get Jacob to shut up and be quiet, but when Jacob is on a roll, it's hard to get the boy to shut his trap. He had no choice but to cover his mouth with his hand.

Little Joey had to get his say in and that was when Joey knew he was in trouble.

"My uncle will kick your ass. I bet your chicken to take him on in a fight. If he wins, we walk, you win, he'll go get you the cash. What do you say, you scared or something?"

Joey really wished little Joey would keep his big mouth shut. He was not a fighter. Never was really very good at it. He just had a knack of ending up on the winning end of a conflict. That wasn't to say he didn't get his ass kicked more than a few times, like he thought was about to happen now.

"The boy says your name is Joey. You're Joey Bats. Oh, my God! I'm in the company of the great Joey Hopkins," he said while looking around nervously.

The gangbanger began to scan all the places a sniper might have taken cover. The last thing he wanted to do was piss off Diablo. He knew by the word on the street that these two worked hand and hand.

"I have changed my mind. You can go now and have a nice day. Make sure you tell Diablo what I have done for you. My name is Sanchez Estrado. Make sure you tell him I saved you." He quickly ducked his head down and sought shelter and the rest of his crew did the same.

Joey walked away from the scene with a child in each arm, but the day was just beginning, for inside the case was about to be opened.

R.J. was doing his skit when he saw Sophia walk out on stage and take her place. The others would soon follow as he was about to wrap it up. Sophia's body language was all off, something was up. He decided he would use his final minutes on stage to make his proposal. Something he was planning to do after the show, but the timeline had to be moved up. He begged her to join him at the microphone.

She just sat down and began to cry as she was reaching to open the case. R.J. sprinted to her and pulled her to her feet. He whispered in her ear.

"What's wrong, honey? I have some splendid news for you."

"Not now R.J., I have some bad news for you. I have a bomb in that case and if I don't open it we're all dead, and if I do, we're all dead," she sobbed.

R.J. felt this was indeed quite a conundrum. He was not going to let her open that case and he had to make sure she stayed safe. A problem he knew he had no answer for. He got on his knee and was about to pull the ring from his pocket when she reached down to open the case. He slapped her hand away from it. She stood up and yelled at him to walk away from her, slapped him in the face, and reached for the case once again. He grabbed it from her and walked away. She screamed at him for all to hear that it contained a bomb. It was all that was needed for complete chaos to ensue.

The good and the bad agents were on stage in a flash. The good ones trying to get the case away from him, the bad trying to get it open. The good we're all over him, the bad we're at the case. Bodies were flying around the stage as R.J. shrugged the agents off. He had to prevent that case from being opened at all cost. He dove into the agents as they were about to open it causing more bodies to fly around and a gun to be sent skittering across the stage. The case went flying along with another agent. They were going to need more men if they were going to contain R.J. when he was on the warpath.

Joey had gotten the boys back into the dressing room and found Lori tied up with little Maria. His first mistake was to untie her. She was out the door in a flash heading for the stage. The noise coming from the stage was hard to block out. Joey stayed with the children keeping them safe. Lori went to get into the fiasco.

Sophia had crawled over to the case and was about to open it when she heard a warning from above her.

"Step away from the case and nobody will get hurt. I know how to use this and I'm not afraid to use it."

Sophia laughed at her and told Lori she was out of her league. She would never have R.J.'s love if she were to shoot her. Sophia had greatly underestimated Lori. She hadn't known how much Karma had rubbed off on Lori. She was about to find out. She reached to open the case. A bullet hole formed in the center of her head as she did so.

The agents were trained to take down all threats. A woman had just fired a gun in the vicinity of the President. They returned fire. Lori took several rounds as she scrambled back to where Joey was hiding with the kids.

Blood was flowing freely as she entered the dressing room. Joey grabbed some spare garments and put pressure on her wounds. The children tried to be strong for her, but in the end, Lori faded away, meeting her destiny that she had only just postponed.

Joey wondered if this was the person that had to pay the price for his own life. This amazing woman that he barely knew had sacrificed her life to save so many others. He and the children wept over her now still body.

Karma was there to guide her home along with Ryan. They told her she had done some fine work, but the journey had just begun. There was so much left to do and so little time to do it in. They all laughed as they headed for home, ready to grab their next assignments. Lori was a shoo-in to be an angel of karma.

Owen typed the last of the words and began to cry. He would miss this girl. He so wanted to be a part of her life but never had the chance to commit to it with everything that was going on in his. He felt like he knew what the saying meant, the one that said you needed to take time out to smell the roses.

He stepped away from his laptop, walked outside, and took a deep breath. All he could smell was manure from the barn, so he walked around the house and found Samantha sunbathing with her top off. He quickly turned away and was going to walk back out to the front when she called him over and asked him to put some oil on her back. Well, how could he refuse such a pretty girl? The roses smelled wonderful out back behind the house. He smiled as he applied the oil much to her delight.

"They will all be here soon. I can tell where you're at in the story. I bet it was the part where Lori dies. Am I right?" Samantha inquired.

Owen rubbed the oil on her back and nodded she was correct. He wiped a tear from his eye.

Samantha rolled over on her back and took the oil from him, applied some to her breast and belly. She didn't think Owen would have been able to handle it himself. He had a story to finish.

"Spoiler alert Owen. They still got the case open, only it wasn't inside, it was outside the building and the virus got into the wind. Inside it would have killed most of the politicians that hadn't received the vaccine. Maria says it is going to mutate and when it does, nobody is going to be spared. We're talking tens of millions of people. You know what that means, don't you? The world is going to be cast into total chaos. This virus is airborne, so no place is going to be safe, not even here. Maria says she has a vaccine, but only enough for a few hundred people. We are going to make our stand here until the world is safe for us to once again venture out into. Joey used the word, 'Parabellum.' Do you know what that means Owen?"

Owen nodded his head, "If you want peace, prepare for war."

Samantha stood up, gave him a hug, and said, "Well you better get to it. Those stories aren't going to write themselves. Peace and quiet around here is going to be a thing of the past in about forty-eight hours when they start to arrive. She sat back down and stretched out on her stomach. Owen walked back inside to his computer and listened to the rest of the story he had yet heard.

"Oh, my God," was all he could say after listening to what was coming their way. The sound of rotors cutting through the air could be heard in the distance. The first of the arrivals were about to set foot on this holy ground. The tape finished up with a song Joey had picked out just for this occasion, A song by Passion featuring Kristian Stanfill called, "More To Come."

Joey sure wasn't lying when he picked that song. He looked out at the vastness around him and imagined where he would set up his post and fire down upon the ones that would come and try to take what they had here. It was going to be survival mode for many days to come. He picked up a rifle and found a spot in the hill above the ranch, best to be prepared if these weren't friendly arrivals. He peered across the way and saw Billy had taken up a similar position. Never could be too careful. He waved and took his position and waited.

Time will tell as he wiped away the first sweat that had begun to run into his eyes. He closed his eyes and prayed, and then he readied himself.

CPSIA information can be obtained
at www.ICGtesting.com
Printed in the USA
LVHW052031021021
699315LV00005B/19

9 781949 735772